# SONIC THE HEDGEHOG / MAN

# WORLDS COLLIDE

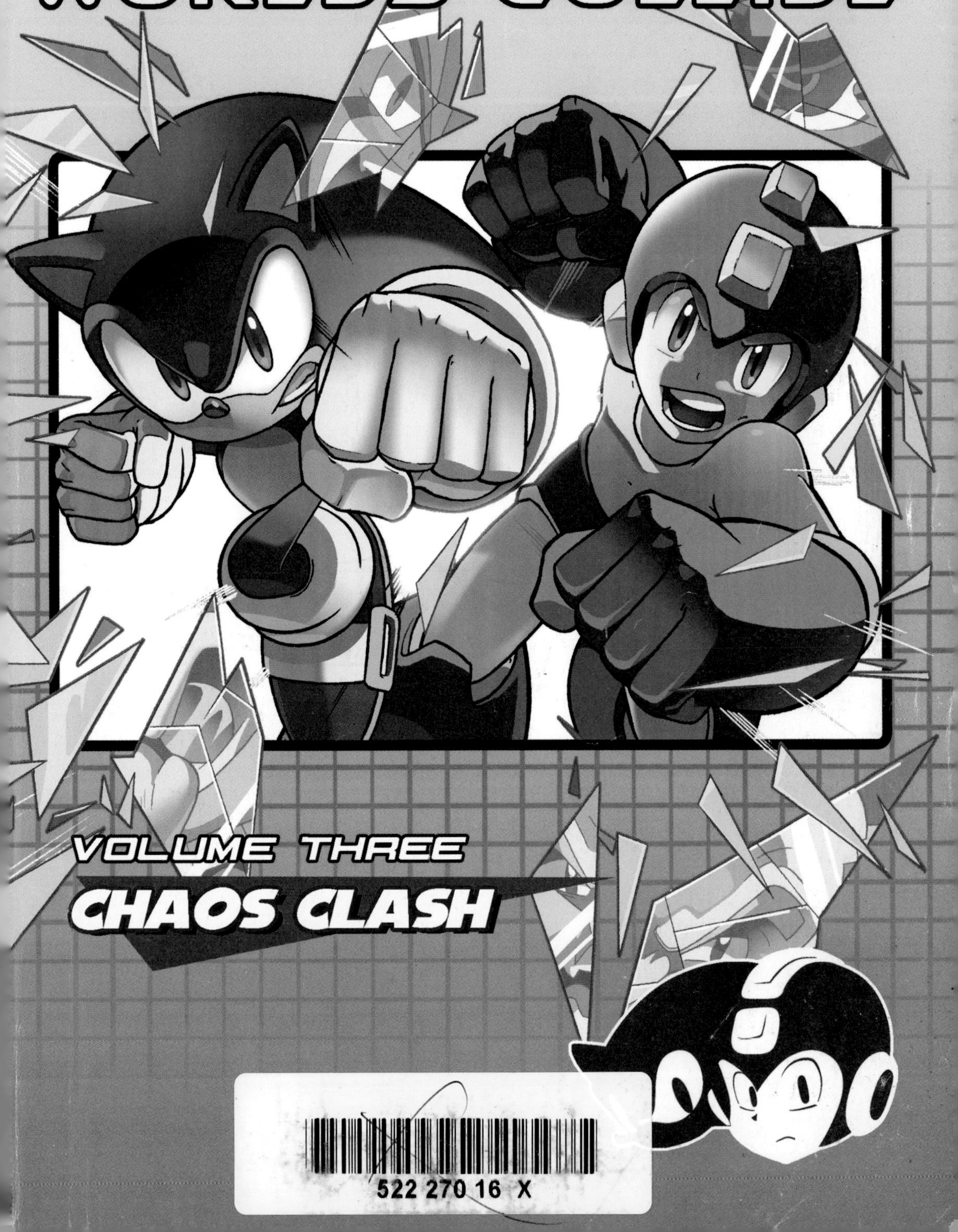

## VOLUME THREE

## CHAOS CLASH

WELCOME TO THE COMIC BOOK
ADVENTURES OF SONIC THE
HEDGEHOG AND MEGA MAN --
A WORLD UNIQUE & BEYOND
WHAT YOU KNOW FROM THE
SEGA AND CAPCOM GAMES!

# SONIC THE HEDGEHOG / MEGA MAN
## WORLDS COLLIDE
### -VOLUME THREE-

**IAN FLYNN**
SCRIPT

**BEN BATES**
PENCILS

**GARY MARTIN**
INKS

**MATT HERMS**
SONIC THE HEDGEHOG
#250 & #251
SONIC UNIVERSE #54

**STEVE DOWNER**
MEGA MAN #27
COLORS

**JOHN WORKMAN**
LETTERS

COVER BY
**PATRICK SPAZIANTE
& BEN HUNZEKER**

SPAZ
Hunzeker

## SPECIAL THANKS TO

ANTHONY GACCIONE and to
Character Business and
Licensing Department of
SEGA Corporation

BRIAN OLIVEIRA
AT CAPCOM MEDIA AND
CONSUMER PRODUCTS
AND TO 飛田 栄実

ARCHIE COMIC PUBLICATIONS, INC.
JONATHAN GOLDWATER, publisher/co-ceo
NANCY SILBERKLEIT, co-ceo
MIKE PELLERITO, president
VICTOR GORELICK, co-president, e-i-c
ROBERTO AGUIRRE-SACASA, chief creative officer
JIM SOKOLOWSKI, senior vice president of sales
and business development
HAROLD BUCHHOLZ, senior vice president of
publishing and operations
ALEX SEGURA, senior vice president
of publicity and marketing
PAUL KAMINSKI, exec. director of
editorial/compilation editor
VINCENT LOVALLO, assistant editor
STEPHEN OSWALD, production manager
JAMIE LEE ROTANTE, editorial assistant/
proofreader
ELIZABETH BORGATTI, book design

# TABLE OF CONTENTS

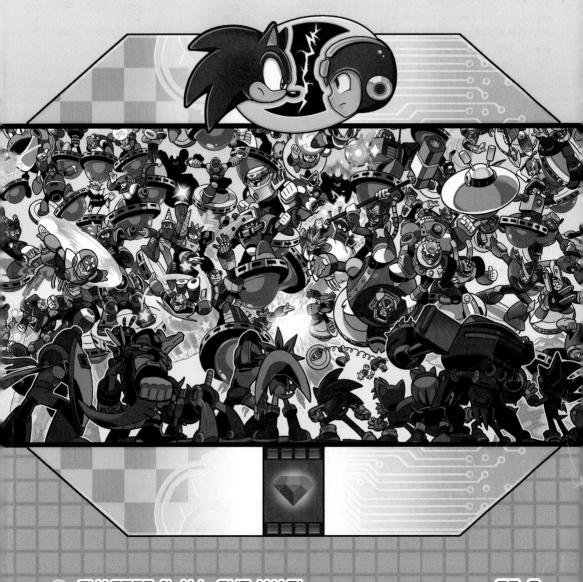

# PREVIOUSLY IN WORLDS COLLIDE

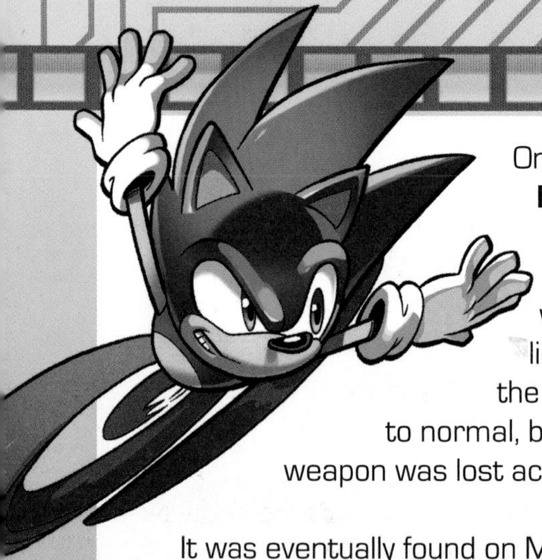

On Sonic's world, the mad scientist **Dr. Eggman** used the power of a **Chaos Emerald** to produce the **Genesis Wave** – a reality-warping energy event that he would use to reshape the world to his liking! Through the heroic efforts of Sonic the Hedgehog, Sonic's world was returned to normal, but the Chaos Emerald used to power the weapon was lost across time and space.

It was eventually found on Mega Man's world by **Dr. Wily**. The equally-mad scientist tapped into its energy and made contact with Dr. Eggman. The two mustachioed malcontents found they had much in common – their love for machines, a desire to conquer their worlds, and unending trouble from blue heroes!

Drs. Eggman and Wily joined forces and used the Chaos Emerald to create the **Skull Egg Zone** – a pocket dimension where time runs differently! Together they built an army of **badniks** and **Robot Masters** and housed them all in their flying fortress: the **Wily Egg!** Then they kidnapped Sonic's friends and turned them into the fearsome **Roboticized Masters!**

With all their forces gathered, the doctors sent the Roboticized Masters out into the two worlds to hunt down the remaining Chaos Emeralds. Their thievery eventually caught the attention of Sonic and Mega Man. The Blue Blur and Blue Bomber were tricked into fighting each other, and their battle raged across dimensions!

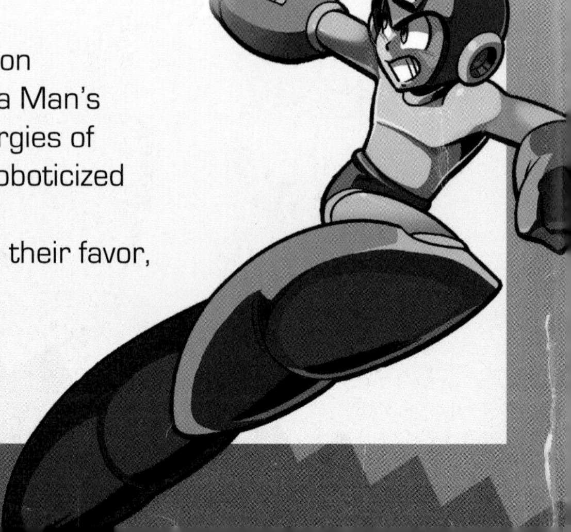

But our heroes figured out the deception and united. They discovered that Mega Man's **Charged Shot**, combined with the energies of Sonic's **Spin Dash**, transformed the Roboticized Masters back into their original forms.
Just as things seemed to be turning in their favor, the evil doctors had Mega Man's father – **Dr. Light** – kidnapped!

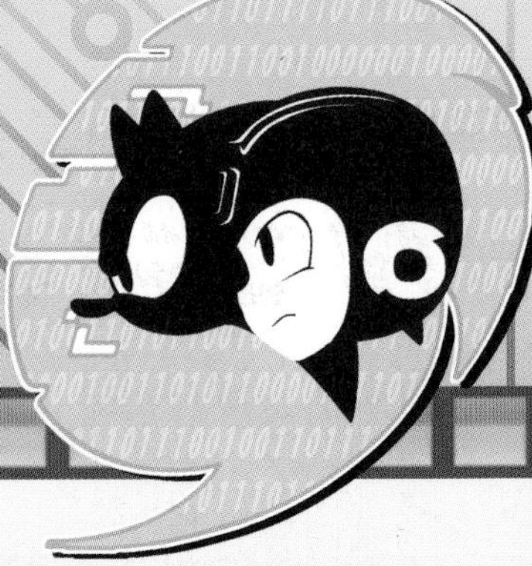

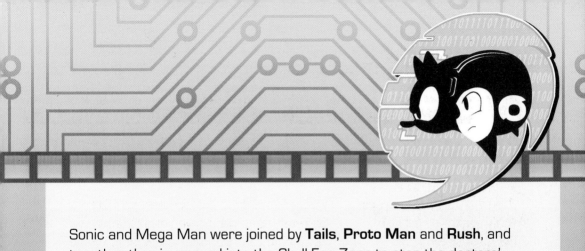

Sonic and Mega Man were joined by **Tails**, **Proto Man** and **Rush**, and together they journeyed into the Skull Egg Zone to stop the doctors' schemes and to rescue both Dr. Light and the rest of Sonic's friends! There they fought numerous foes, dodged dangerous traps, and tracked down the Roboticized Masters. With every victory, Sonic regained a friend and Mega Man gained a new special weapon.

Now the stage is set! Sonic and Mega Man stand shoulder-to-shoulder with a small army of allies behind them, ready to storm the Wily Egg, stop the mad mechanics, and save Dr. Light. But Drs. Eggman and Wily have ten times the forces, all seven Chaos Emeralds, and are preparing to unleash the power of the

**Super Genesis Wave**...

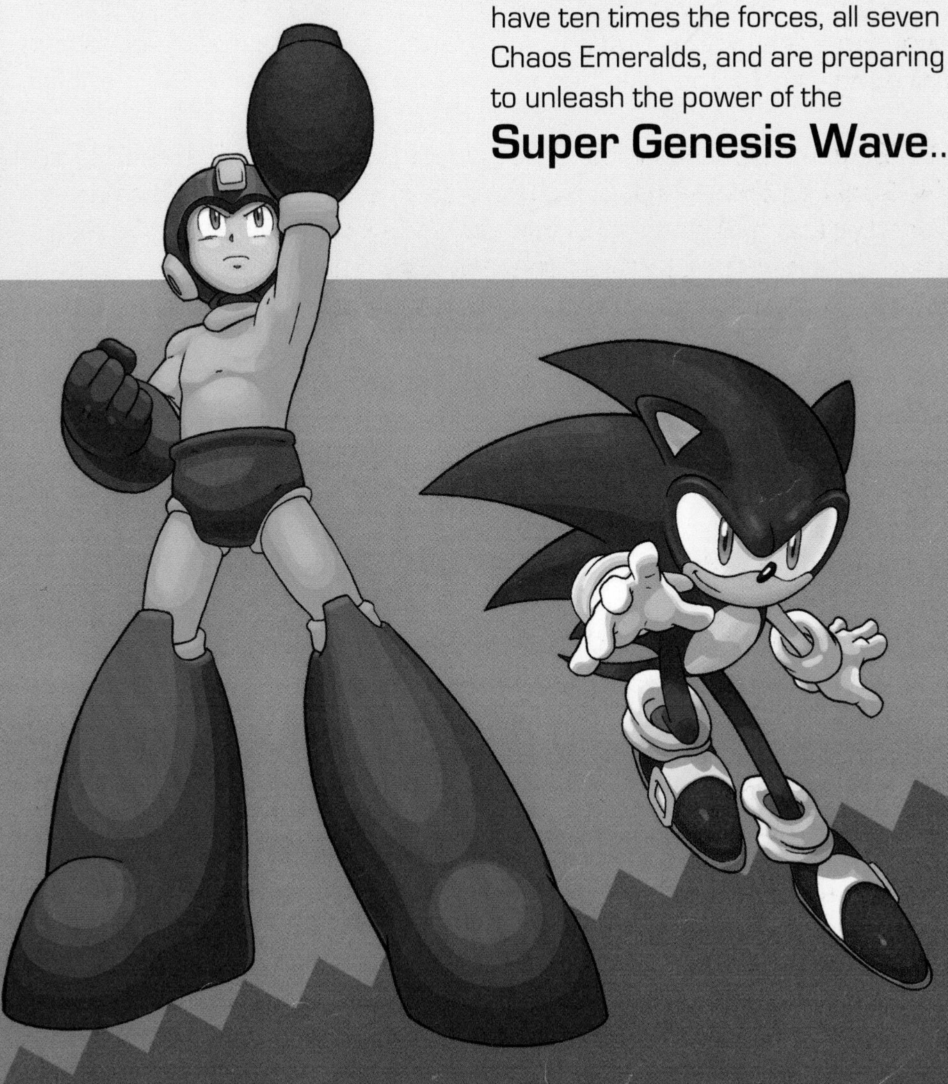

# CHAPTER 1

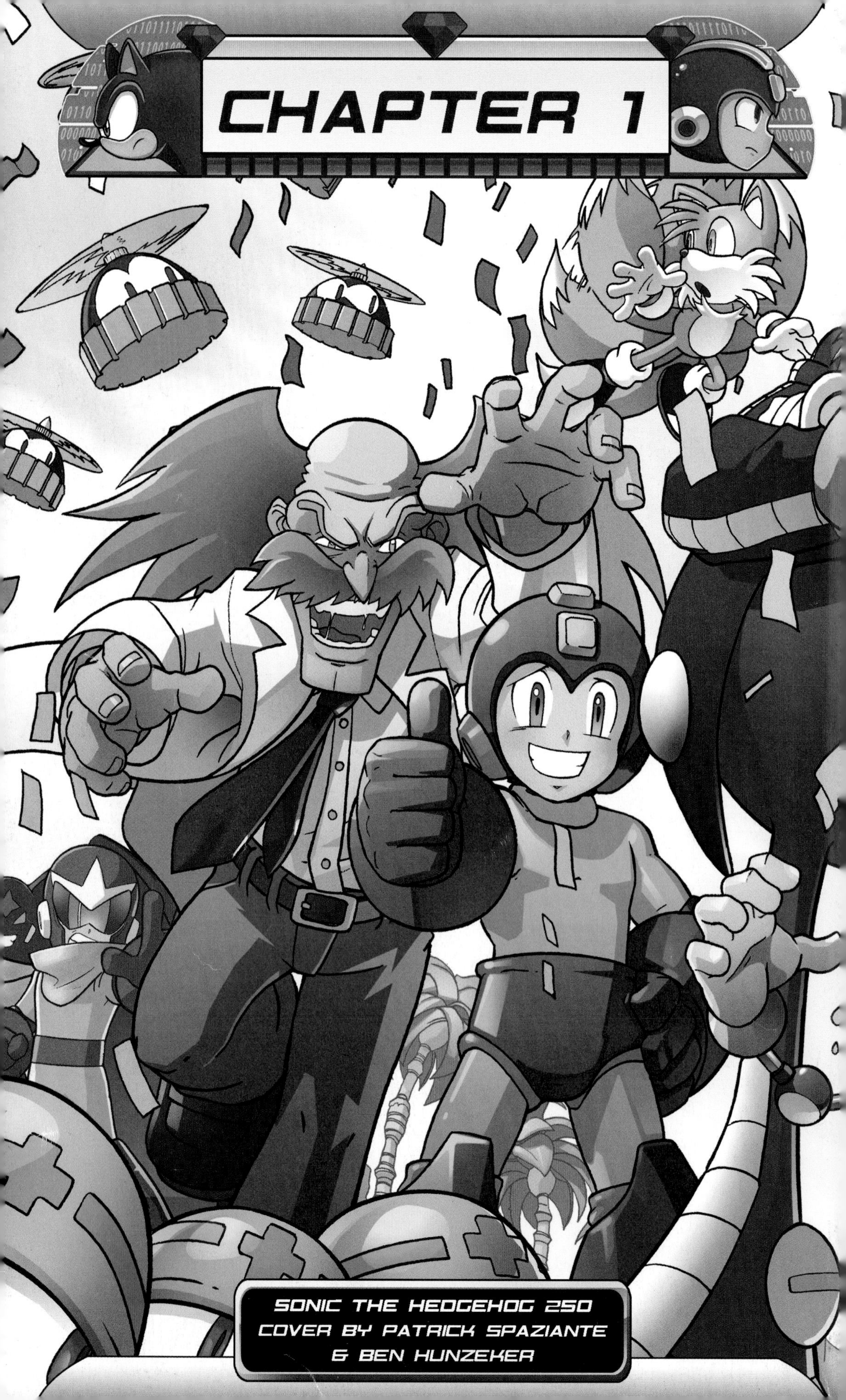

SONIC THE HEDGEHOG 250
COVER BY PATRICK SPAZIANTE
& BEN HUNZEKER

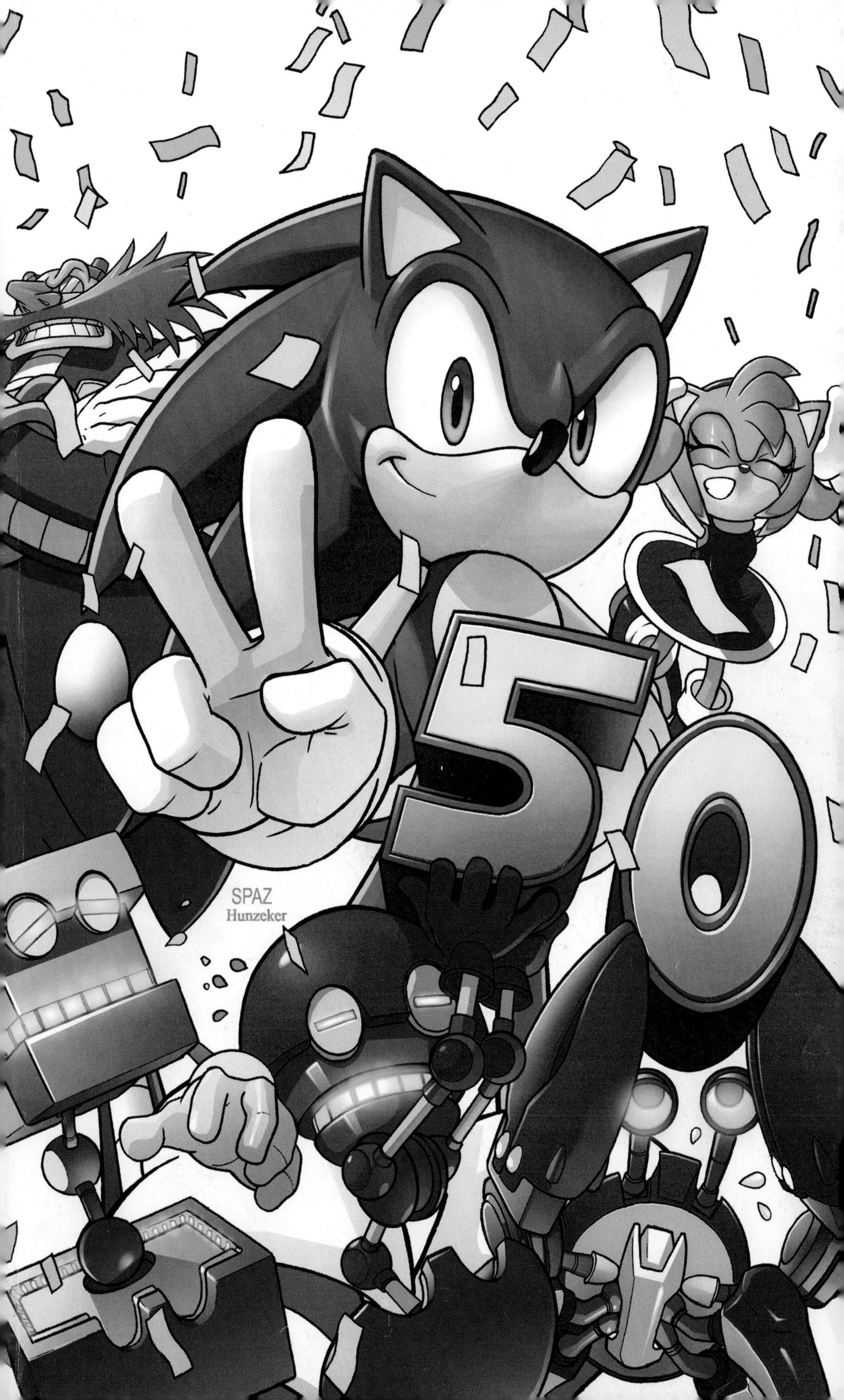
50
SPAZ
Hunzeker

# CHIBI VARIANT COVERS

BY RYAN JAMPOLE, GARY MARTIN & MATT HERMS

## SONIC THE HEDGEHOG 250

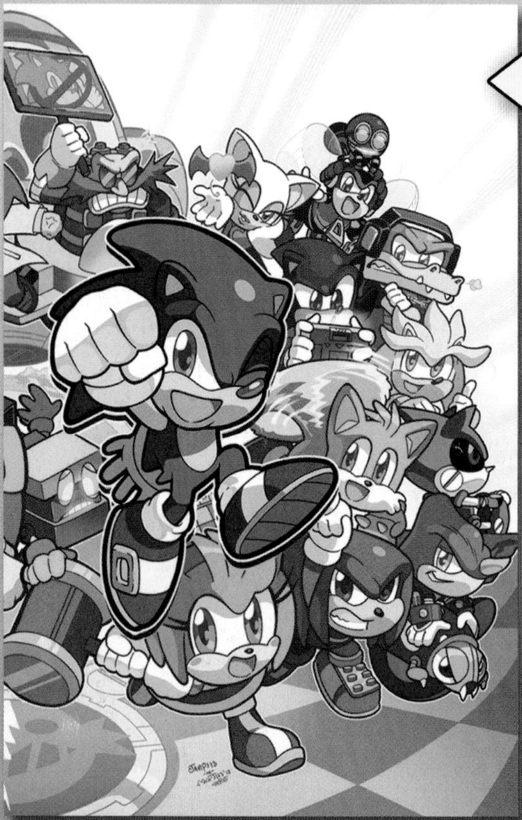

### TEAM SONIC

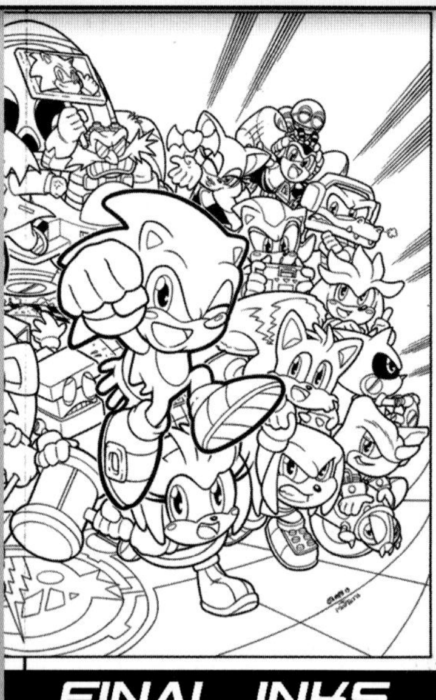

FINAL INKS

### TEAM MEGA MAN

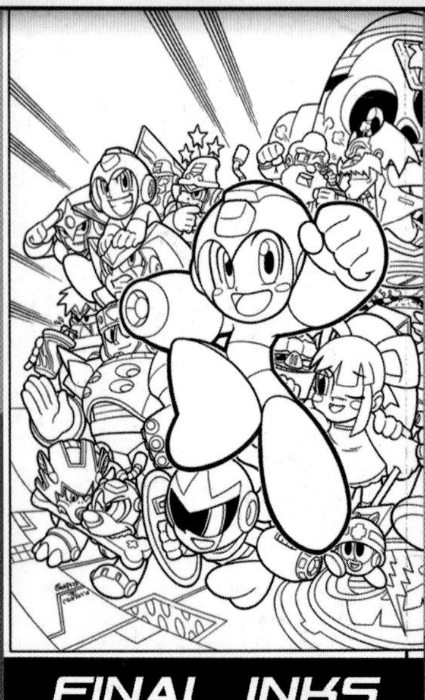

FINAL INKS

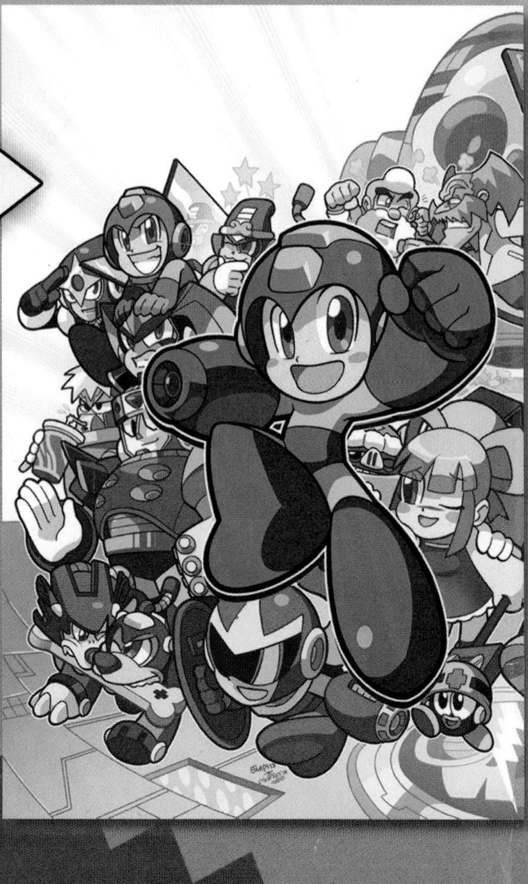

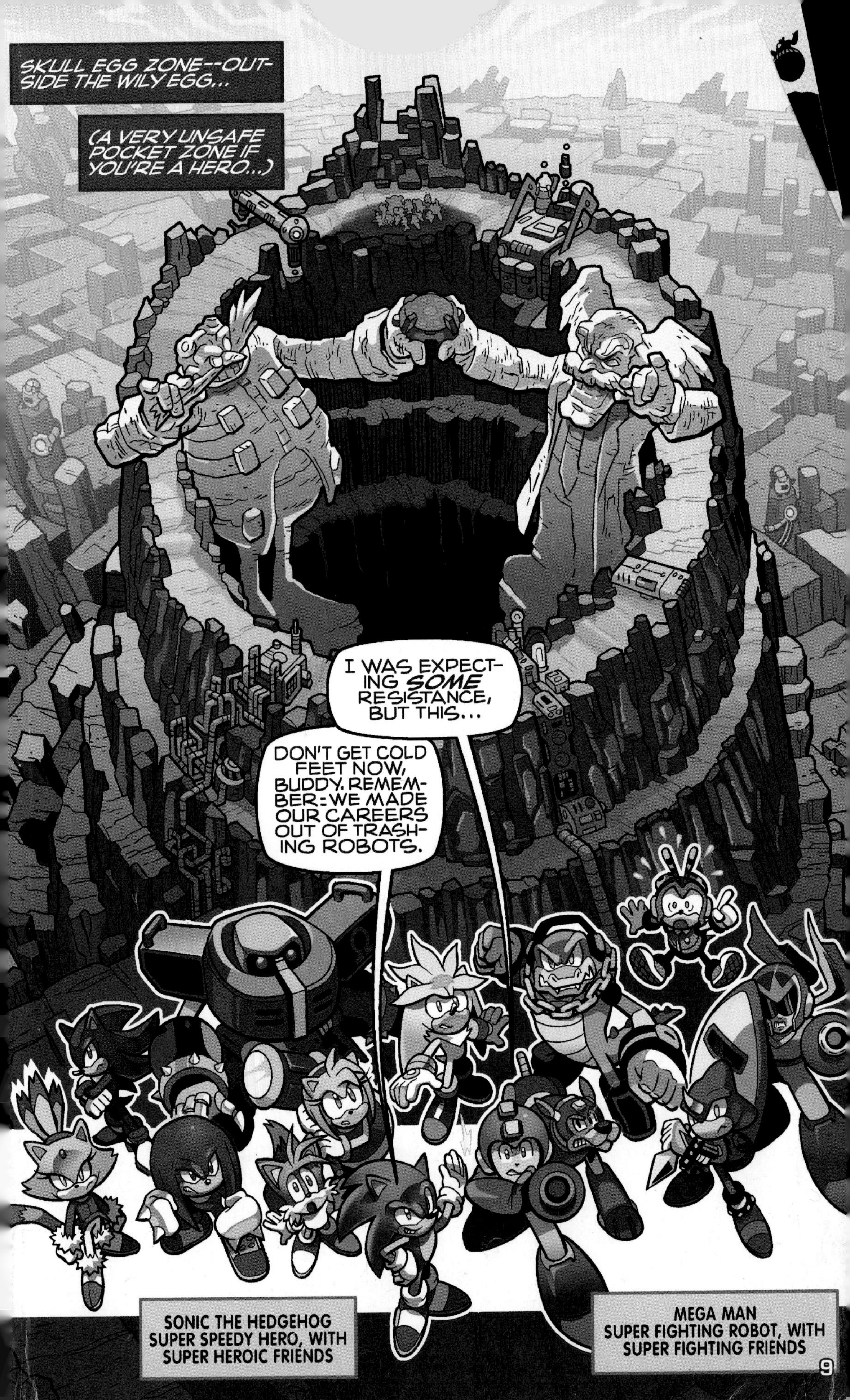

SKULL EGG ZONE--OUTSIDE THE WILY EGG...
(A VERY UNSAFE POCKET ZONE IF YOU'RE A HERO...)
I WAS EXPECTING SOME RESISTANCE, BUT THIS...
DON'T GET COLD FEET NOW, BUDDY. REMEMBER: WE MADE OUR CAREERS OUT OF TRASHING ROBOTS.
SONIC THE HEDGEHOG SUPER SPEEDY HERO, WITH SUPER HEROIC FRIENDS
MEGA MAN SUPER FIGHTING ROBOT, WITH SUPER FIGHTING FRIENDS

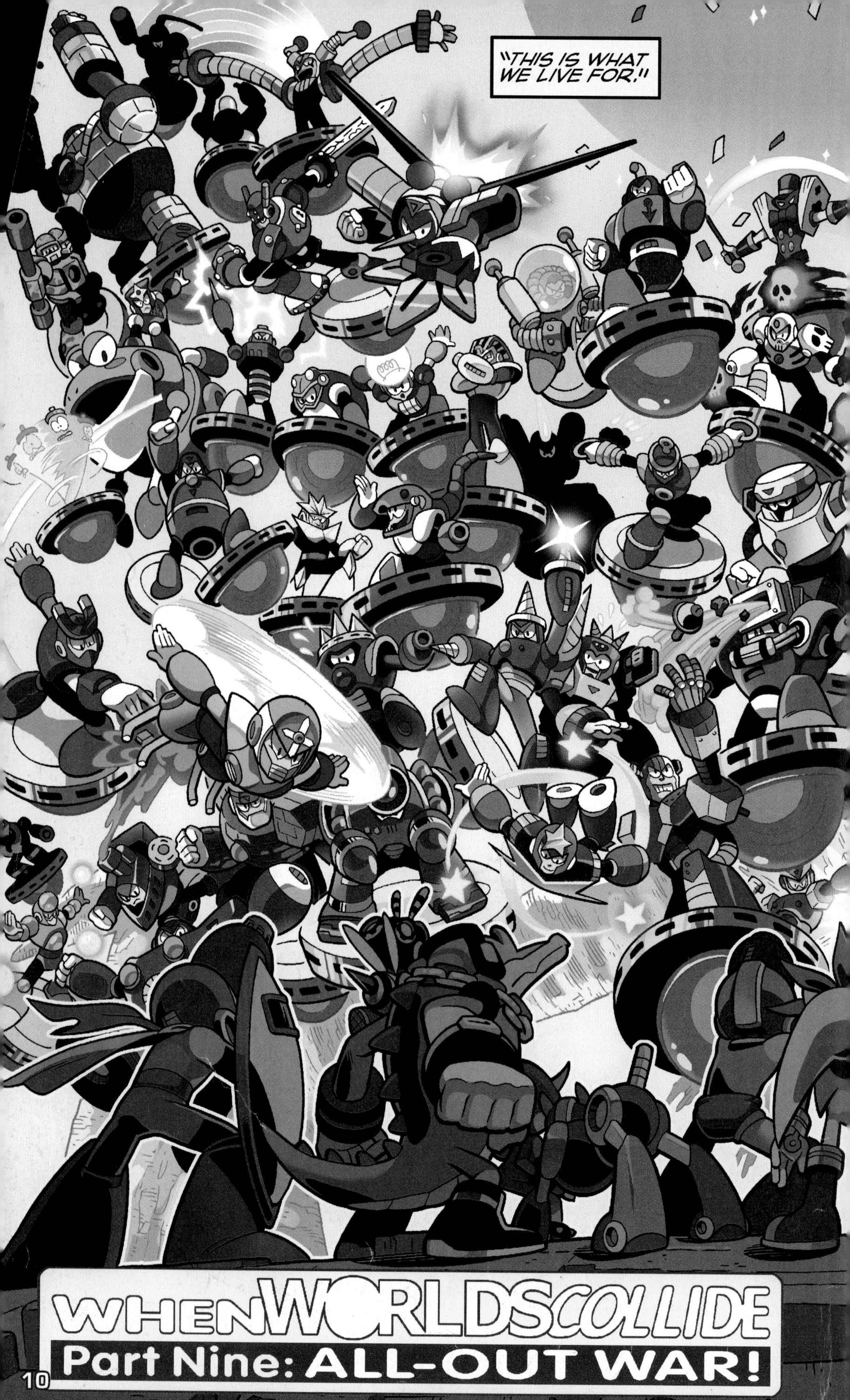

"THIS IS WHAT WE LIVE FOR."
WHEN WORLDS COLLIDE
Part Nine: ALL-OUT WAR!

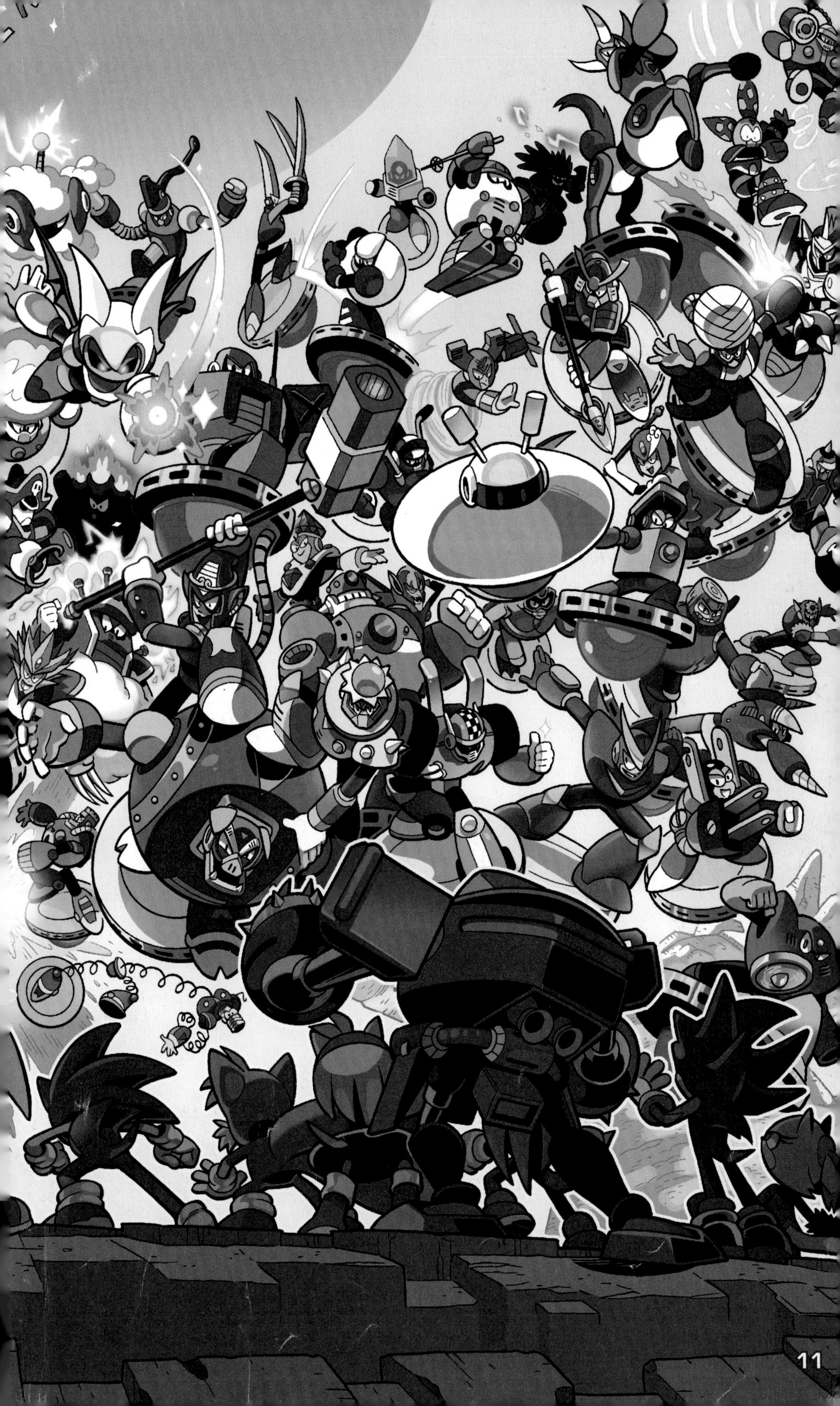

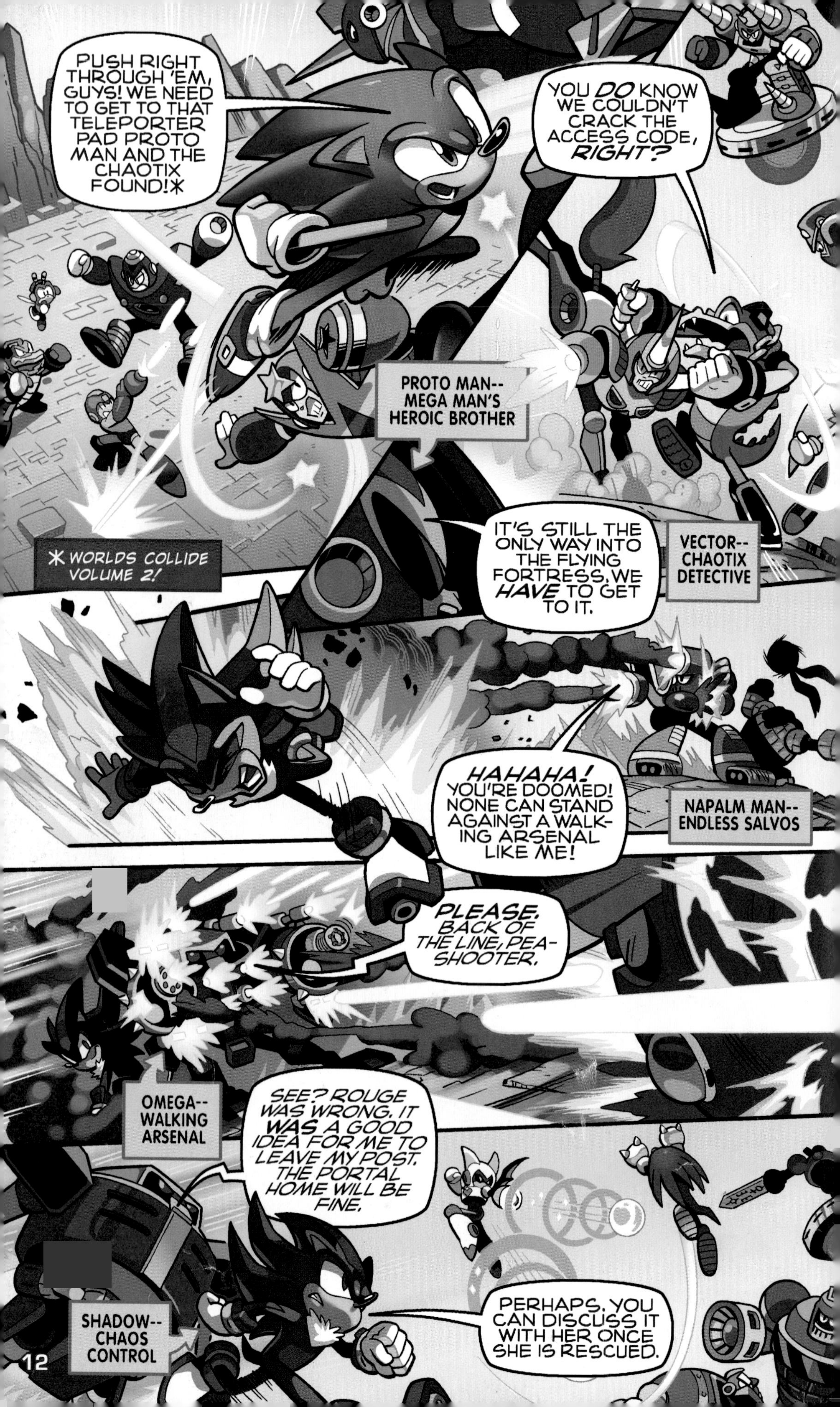
PUSH RIGHT THROUGH 'EM, GUYS! WE NEED TO GET TO THAT TELEPORTER PAD PROTO MAN AND THE CHAOTIX FOUND!*
YOU *DO* KNOW WE COULDN'T CRACK THE ACCESS CODE, *RIGHT?*
PROTO MAN--MEGA MAN'S HEROIC BROTHER
* *WORLDS COLLIDE VOLUME 2!*
IT'S STILL THE ONLY WAY INTO THE FLYING FORTRESS, WE *HAVE* TO GET TO IT.
VECTOR--CHAOTIX DETECTIVE
*HAHAHA!* YOU'RE DOOMED! NONE CAN STAND AGAINST A WALKING ARSENAL LIKE ME!
NAPALM MAN--ENDLESS SALVOS
*PLEASE.* *BACK OF THE LINE, PEA-SHOOTER.*
OMEGA--WALKING ARSENAL
*SEE? ROUGE WAS WRONG. IT* ***WAS*** *A GOOD IDEA FOR ME TO LEAVE MY POST. THE PORTAL HOME WILL BE FINE.*
SHADOW--CHAOS CONTROL
PERHAPS. YOU CAN DISCUSS IT WITH HER ONCE SHE IS RESCUED.

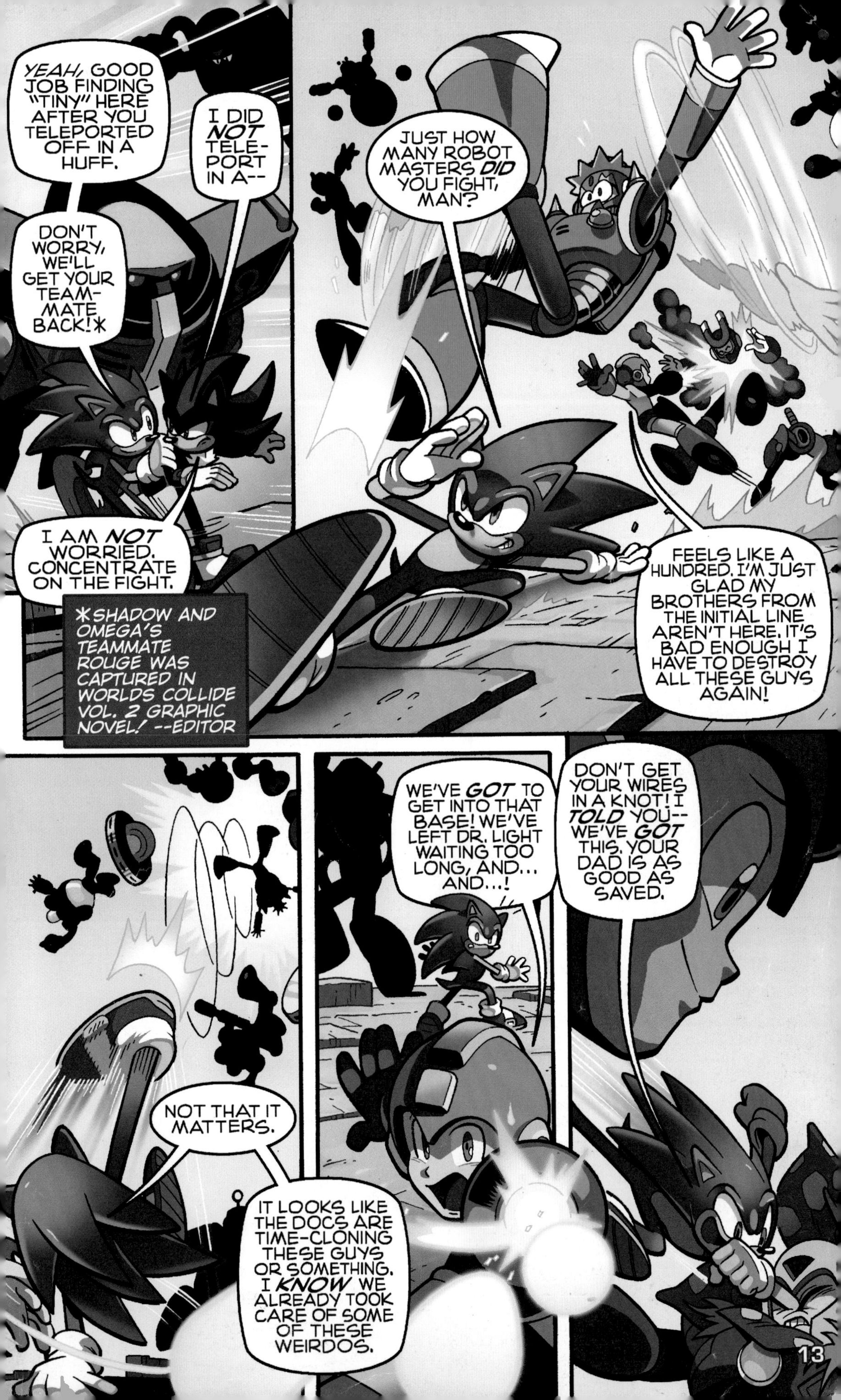
YEAH, GOOD JOB FINDING "TINY" HERE AFTER YOU TELEPORTED OFF IN A HUFF.
I DID NOT TELE-PORT IN A--
DON'T WORRY, WE'LL GET YOUR TEAM-MATE BACK!*
I AM NOT WORRIED. CONCENTRATE ON THE FIGHT.
*SHADOW AND OMEGA'S TEAMMATE ROUGE WAS CAPTURED IN WORLDS COLLIDE VOL. 2 GRAPHIC NOVEL! --EDITOR
JUST HOW MANY ROBOT MASTERS DID YOU FIGHT, MAN?
FEELS LIKE A HUNDRED. I'M JUST GLAD MY BROTHERS FROM THE INITIAL LINE AREN'T HERE. IT'S BAD ENOUGH I HAVE TO DESTROY ALL THESE GUYS AGAIN!
NOT THAT IT MATTERS.
IT LOOKS LIKE THE DOCS ARE TIME-CLONING THESE GUYS OR SOMETHING. I KNOW WE ALREADY TOOK CARE OF SOME OF THESE WEIRDOS.
WE'VE GOT TO GET INTO THAT BASE! WE'VE LEFT DR. LIGHT WAITING TOO LONG, AND... AND...!
DON'T GET YOUR WIRES IN A KNOT! I TOLD YOU-- WE'VE GOT THIS. YOUR DAD IS AS GOOD AS SAVED.

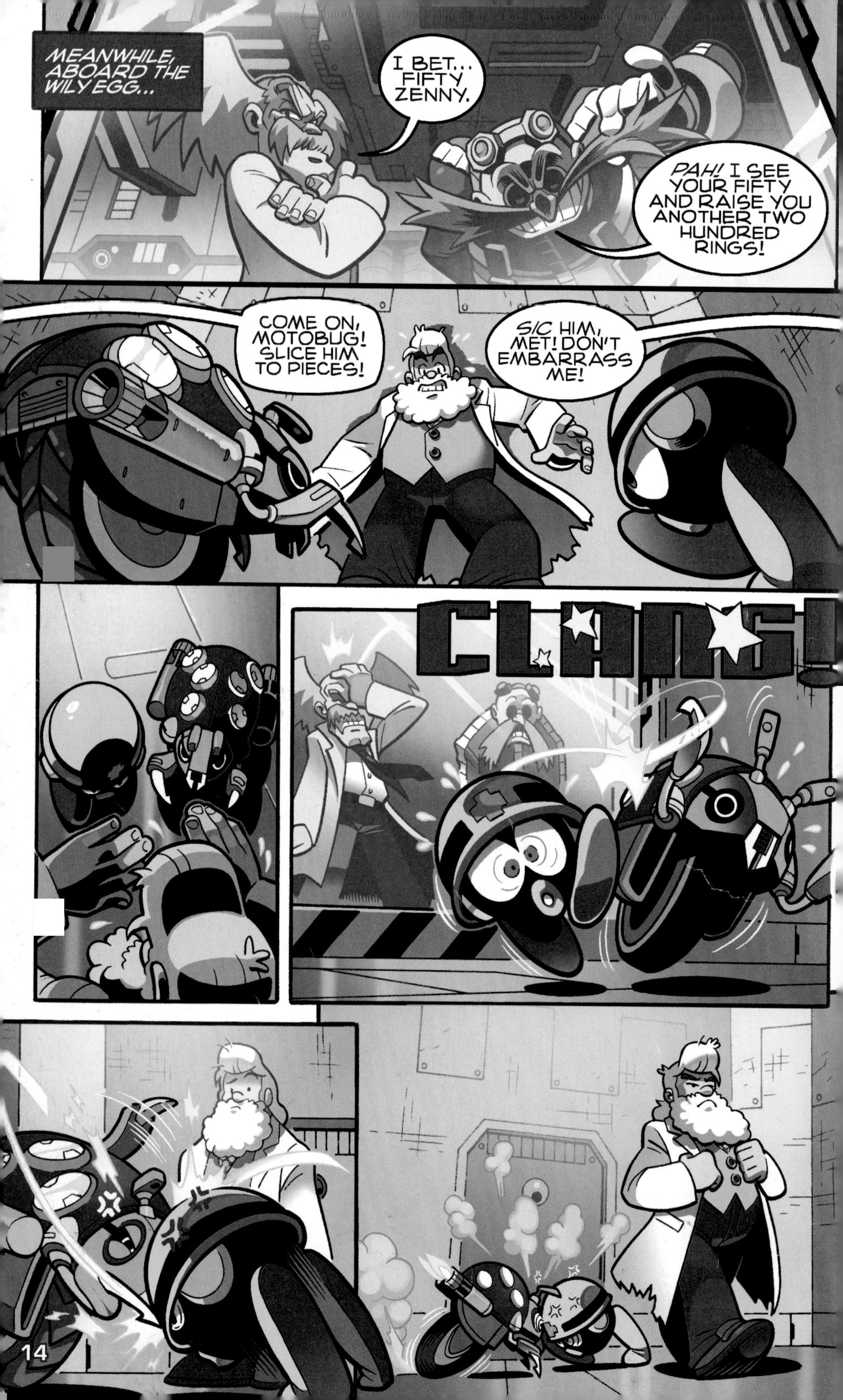
MEANWHILE, ABOARD THE WILY EGG...
I BET... FIFTY ZENNY.
PAH! I SEE YOUR FIFTY AND RAISE YOU ANOTHER TWO HUNDRED RINGS!
COME ON, MOTOBUG! SLICE HIM TO PIECES!
SIC HIM, MET! DON'T EMBARRASS ME!
CLANG!

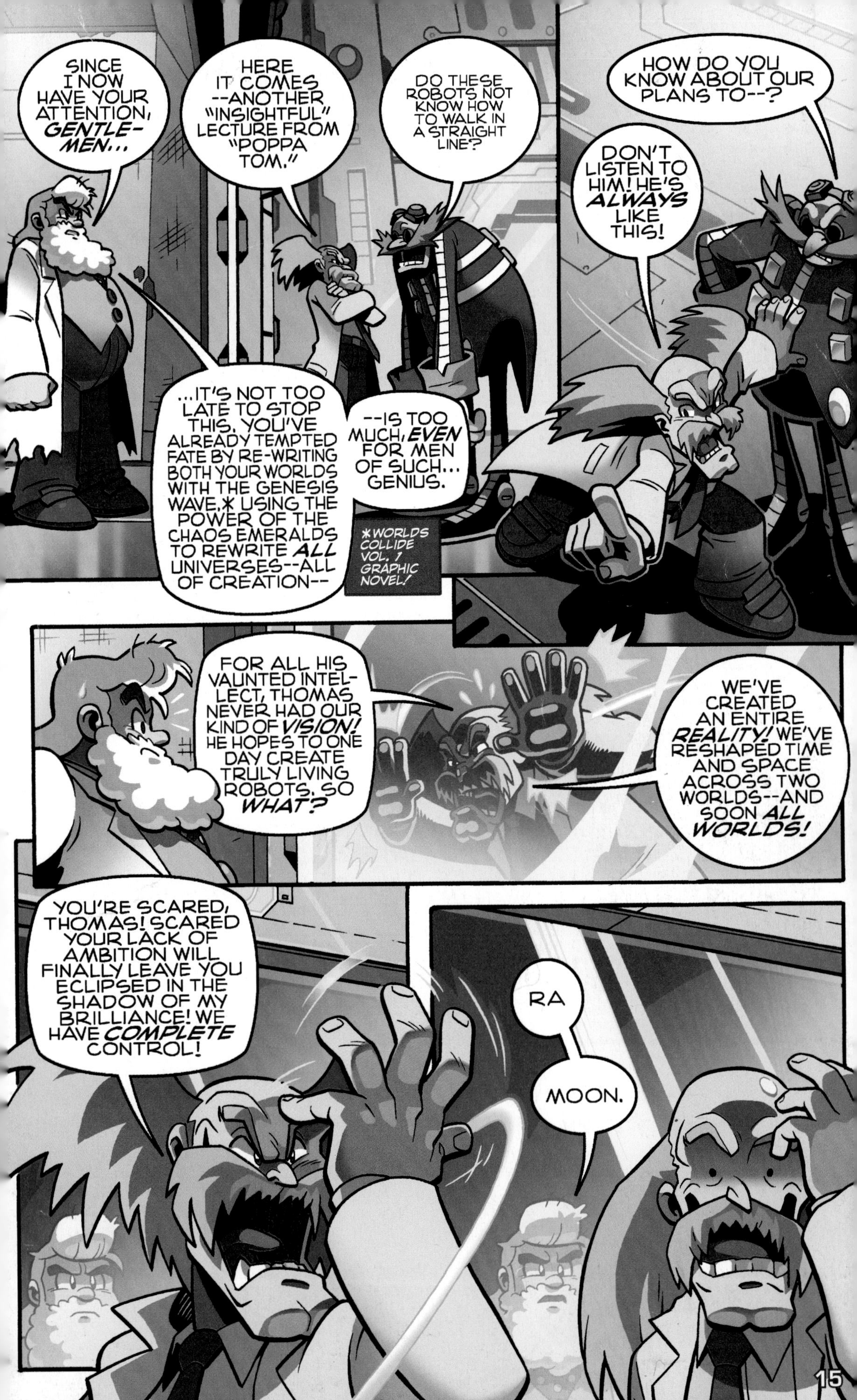

SINCE I NOW HAVE YOUR ATTENTION, GENTLE-MEN...
HERE IT COMES --ANOTHER "INSIGHTFUL" LECTURE FROM "POPPA TOM."
DO THESE ROBOTS NOT KNOW HOW TO WALK IN A STRAIGHT LINE?
...IT'S NOT TOO LATE TO STOP THIS. YOU'VE ALREADY TEMPTED FATE BY RE-WRITING BOTH YOUR WORLDS WITH THE GENESIS WAVE.* USING THE POWER OF THE CHAOS EMERALDS TO REWRITE ALL UNIVERSES--ALL OF CREATION--
--IS TOO MUCH, EVEN FOR MEN OF SUCH... GENIUS.
*WORLDS COLLIDE VOL. 1 GRAPHIC NOVEL!
HOW DO YOU KNOW ABOUT OUR PLANS TO--?
DON'T LISTEN TO HIM! HE'S ALWAYS LIKE THIS!
FOR ALL HIS VAUNTED INTEL-LECT, THOMAS NEVER HAD OUR KIND OF VISION! HE HOPES TO ONE DAY CREATE TRULY LIVING ROBOTS. SO WHAT?
WE'VE CREATED AN ENTIRE REALITY! WE'VE RESHAPED TIME AND SPACE ACROSS TWO WORLDS--AND SOON ALL WORLDS!
YOU'RE SCARED, THOMAS! SCARED YOUR LACK OF AMBITION WILL FINALLY LEAVE YOU ECLIPSED IN THE SHADOW OF MY BRILLIANCE! WE HAVE COMPLETE CONTROL!
RA
MOON.

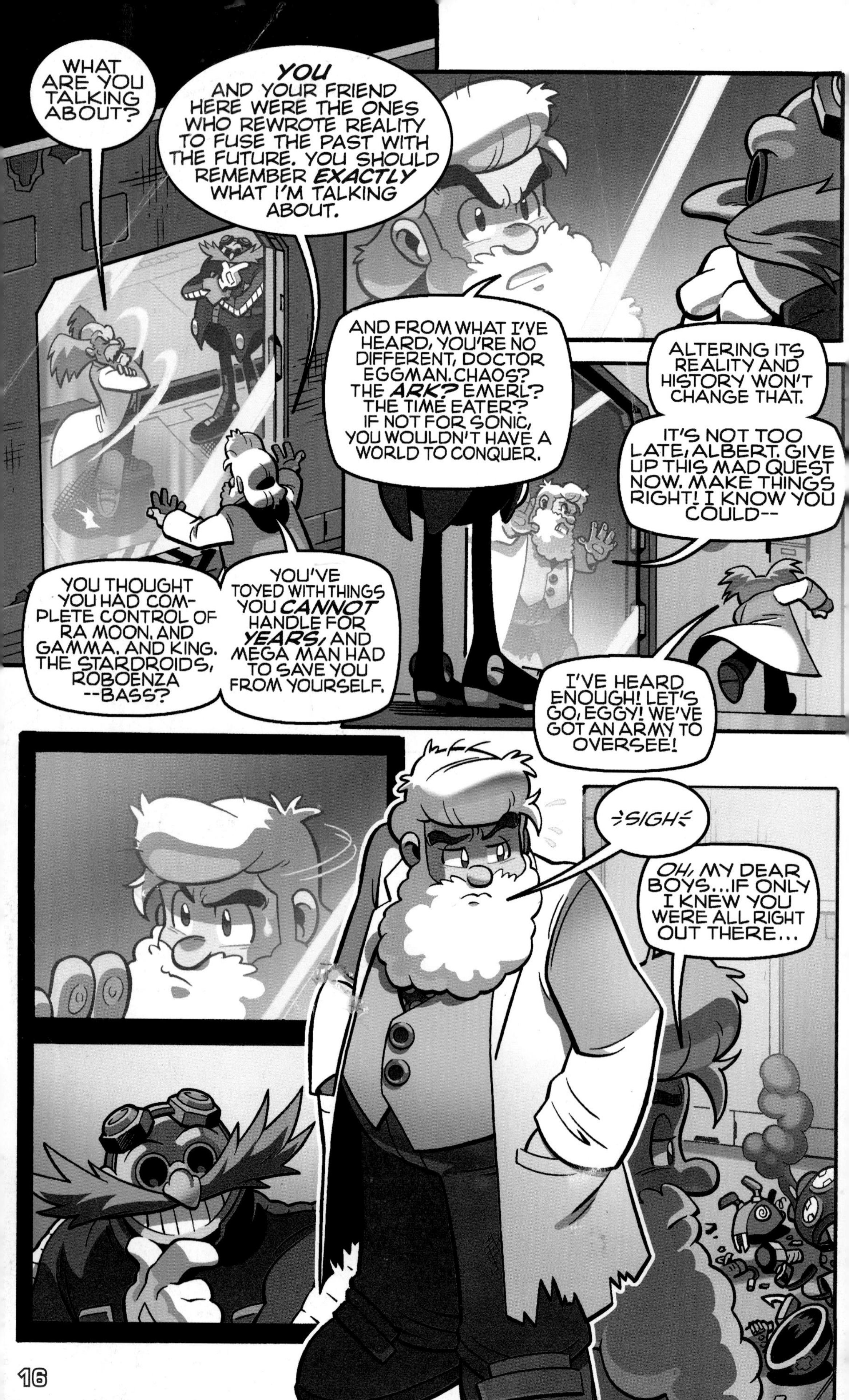

WHAT ARE YOU TALKING ABOUT?
YOU AND YOUR FRIEND HERE WERE THE ONES WHO REWROTE REALITY TO FUSE THE PAST WITH THE FUTURE. YOU SHOULD REMEMBER EXACTLY WHAT I'M TALKING ABOUT.
AND FROM WHAT I'VE HEARD, YOU'RE NO DIFFERENT, DOCTOR EGGMAN. CHAOS? THE ARK? EMERL? THE TIME EATER? IF NOT FOR SONIC, YOU WOULDN'T HAVE A WORLD TO CONQUER.
YOU THOUGHT YOU HAD COM-PLETE CONTROL OF RA MOON. AND GAMMA. AND KING. THE STARDROIDS, ROBOENZA --BASS?
YOU'VE TOYED WITH THINGS YOU CANNOT HANDLE FOR YEARS, AND MEGA MAN HAD TO SAVE YOU FROM YOURSELF.
ALTERING ITS REALITY AND HISTORY WON'T CHANGE THAT.
IT'S NOT TOO LATE, ALBERT. GIVE UP THIS MAD QUEST NOW. MAKE THINGS RIGHT! I KNOW YOU COULD--
I'VE HEARD ENOUGH! LET'S GO, EGGY! WE'VE GOT AN ARMY TO OVERSEE!
SIGH
OH, MY DEAR BOYS...IF ONLY I KNEW YOU WERE ALL RIGHT OUT THERE...

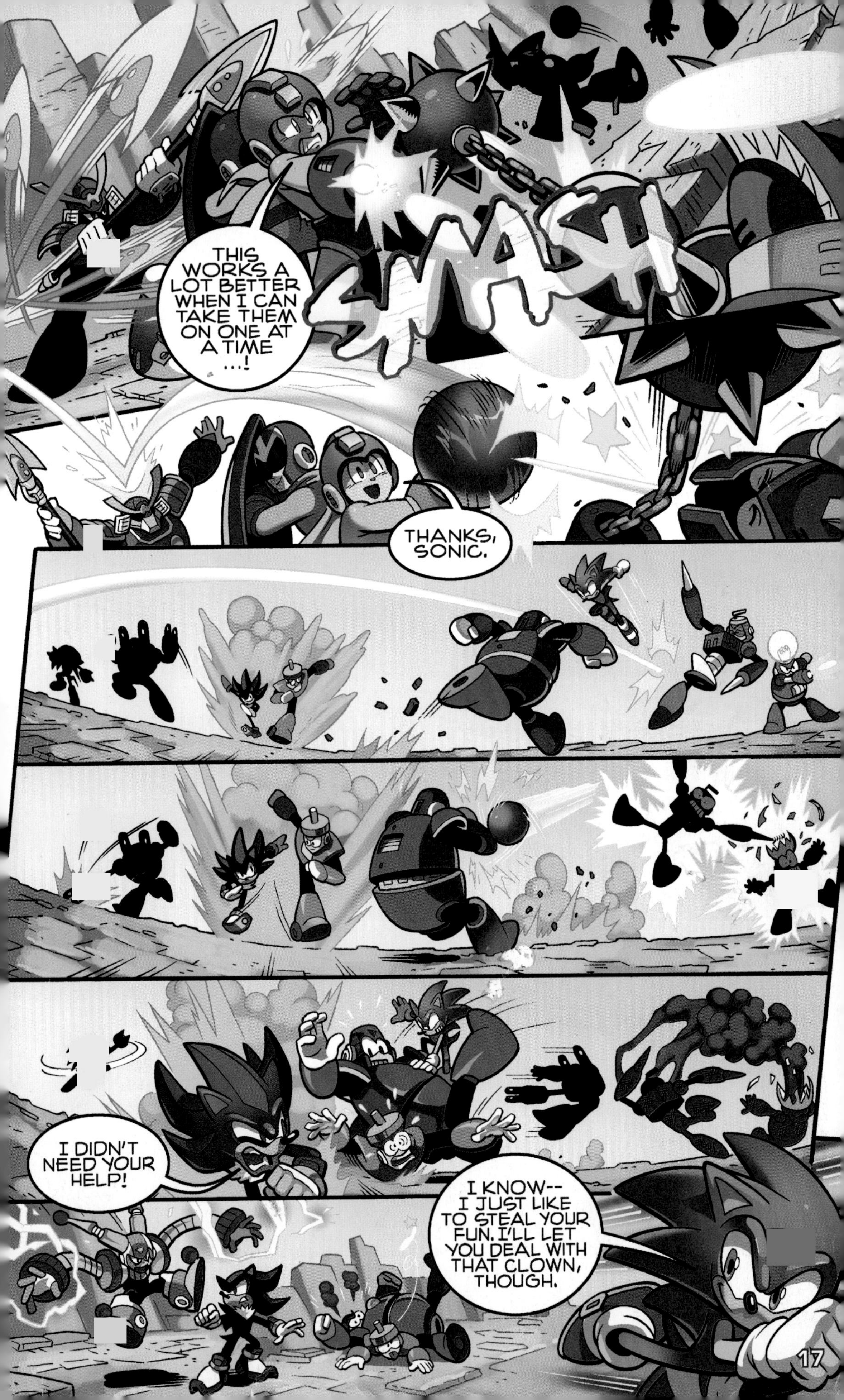
THIS WORKS A LOT BETTER WHEN I CAN TAKE THEM ON ONE AT A TIME ...!
SMASH
THANKS, SONIC.
I DIDN'T NEED YOUR HELP!
I KNOW-- I JUST LIKE TO STEAL YOUR FUN. I'LL LET YOU DEAL WITH THAT CLOWN, THOUGH.

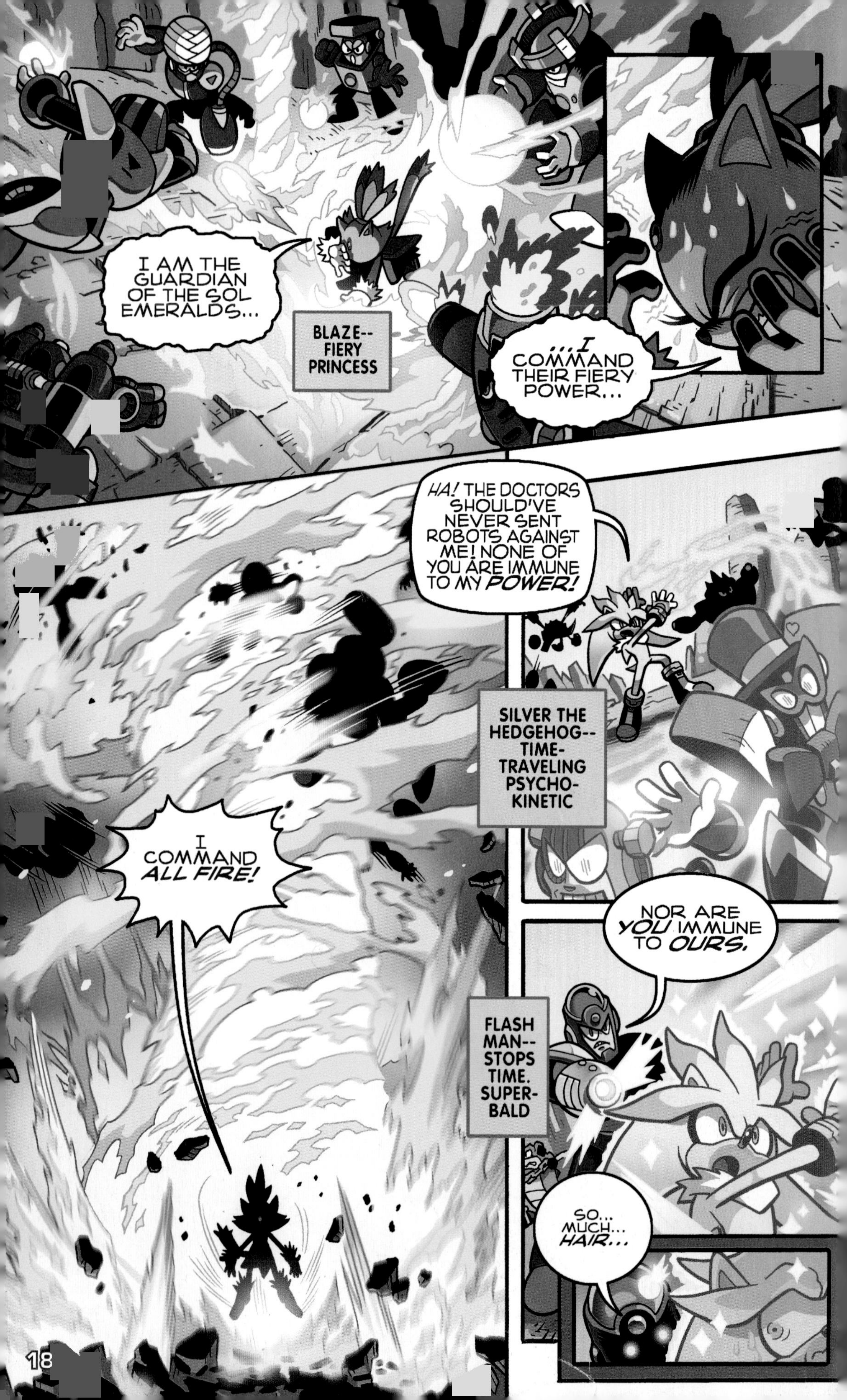

I AM THE GUARDIAN OF THE SOL EMERALDS...
BLAZE-- FIERY PRINCESS
...I COMMAND THEIR FIERY POWER...
I COMMAND *ALL FIRE!*
*HA!* THE DOCTORS SHOULD'VE NEVER SENT ROBOTS AGAINST ME! NONE OF YOU ARE IMMUNE TO MY *POWER!*
SILVER THE HEDGEHOG-- TIME-TRAVELING PSYCHO-KINETIC
NOR ARE *YOU* IMMUNE TO *OURS.*
FLASH MAN-- STOPS TIME. SUPER-BALD
SO... MUCH... *HAIR...*

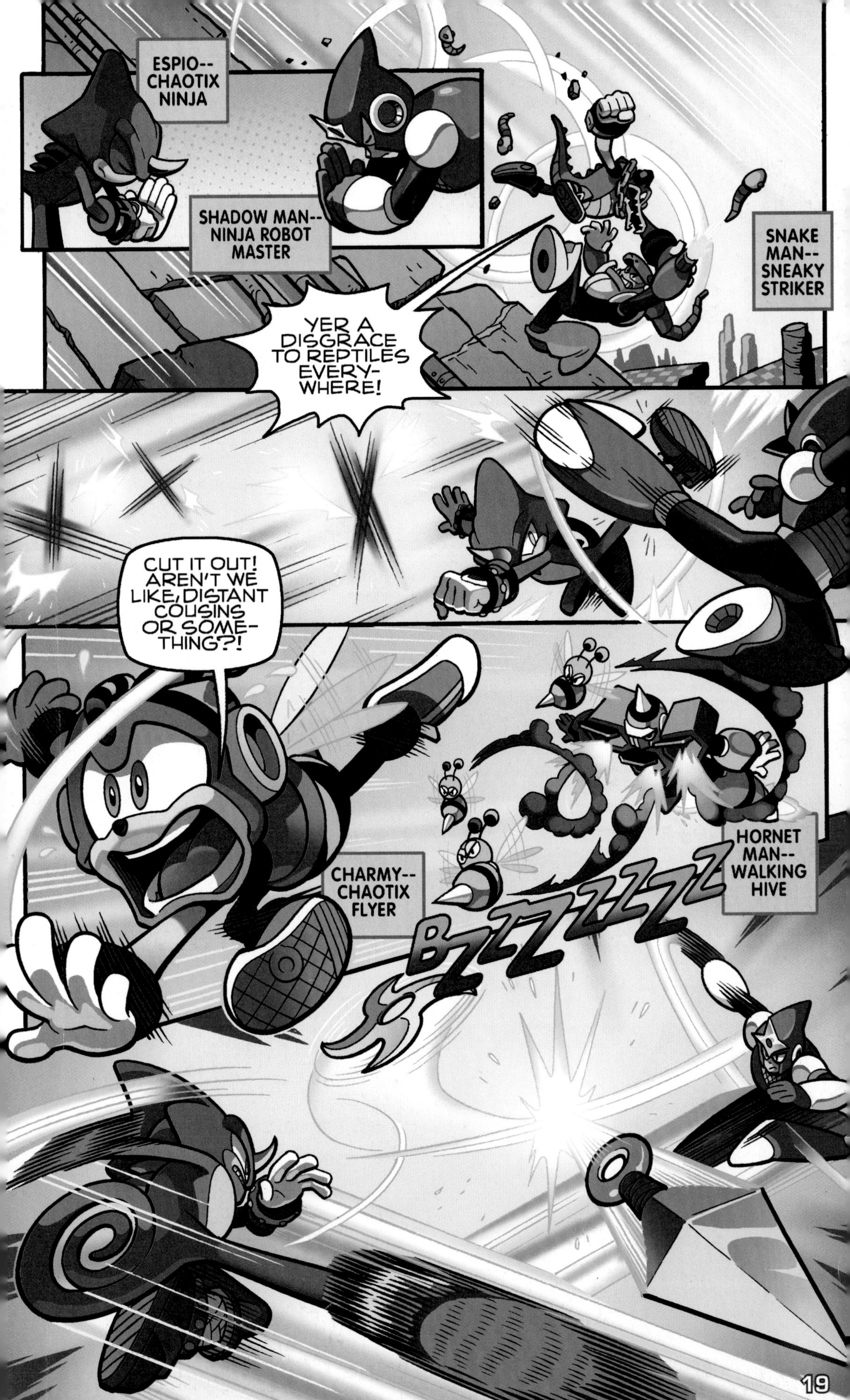
ESPIO--
CHAOTIX
NINJA
SHADOW MAN--
NINJA ROBOT
MASTER
SNAKE
MAN--
SNEAKY
STRIKER
YER A
DISGRACE
TO REPTILES
EVERY-
WHERE!
CUT IT OUT!
AREN'T WE
LIKE, DISTANT
COUSINS
OR SOME-
THING?!
CHARMY--
CHAOTIX
FLYER
HORNET
MAN--
WALKING
HIVE
BZZZZZZZ

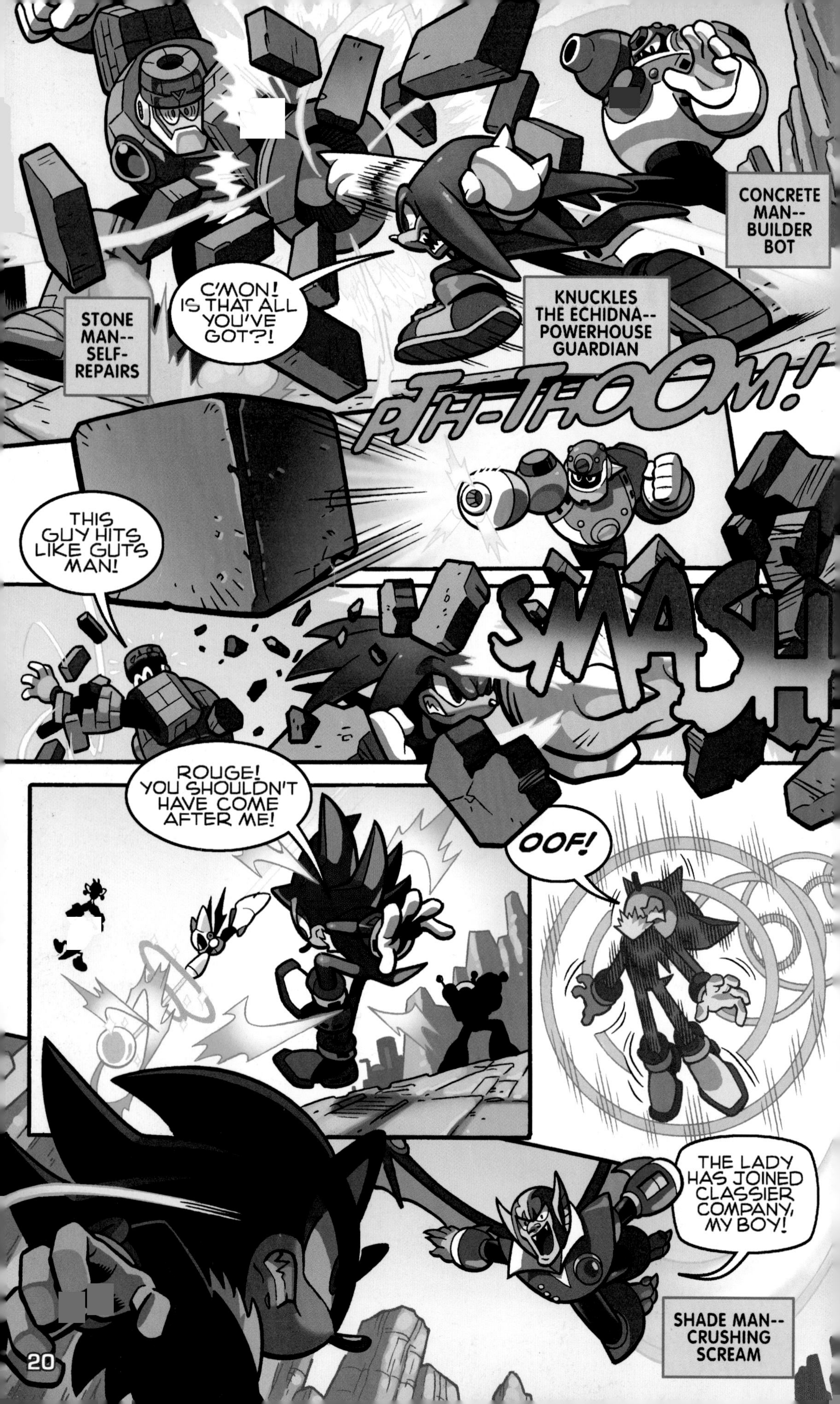
STONE MAN-- SELF-REPAIRS
C'MON! IS THAT ALL YOU'VE GOT?!
KNUCKLES THE ECHIDNA-- POWERHOUSE GUARDIAN
CONCRETE MAN-- BUILDER BOT
PTH-THOOM!
THIS GUY HITS LIKE GUTS MAN!
SMASH
ROUGE! YOU SHOULDN'T HAVE COME AFTER ME!
OOF!
THE LADY HAS JOINED CLASSIER COMPANY, MY BOY!
SHADE MAN-- CRUSHING SCREAM

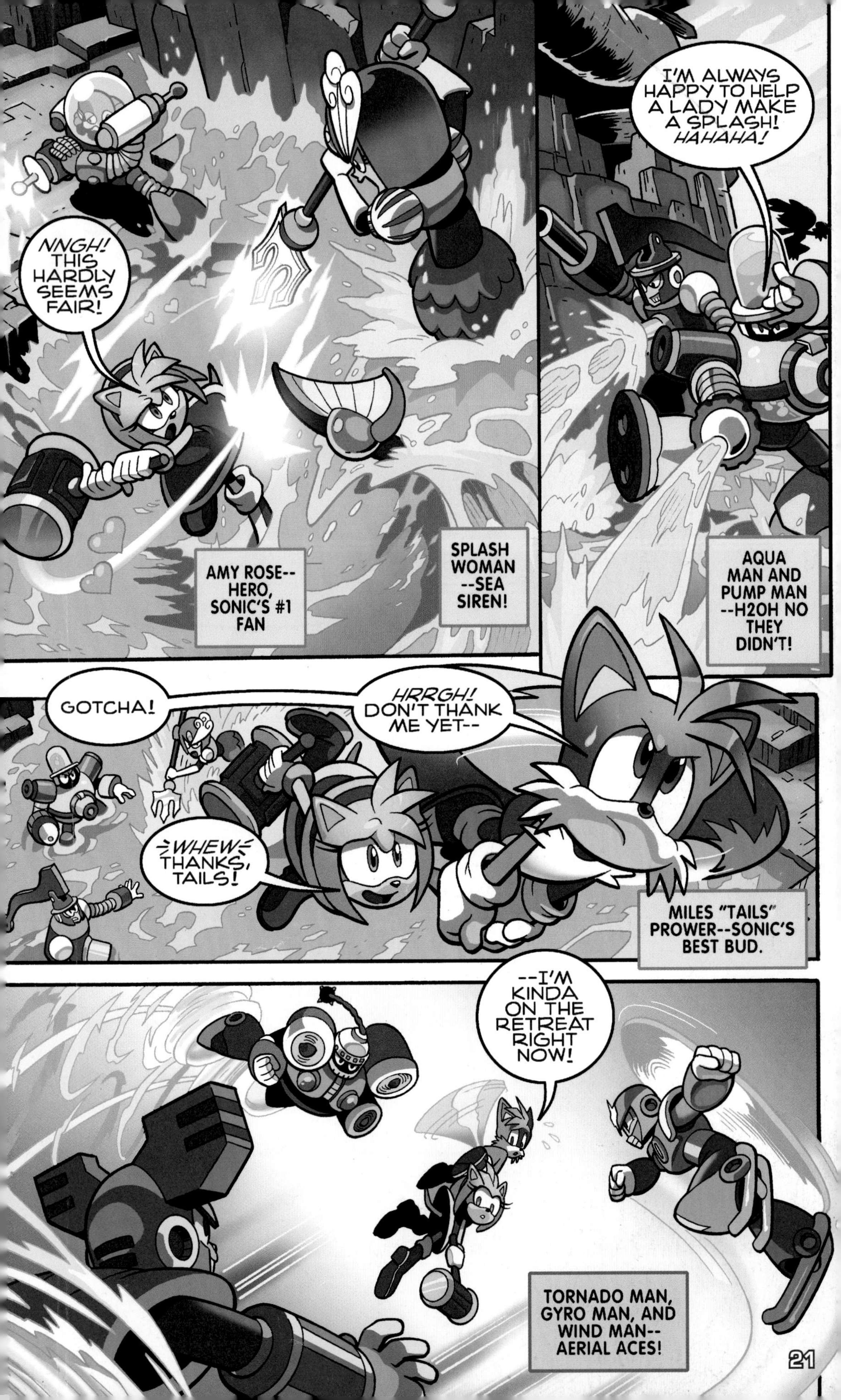
NNGH! THIS HARDLY SEEMS FAIR!
AMY ROSE--HERO, SONIC'S #1 FAN
SPLASH WOMAN--SEA SIREN!
I'M ALWAYS HAPPY TO HELP A LADY MAKE A SPLASH! HAHAHA!
AQUA MAN AND PUMP MAN--H2OH NO THEY DIDN'T!
GOTCHA!
HRRGH! DON'T THANK ME YET--
WHEW THANKS, TAILS!
MILES "TAILS" PROWER--SONIC'S BEST BUD.
--I'M KINDA ON THE RETREAT RIGHT NOW!
TORNADO MAN, GYRO MAN, AND WIND MAN--AERIAL ACES!

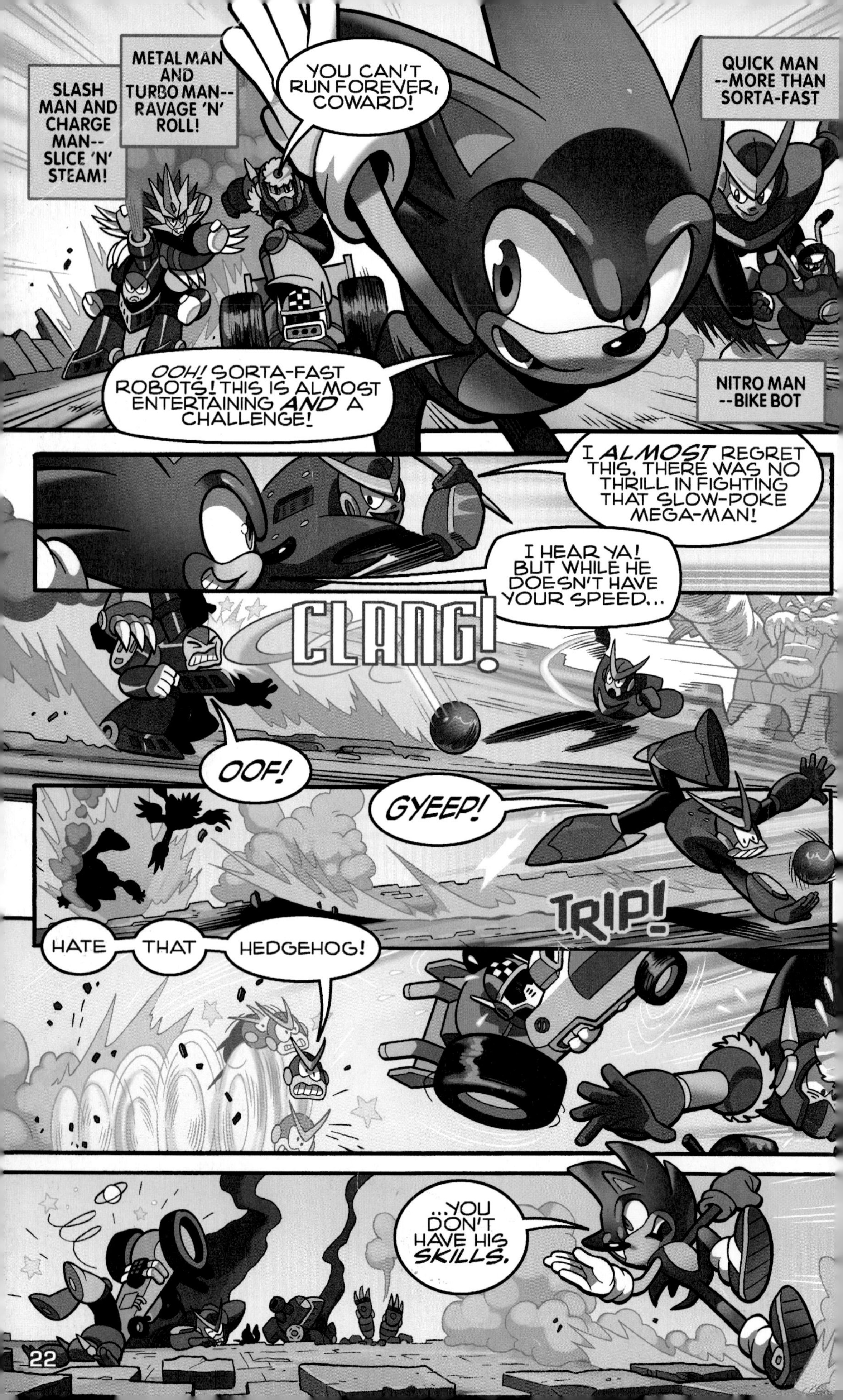

SLASH MAN AND CHARGE MAN-- SLICE 'N' STEAM!
METAL MAN AND TURBO MAN-- RAVAGE 'N' ROLL!
YOU CAN'T RUN FOREVER, COWARD!
QUICK MAN --MORE THAN SORTA-FAST
OOH! SORTA-FAST ROBOTS! THIS IS ALMOST ENTERTAINING AND A CHALLENGE!
NITRO MAN --BIKE BOT
I ALMOST REGRET THIS. THERE WAS NO THRILL IN FIGHTING THAT SLOW-POKE MEGA-MAN!
I HEAR YA! BUT WHILE HE DOESN'T HAVE YOUR SPEED...
CLANG!
OOF!
GYEEP!
TRIP!
HATE
THAT
HEDGEHOG!
...YOU DON'T HAVE HIS SKILLS.

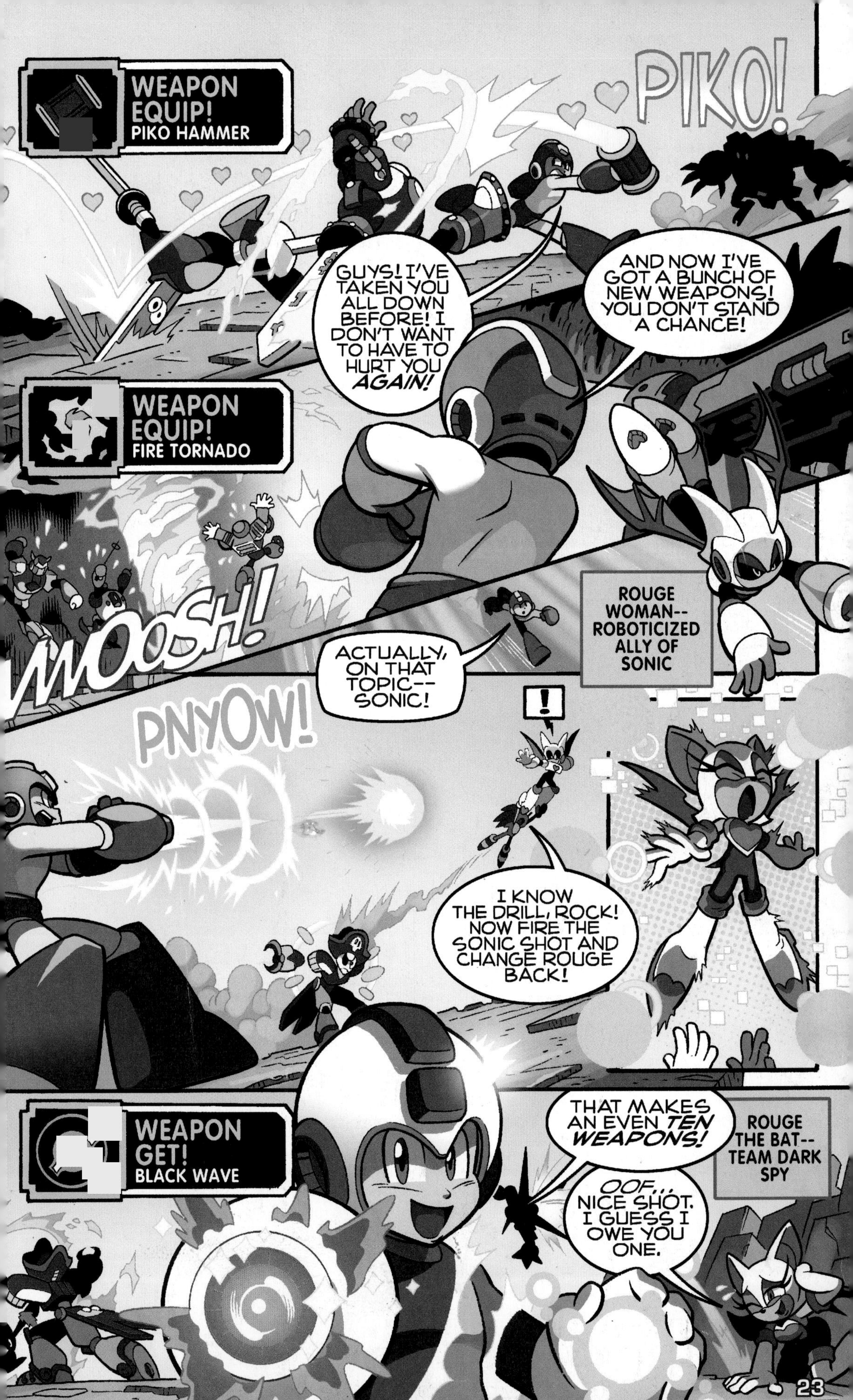
WEAPON EQUIP! PIKO HAMMER
PIKO!
GUYS! I'VE TAKEN YOU ALL DOWN BEFORE! I DON'T WANT TO HAVE TO HURT YOU *AGAIN!*
AND NOW I'VE GOT A BUNCH OF NEW WEAPONS! YOU DON'T STAND A CHANCE!
WEAPON EQUIP! FIRE TORNADO
WOOSH!
ROUGE WOMAN-- ROBOTICIZED ALLY OF SONIC
ACTUALLY, ON THAT TOPIC-- SONIC!
PNYOW!
!
I KNOW THE DRILL, ROCK! NOW FIRE THE SONIC SHOT AND CHANGE ROUGE BACK!
WEAPON GET! BLACK WAVE
THAT MAKES AN EVEN *TEN WEAPONS!*
ROUGE THE BAT-- TEAM DARK SPY
*OOF*... NICE SHOT. I GUESS I OWE YOU ONE.

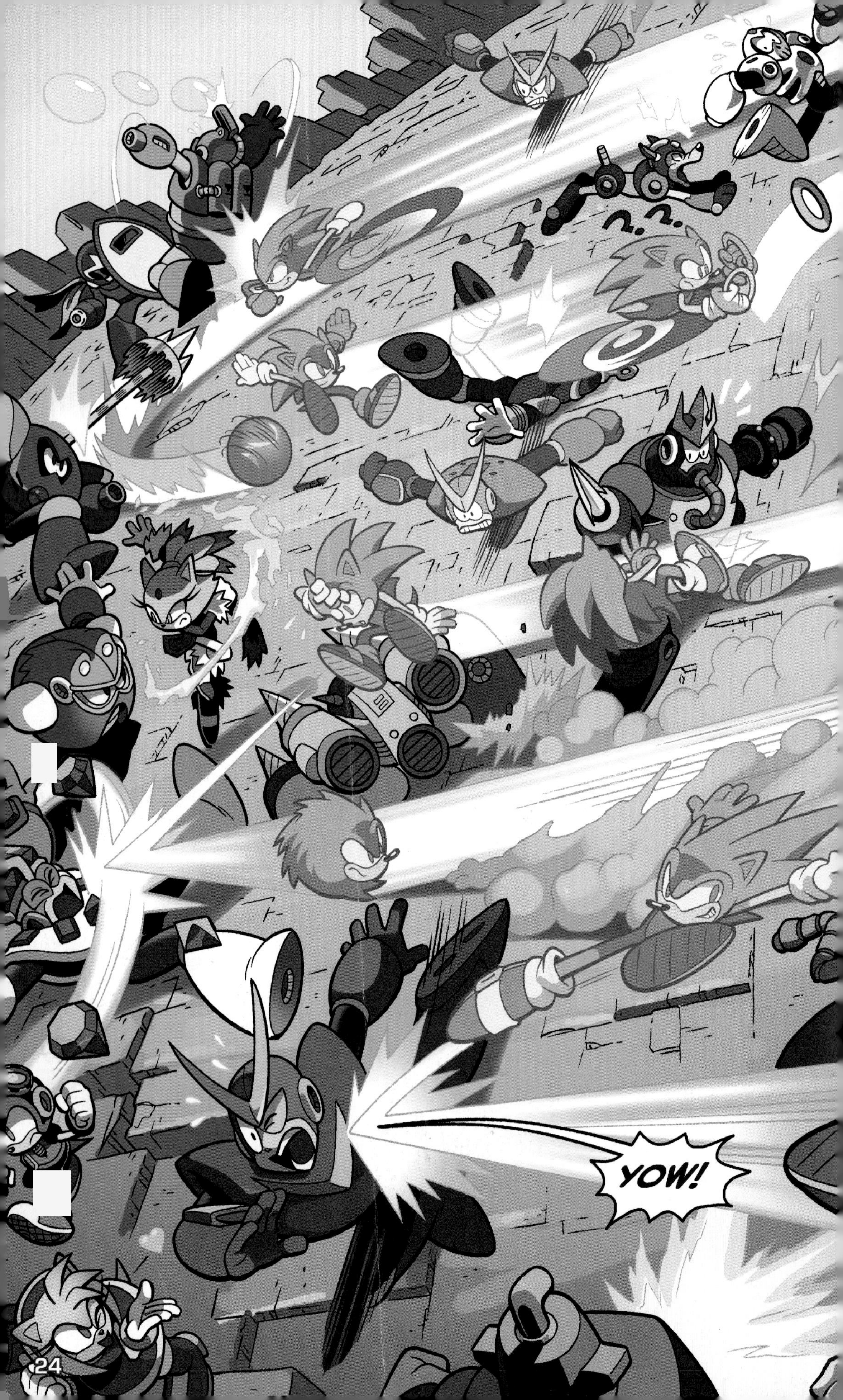
YOW!

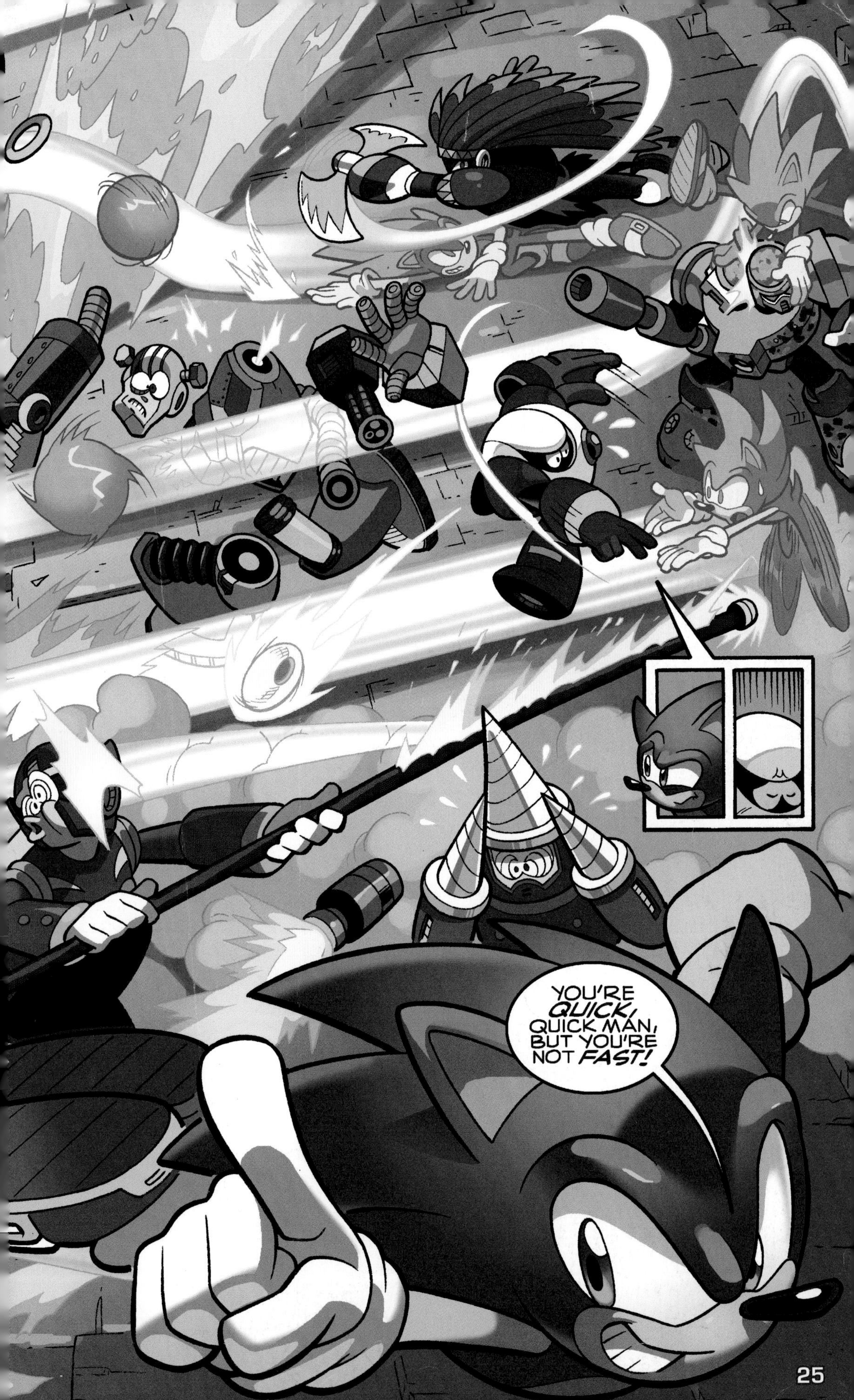
YOU'RE *QUICK*, QUICK MAN, BUT YOU'RE NOT *FAST*!

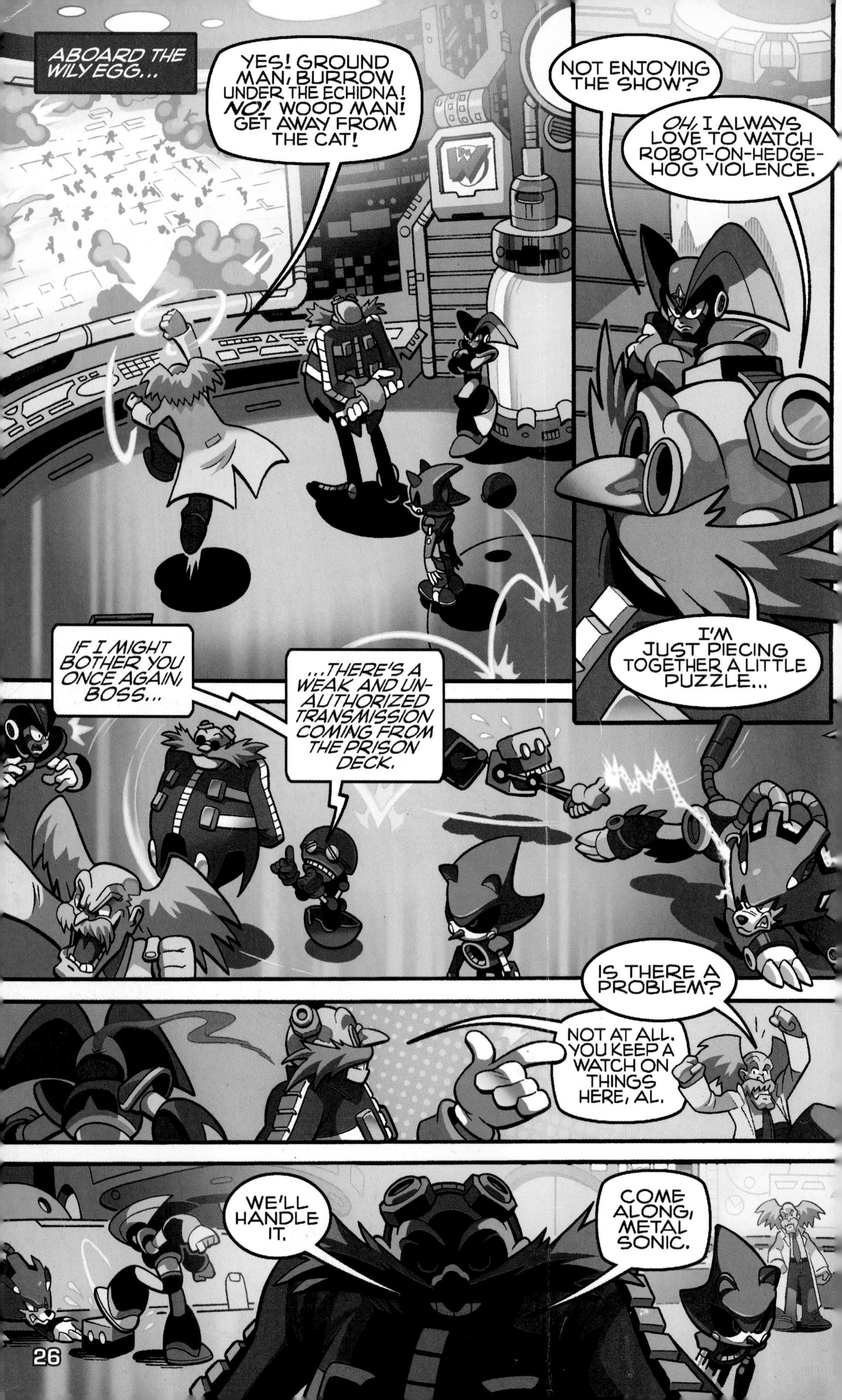
ABOARD THE WILY EGG...
YES! GROUND MAN, BURROW UNDER THE ECHIDNA! NO! WOOD MAN! GET AWAY FROM THE CAT!
NOT ENJOYING THE SHOW?
OH, I ALWAYS LOVE TO WATCH ROBOT-ON-HEDGE-HOG VIOLENCE.
I'M JUST PIECING TOGETHER A LITTLE PUZZLE...
IF I MIGHT BOTHER YOU ONCE AGAIN, BOSS...
...THERE'S A WEAK AND UN-AUTHORIZED TRANSMISSION COMING FROM THE PRISON DECK.
IS THERE A PROBLEM?
NOT AT ALL. YOU KEEP A WATCH ON THINGS HERE, AL.
WE'LL HANDLE IT.
COME ALONG, METAL SONIC.
26

# P.I.C. VARIANT COVERS
## BY PATRICK SPAZIANTE & MATT HERMS

## MEGA MAN 27

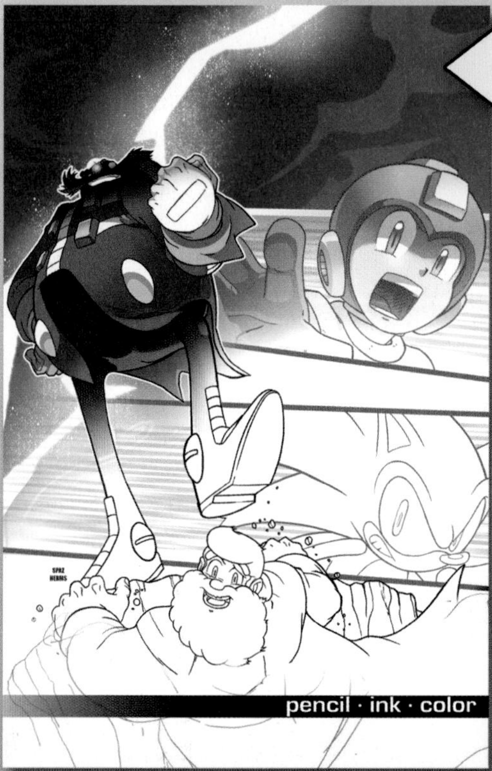
pencil · ink · color

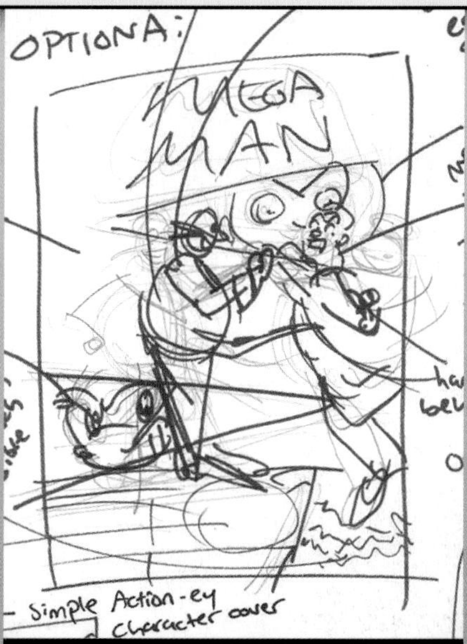
OPTION A:
MEGA MAN
simple Action-ey character cover

THUMBNAIL SKETCH BY PAUL KAMINSKI

## SONIC UNIVERSE 54

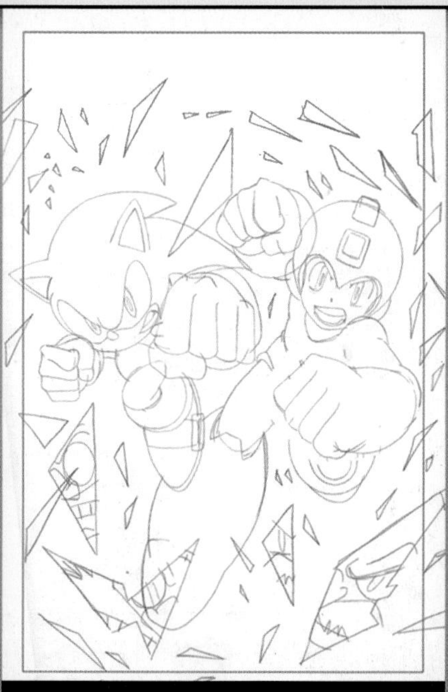

PENCIL SKETCH

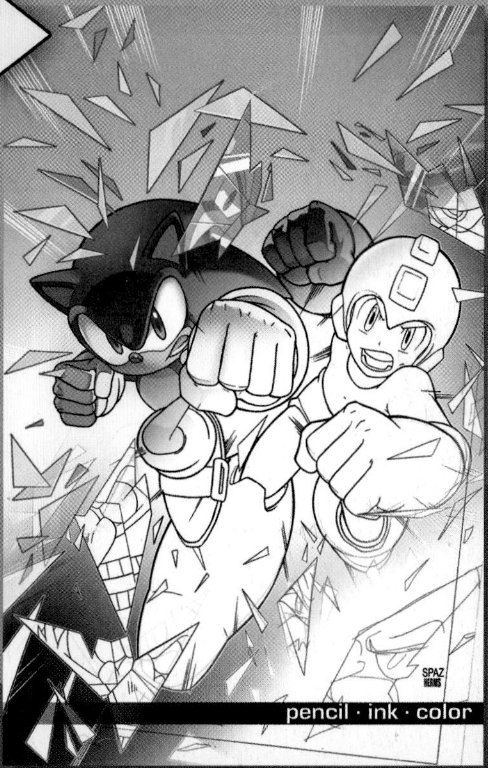
SPAZ HERMS
pencil · ink · color

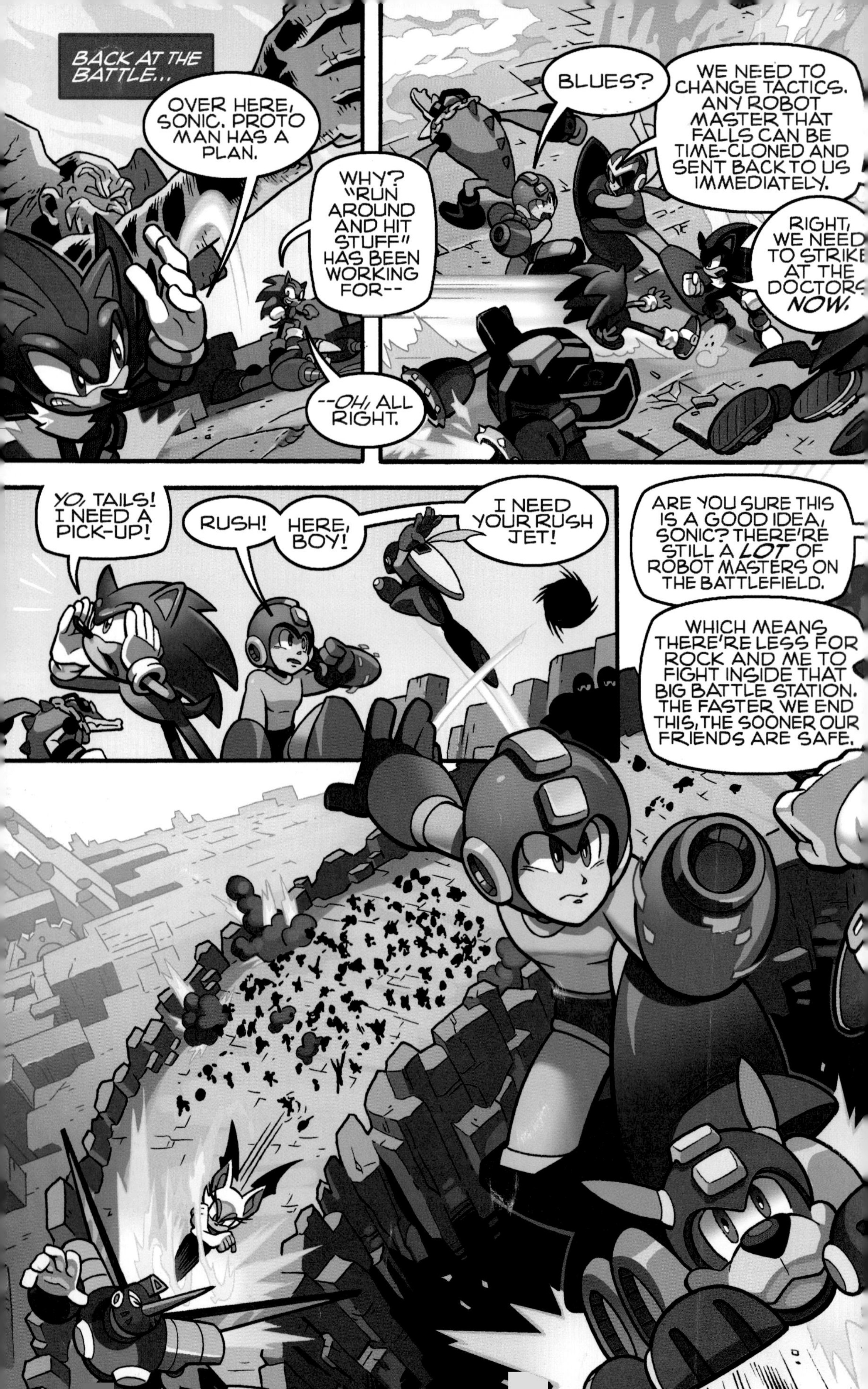
BACK AT THE BATTLE...
OVER HERE, SONIC. PROTO MAN HAS A PLAN.
WHY? "RUN AROUND AND HIT STUFF" HAS BEEN WORKING FOR--
--OH, ALL RIGHT.
BLUES?
WE NEED TO CHANGE TACTICS. ANY ROBOT MASTER THAT FALLS CAN BE TIME-CLONED AND SENT BACK TO US IMMEDIATELY.
RIGHT, WE NEED TO STRIKE AT THE DOCTORS NOW.
YO, TAILS! I NEED A PICK-UP!
RUSH!
HERE, BOY!
I NEED YOUR RUSH JET!
ARE YOU SURE THIS IS A GOOD IDEA, SONIC? THERE'RE STILL A LOT OF ROBOT MASTERS ON THE BATTLEFIELD.
WHICH MEANS THERE'RE LESS FOR ROCK AND ME TO FIGHT INSIDE THAT BIG BATTLE STATION. THE FASTER WE END THIS, THE SOONER OUR FRIENDS ARE SAFE.

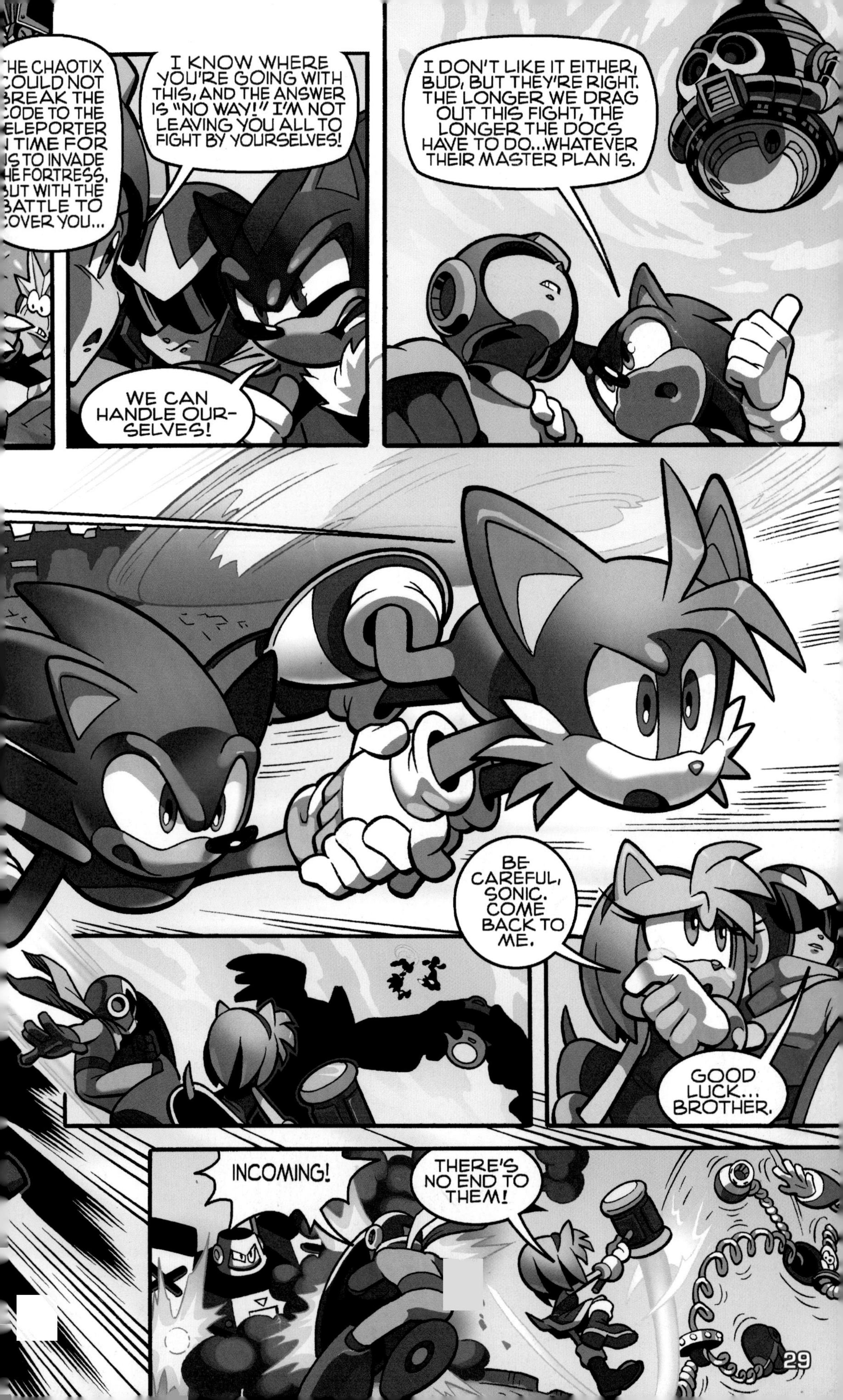

THE CHAOTIX COULD NOT BREAK THE CODE TO THE TELEPORTER IN TIME FOR US TO INVADE THE FORTRESS, BUT WITH THE BATTLE TO COVER YOU...
I KNOW WHERE YOU'RE GOING WITH THIS, AND THE ANSWER IS "NO WAY!" I'M NOT LEAVING YOU ALL TO FIGHT BY YOURSELVES!
WE CAN HANDLE OUR-SELVES!
I DON'T LIKE IT EITHER, BUD, BUT THEY'RE RIGHT. THE LONGER WE DRAG OUT THIS FIGHT, THE LONGER THE DOCS HAVE TO DO...WHATEVER THEIR MASTER PLAN IS.
BE CAREFUL, SONIC. COME BACK TO ME.
GOOD LUCK... BROTHER.
INCOMING!
THERE'S NO END TO THEM!

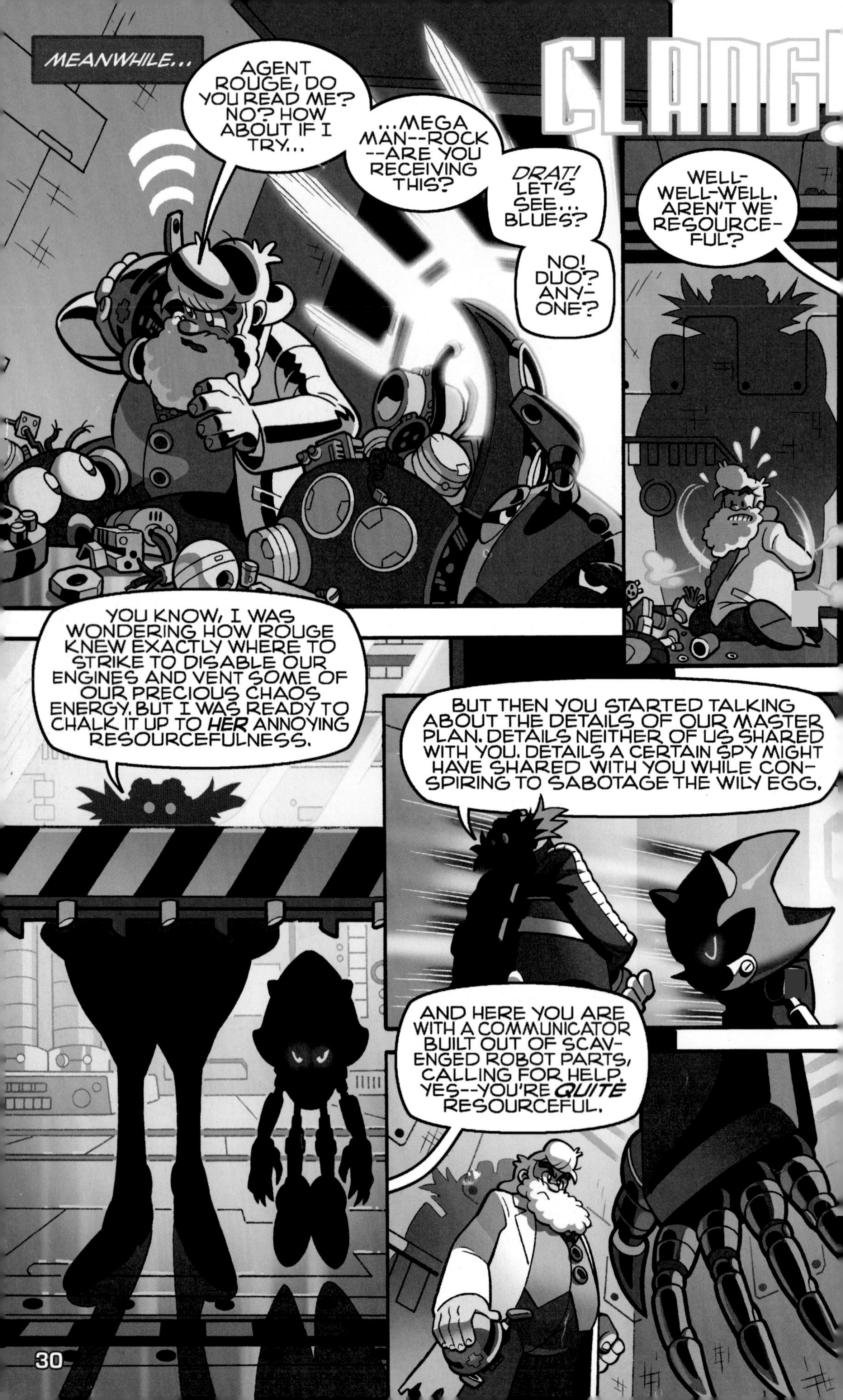

MEANWHILE...
AGENT ROUGE, DO YOU READ ME? NO? HOW ABOUT IF I TRY...
...MEGA MAN--ROCK --ARE YOU RECEIVING THIS?
DRAT! LET'S SEE... BLUES?
NO! DUO? ANY-ONE?
CLANG!
WELL-WELL-WELL. AREN'T WE RESOURCE-FUL?
YOU KNOW, I WAS WONDERING HOW ROUGE KNEW EXACTLY WHERE TO STRIKE TO DISABLE OUR ENGINES AND VENT SOME OF OUR PRECIOUS CHAOS ENERGY. BUT I WAS READY TO CHALK IT UP TO HER ANNOYING RESOURCEFULNESS.
BUT THEN YOU STARTED TALKING ABOUT THE DETAILS OF OUR MASTER PLAN. DETAILS NEITHER OF US SHARED WITH YOU. DETAILS A CERTAIN SPY MIGHT HAVE SHARED WITH YOU WHILE CON-SPIRING TO SABOTAGE THE WILY EGG.
AND HERE YOU ARE WITH A COMMUNICATOR BUILT OUT OF SCAV-ENGED ROBOT PARTS, CALLING FOR HELP. YES--YOU'RE QUITE RESOURCEFUL.

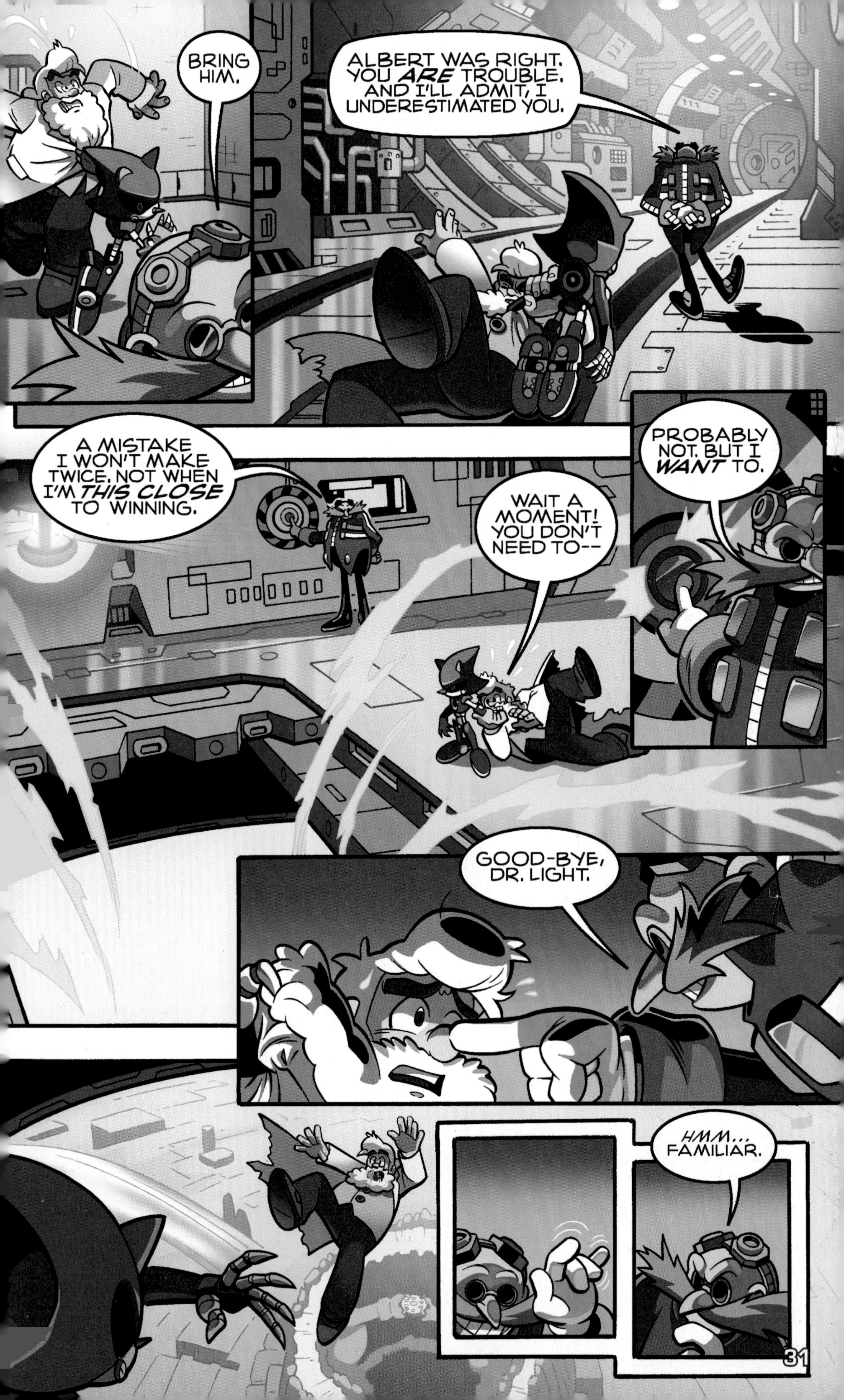
BRING HIM.
ALBERT WAS RIGHT. YOU ARE TROUBLE. AND I'LL ADMIT, I UNDERESTIMATED YOU.
A MISTAKE I WON'T MAKE TWICE. NOT WHEN I'M THIS CLOSE TO WINNING.
WAIT A MOMENT! YOU DON'T NEED TO--
PROBABLY NOT. BUT I WANT TO.
GOOD-BYE, DR. LIGHT.
HMM... FAMILIAR.

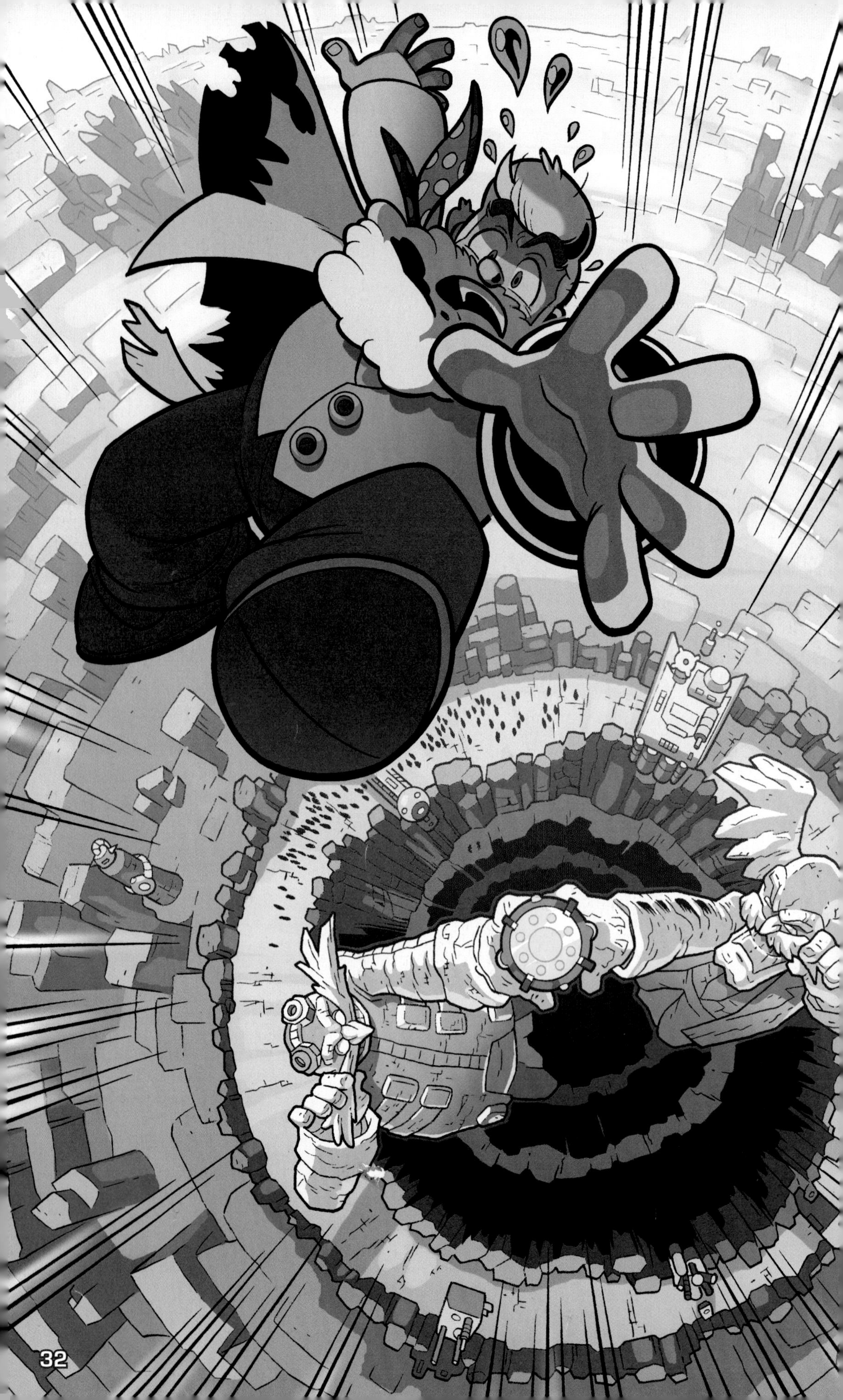

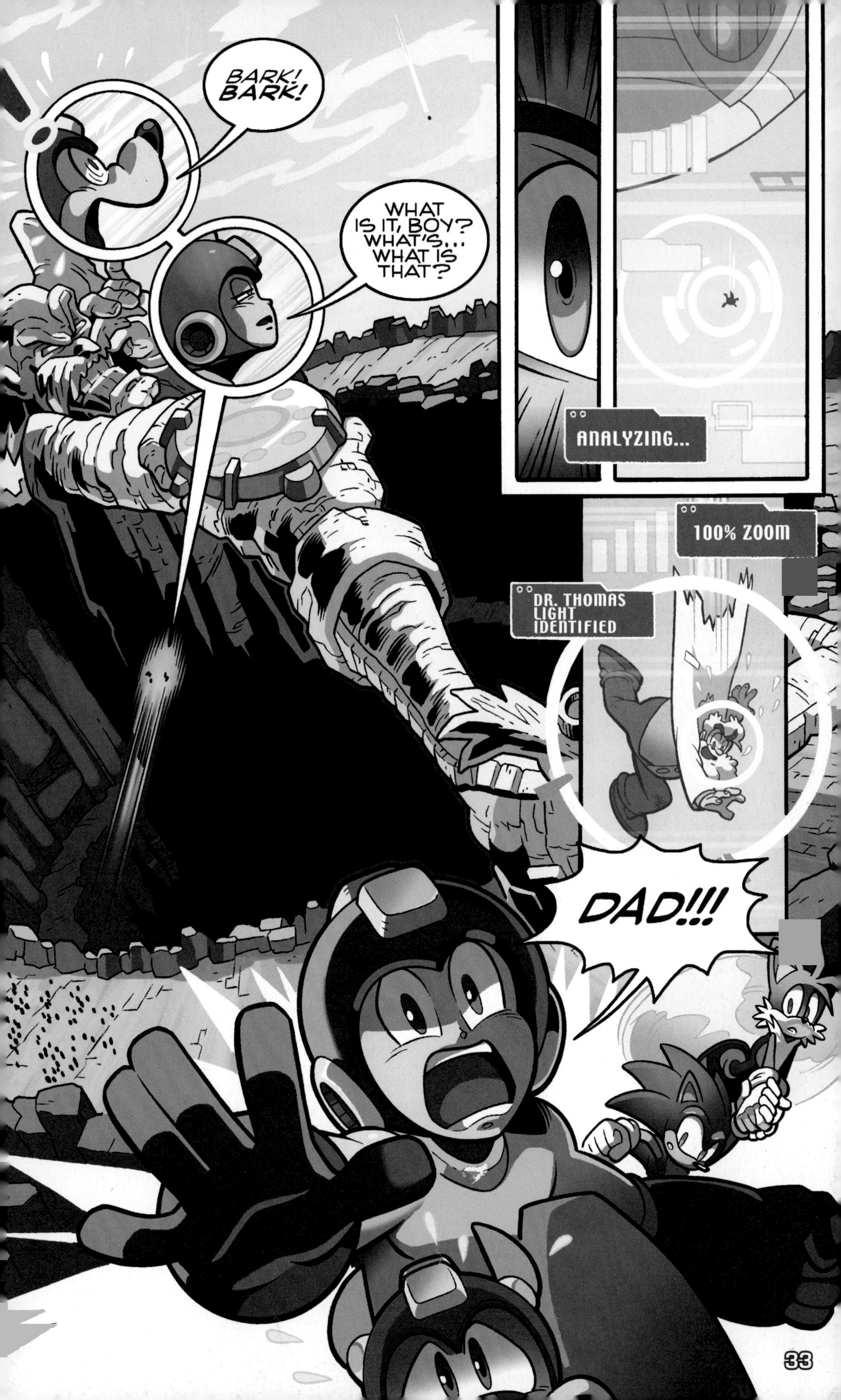

BARK! BARK!
WHAT IS IT, BOY? WHAT'S... WHAT IS THAT?
ANALYZING...
100% ZOOM
DR. THOMAS LIGHT IDENTIFIED
DAD!!!

# CHAPTER 2

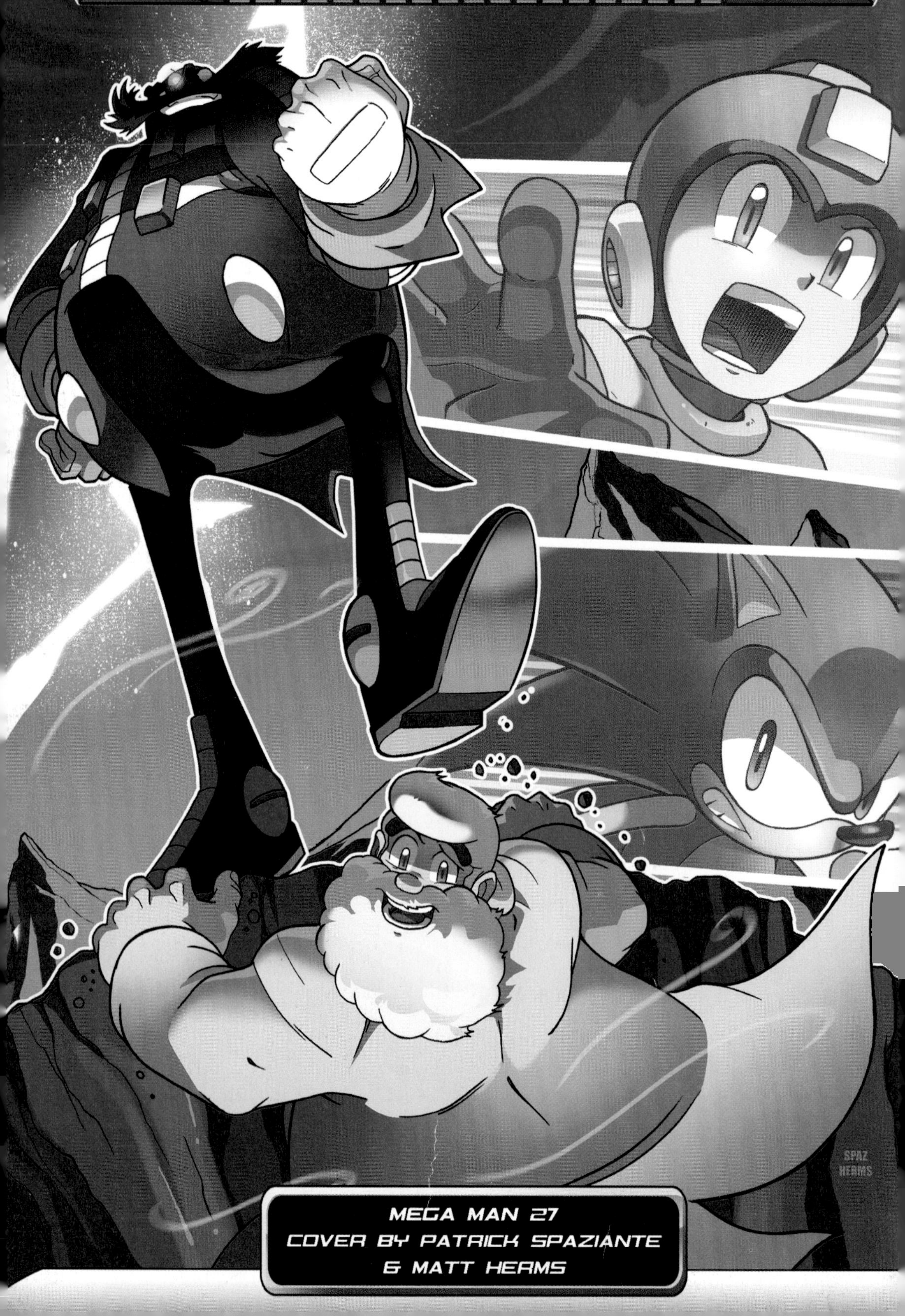
SPAZ
HERMS

MEGA MAN 27
COVER BY PATRICK SPAZIANTE
& MATT HERMS

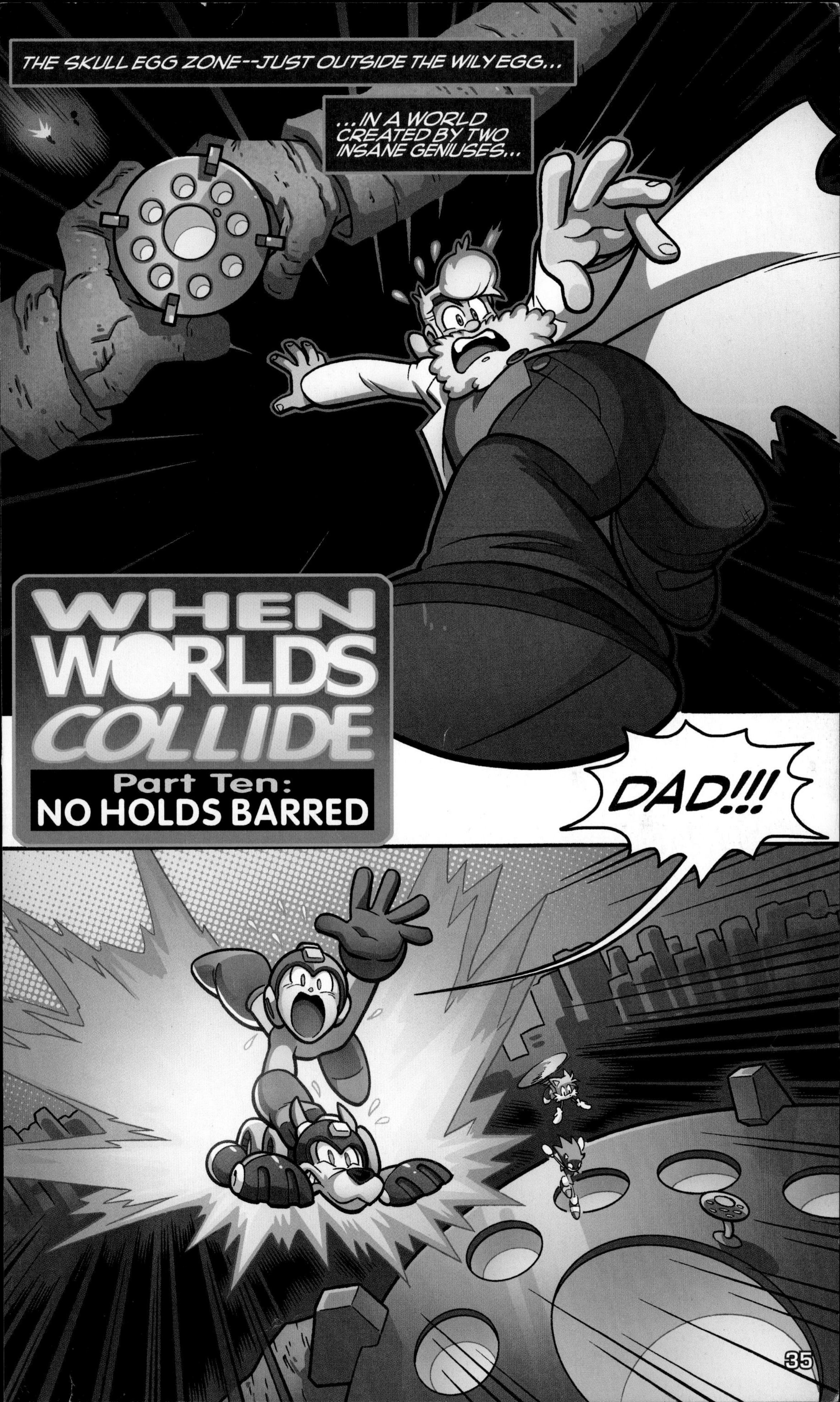
THE SKULL EGG ZONE--JUST OUTSIDE THE WILY EGG...
...IN A WORLD CREATED BY TWO INSANE GENIUSES...
WHEN WORLDS COLLIDE
Part Ten:
NO HOLDS BARRED
DAD!!!

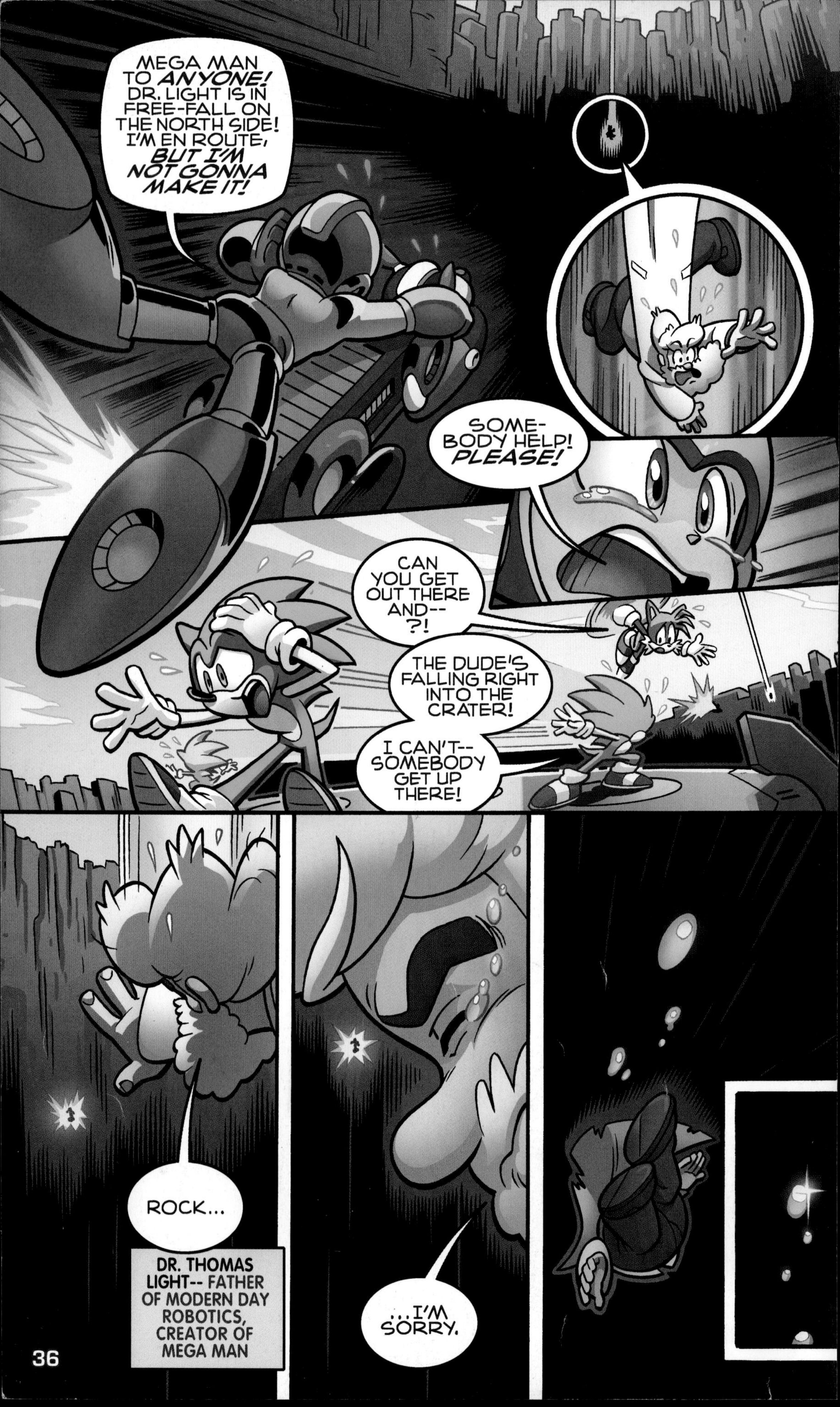
MEGA MAN TO ANYONE! DR. LIGHT IS IN FREE-FALL ON THE NORTH SIDE! I'M EN ROUTE, BUT I'M NOT GONNA MAKE IT!
SOME-BODY HELP! PLEASE!
CAN YOU GET OUT THERE AND-- ?!
THE DUDE'S FALLING RIGHT INTO THE CRATER!
I CAN'T-- SOMEBODY GET UP THERE!
ROCK...
DR. THOMAS LIGHT-- FATHER OF MODERN DAY ROBOTICS, CREATOR OF MEGA MAN
...I'M SORRY.

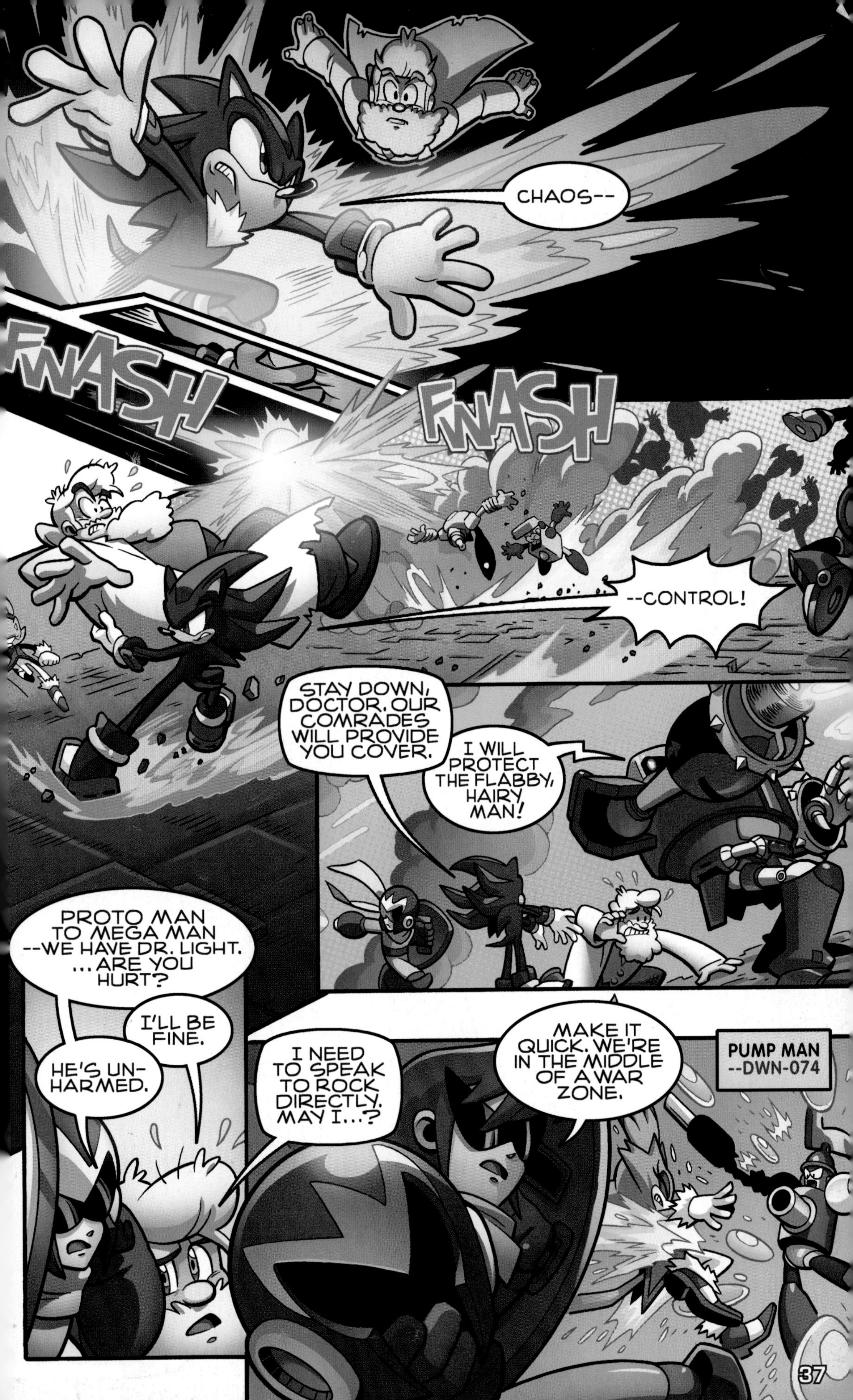

CHAOS--
FWASH
FWASH
--CONTROL!
STAY DOWN, DOCTOR. OUR COMRADES WILL PROVIDE YOU COVER.
I WILL PROTECT THE FLABBY, HAIRY MAN!
PROTO MAN TO MEGA MAN --WE HAVE DR. LIGHT. ...ARE YOU HURT?
HE'S UN-HARMED.
I'LL BE FINE.
I NEED TO SPEAK TO ROCK DIRECTLY. MAY I...?
MAKE IT QUICK. WE'RE IN THE MIDDLE OF A WAR ZONE.
PUMP MAN --DWN-074

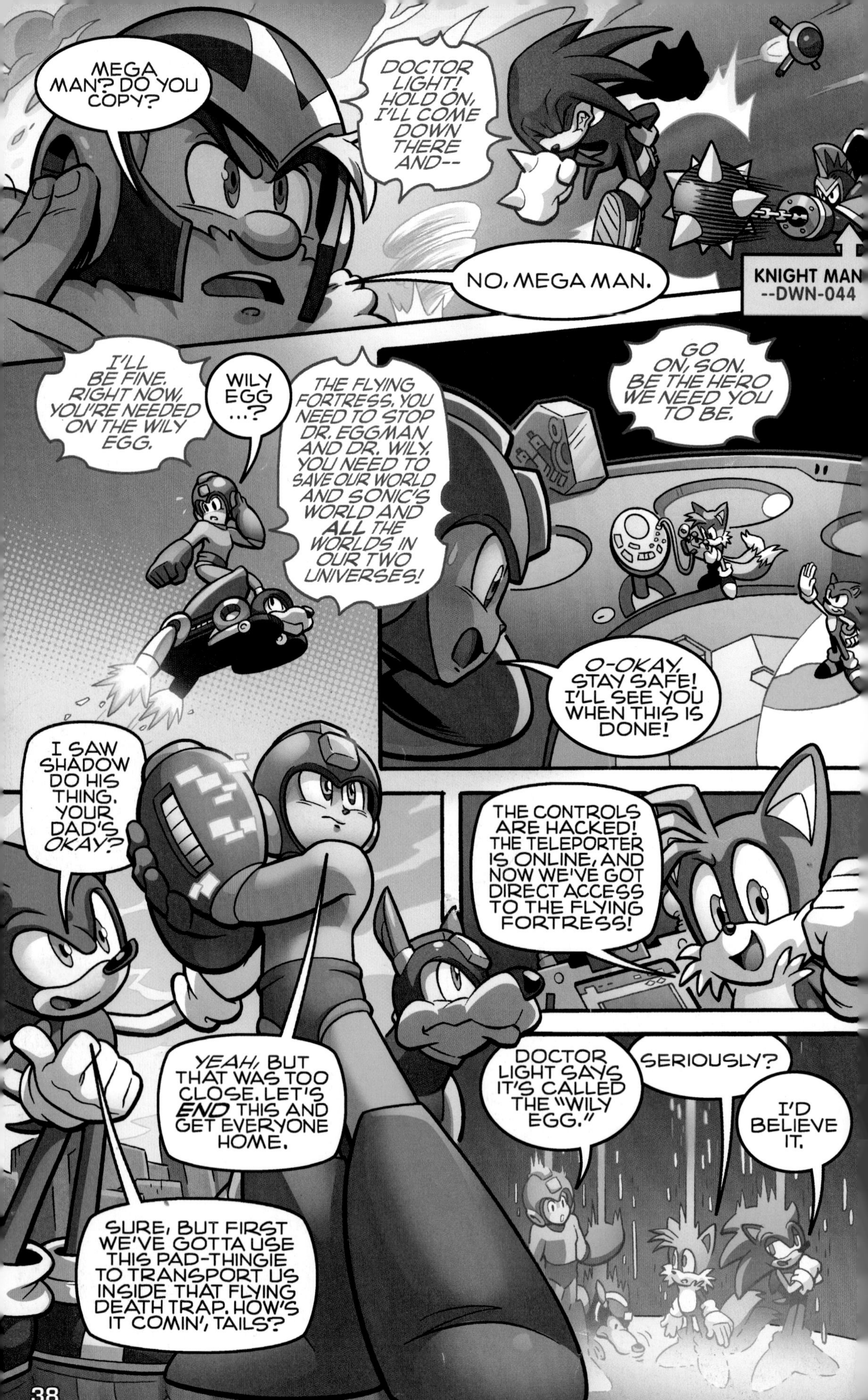
MEGA MAN? DO YOU COPY?
DOCTOR LIGHT! HOLD ON, I'LL COME DOWN THERE AND--
NO, MEGA MAN.
KNIGHT MAN --DWN-044
I'LL BE FINE. RIGHT NOW, YOU'RE NEEDED ON THE WILY EGG.
WILY EGG ...?
THE FLYING FORTRESS. YOU NEED TO STOP DR. EGGMAN AND DR. WILY. YOU NEED TO SAVE OUR WORLD AND SONIC'S WORLD AND ALL THE WORLDS IN OUR TWO UNIVERSES!
GO ON, SON. BE THE HERO WE NEED YOU TO BE.
O-OKAY. STAY SAFE! I'LL SEE YOU WHEN THIS IS DONE!
I SAW SHADOW DO HIS THING. YOUR DAD'S OKAY?
YEAH, BUT THAT WAS TOO CLOSE. LET'S END THIS AND GET EVERYONE HOME.
SURE, BUT FIRST WE'VE GOTTA USE THIS PAD-THINGIE TO TRANSPORT US INSIDE THAT FLYING DEATH TRAP. HOW'S IT COMIN', TAILS?
THE CONTROLS ARE HACKED! THE TELEPORTER IS ONLINE, AND NOW WE'VE GOT DIRECT ACCESS TO THE FLYING FORTRESS!
DOCTOR LIGHT SAYS IT'S CALLED THE "WILY EGG."
SERIOUSLY?
I'D BELIEVE IT.

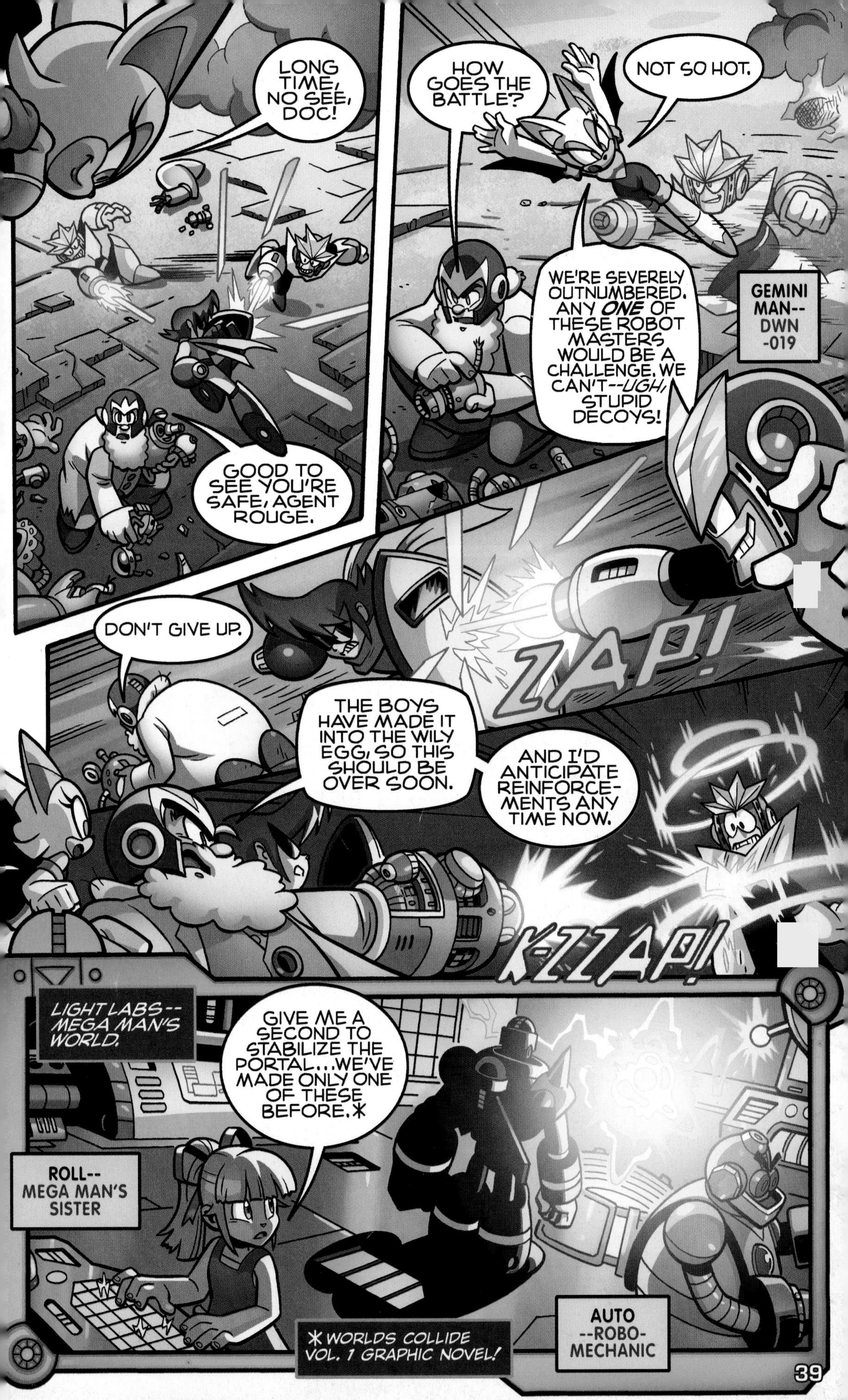
LONG TIME, NO SEE, DOC!
GOOD TO SEE YOU'RE SAFE, AGENT ROUGE.
HOW GOES THE BATTLE?
NOT SO HOT.
WE'RE SEVERELY OUTNUMBERED. ANY ONE OF THESE ROBOT MASTERS WOULD BE A CHALLENGE. WE CAN'T--UGH, STUPID DECOYS!
GEMINI MAN-- DWN -019
ZAP!
DON'T GIVE UP.
THE BOYS HAVE MADE IT INTO THE WILY EGG, SO THIS SHOULD BE OVER SOON.
AND I'D ANTICIPATE REINFORCE-MENTS ANY TIME NOW.
K-ZZAP!
LIGHT LABS-- MEGA MAN'S WORLD.
GIVE ME A SECOND TO STABILIZE THE PORTAL...WE'VE MADE ONLY ONE OF THESE BEFORE.*
ROLL-- MEGA MAN'S SISTER
AUTO --ROBO-MECHANIC
*WORLDS COLLIDE VOL. 1 GRAPHIC NOVEL!

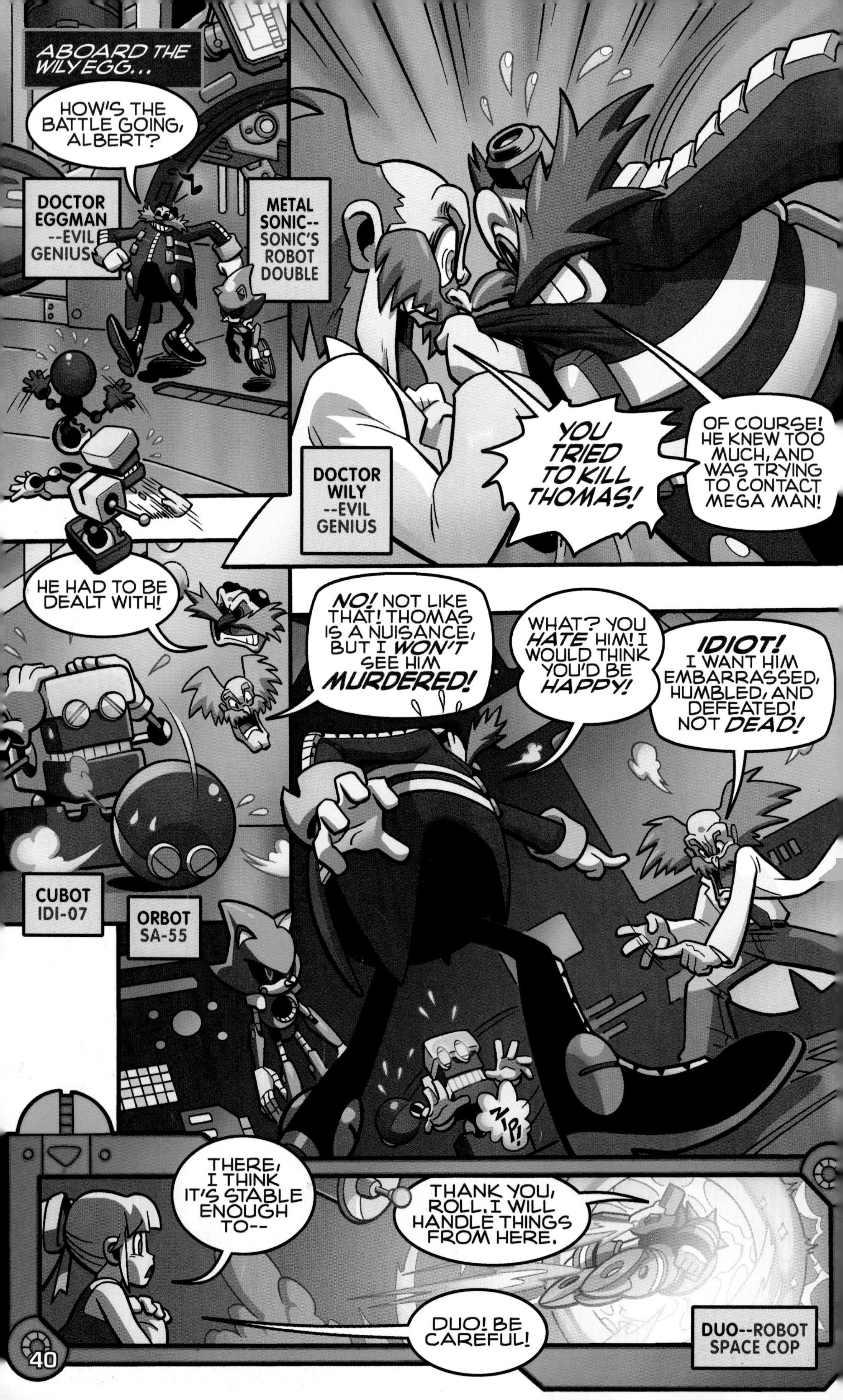
ABOARD THE WILY EGG...
HOW'S THE BATTLE GOING, ALBERT?
DOCTOR EGGMAN --EVIL GENIUS
METAL SONIC-- SONIC'S ROBOT DOUBLE
YOU TRIED TO KILL THOMAS!
DOCTOR WILY --EVIL GENIUS
OF COURSE! HE KNEW TOO MUCH, AND WAS TRYING TO CONTACT MEGA MAN!
HE HAD TO BE DEALT WITH!
NO! NOT LIKE THAT! THOMAS IS A NUISANCE, BUT I WON'T SEE HIM MURDERED!
WHAT? YOU HATE HIM! I WOULD THINK YOU'D BE HAPPY!
IDIOT! I WANT HIM EMBARRASSED, HUMBLED, AND DEFEATED! NOT DEAD!
CUBOT IDI-07
ORBOT SA-55
NIP!
THERE, I THINK IT'S STABLE ENOUGH TO--
THANK YOU, ROLL. I WILL HANDLE THINGS FROM HERE.
DUO! BE CAREFUL!
DUO--ROBOT SPACE COP

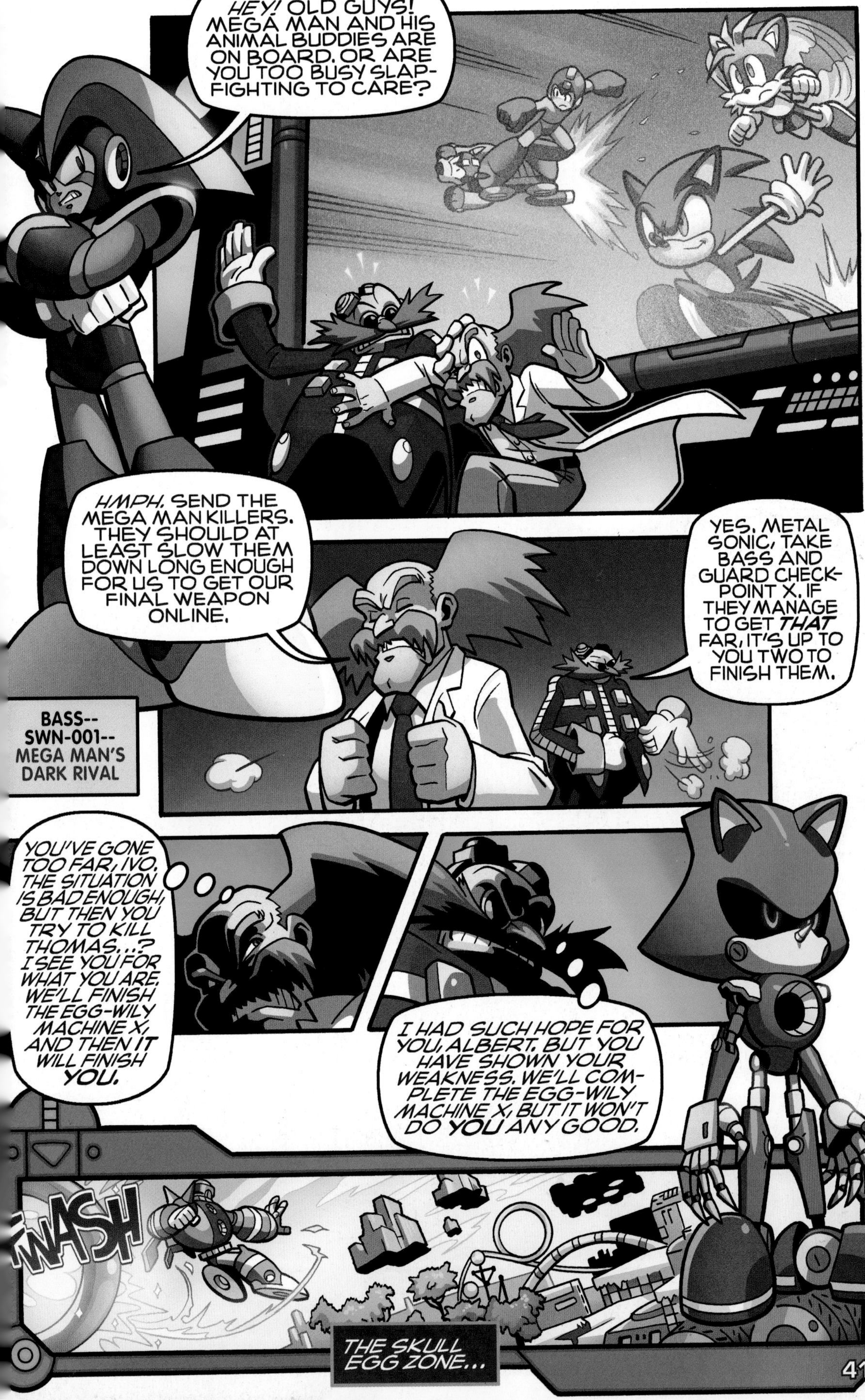

HEY! OLD GUYS! MEGA MAN AND HIS ANIMAL BUDDIES ARE ON BOARD. OR ARE YOU TOO BUSY SLAP-FIGHTING TO CARE?
HMPH. SEND THE MEGA MAN KILLERS. THEY SHOULD AT LEAST SLOW THEM DOWN LONG ENOUGH FOR US TO GET OUR FINAL WEAPON ONLINE.
YES. METAL SONIC, TAKE BASS AND GUARD CHECK-POINT X. IF THEY MANAGE TO GET THAT FAR, IT'S UP TO YOU TWO TO FINISH THEM.
BASS-- SWN-001-- MEGA MAN'S DARK RIVAL
YOU'VE GONE TOO FAR, IVO. THE SITUATION IS BAD ENOUGH, BUT THEN YOU TRY TO KILL THOMAS...? I SEE YOU FOR WHAT YOU ARE. WE'LL FINISH THE EGG-WILY MACHINE X, AND THEN IT WILL FINISH YOU.
I HAD SUCH HOPE FOR YOU, ALBERT. BUT YOU HAVE SHOWN YOUR WEAKNESS. WE'LL COMPLETE THE EGG-WILY MACHINE X, BUT IT WON'T DO YOU ANY GOOD.
FWASH
THE SKULL EGG ZONE...

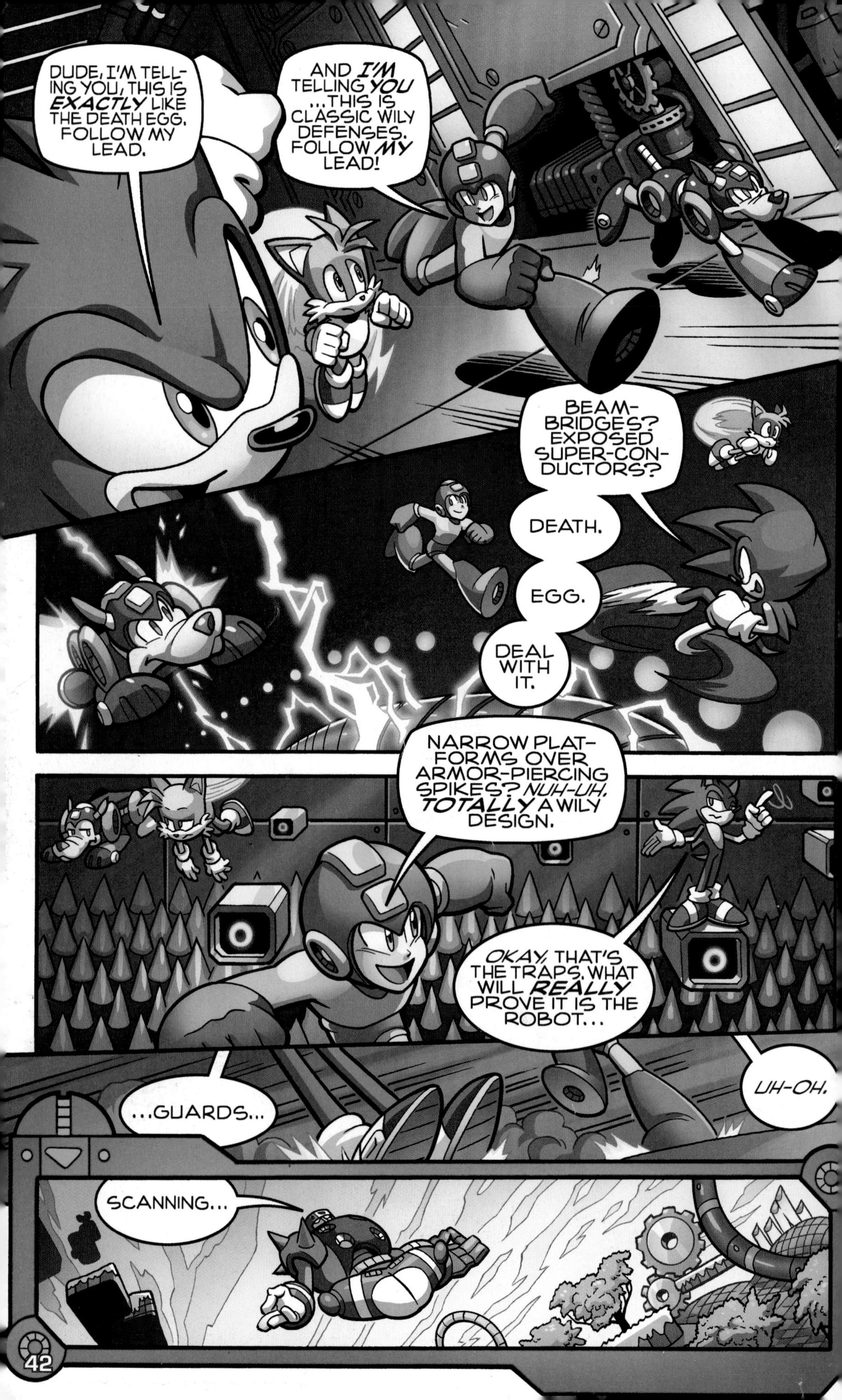
DUDE, I'M TELLING YOU, THIS IS EXACTLY LIKE THE DEATH EGG. FOLLOW MY LEAD.
AND I'M TELLING YOU ...THIS IS CLASSIC WILY DEFENSES. FOLLOW MY LEAD!
BEAM-BRIDGES? EXPOSED SUPER-CONDUCTORS?
DEATH.
EGG.
DEAL WITH IT.
NARROW PLATFORMS OVER ARMOR-PIERCING SPIKES? NUH-UH, TOTALLY A WILY DESIGN.
OKAY, THAT'S THE TRAPS. WHAT WILL REALLY PROVE IT IS THE ROBOT...
...GUARDS...
UH-OH.
SCANNING...

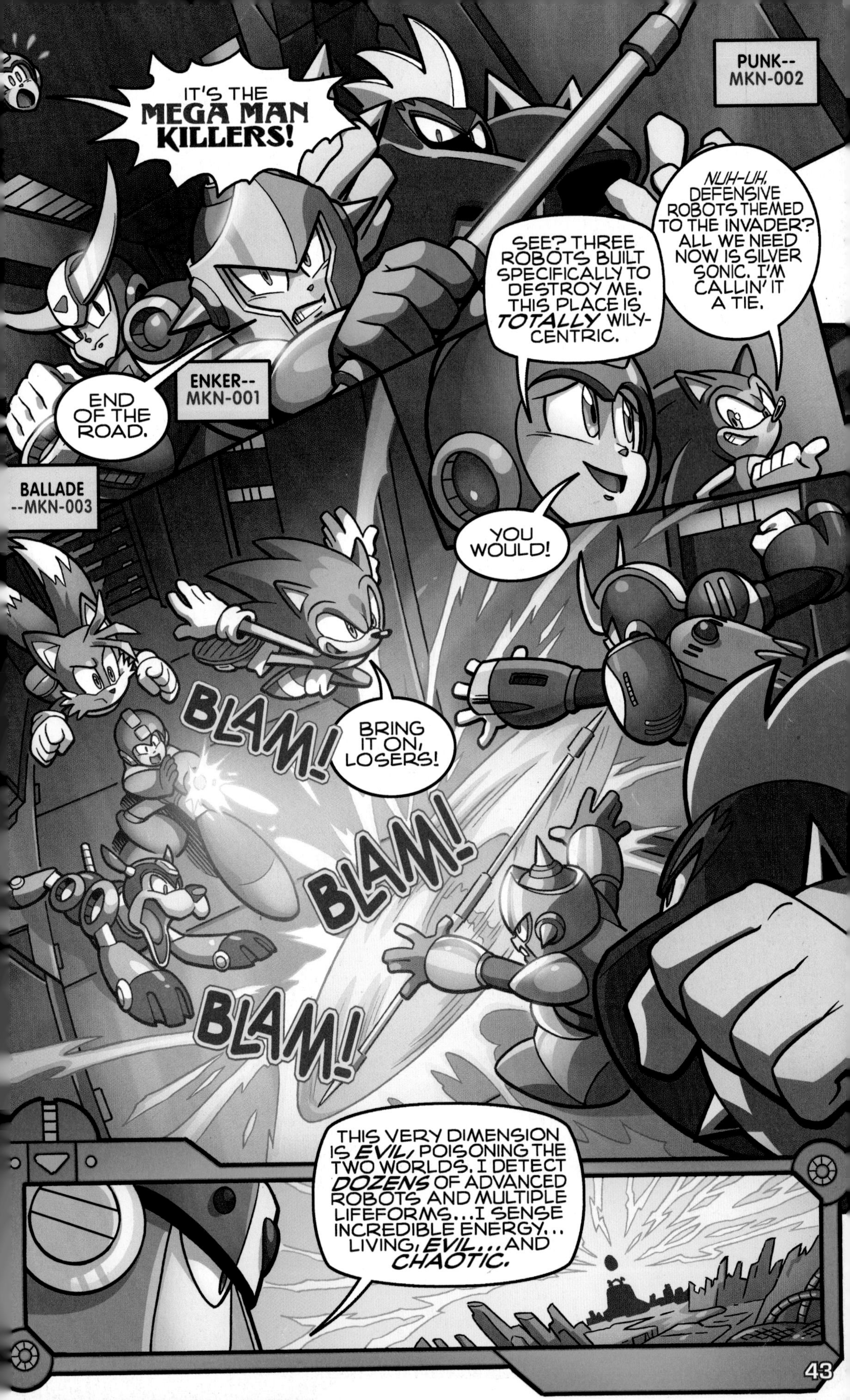
IT'S THE MEGA MAN KILLERS!
PUNK-- MKN-002
SEE? THREE ROBOTS BUILT SPECIFICALLY TO DESTROY ME. THIS PLACE IS TOTALLY WILY-CENTRIC.
NUH-UH. DEFENSIVE ROBOTS THEMED TO THE INVADER? ALL WE NEED NOW IS SILVER SONIC. I'M CALLIN' IT A TIE.
END OF THE ROAD.
ENKER-- MKN-001
YOU WOULD!
BALLADE --MKN-003
BLAM!
BRING IT ON, LOSERS!
BLAM!
BLAM!
THIS VERY DIMENSION IS EVIL, POISONING THE TWO WORLDS. I DETECT DOZENS OF ADVANCED ROBOTS AND MULTIPLE LIFEFORMS...I SENSE INCREDIBLE ENERGY... LIVING, EVIL... AND CHAOTIC.

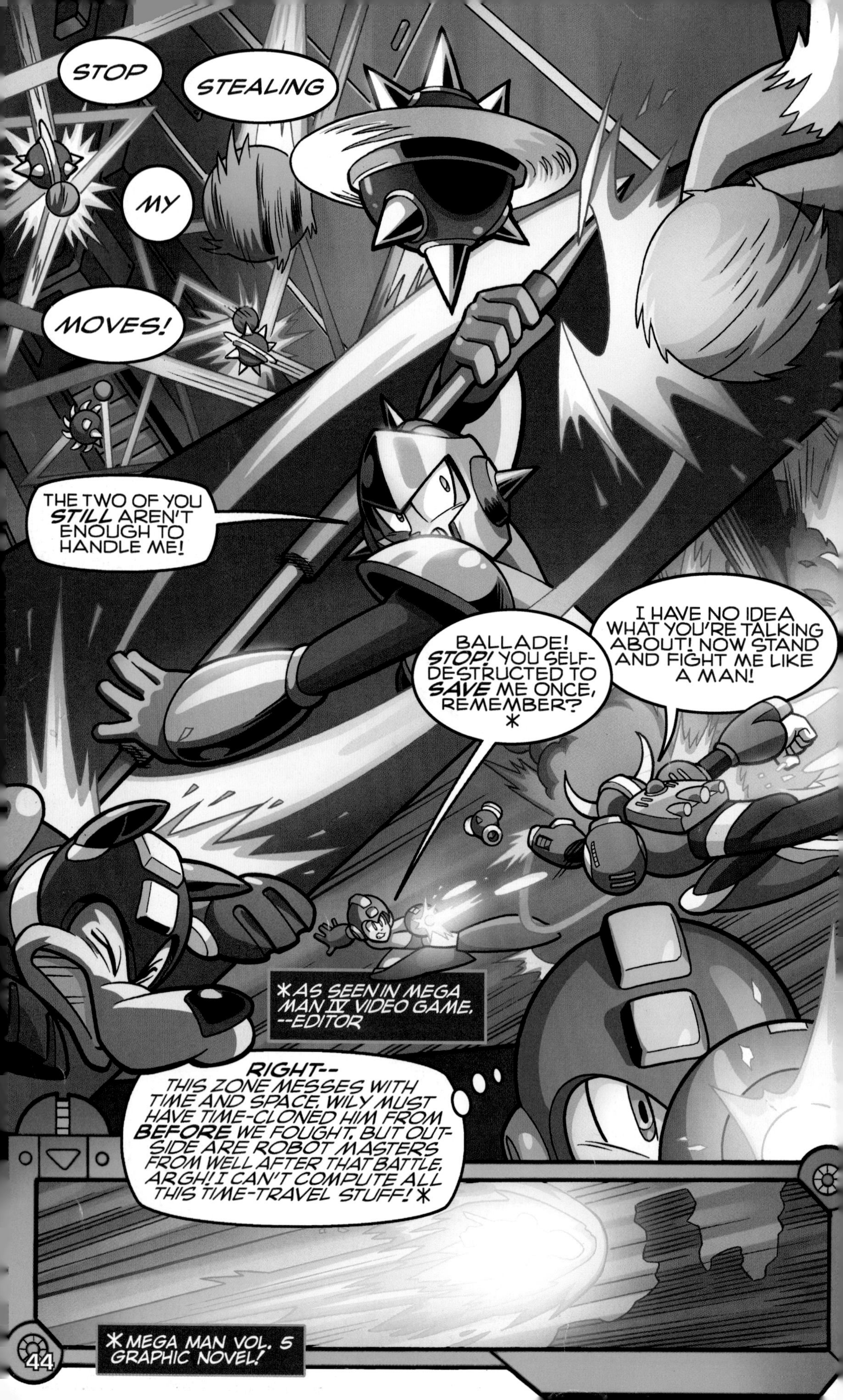
STOP
STEALING
MY
MOVES!
THE TWO OF YOU STILL AREN'T ENOUGH TO HANDLE ME!
BALLADE! STOP! YOU SELF-DESTRUCTED TO SAVE ME ONCE, REMEMBER? *
I HAVE NO IDEA WHAT YOU'RE TALKING ABOUT! NOW STAND AND FIGHT ME LIKE A MAN!
*AS SEEN IN MEGA MAN IV VIDEO GAME. --EDITOR
RIGHT-- THIS ZONE MESSES WITH TIME AND SPACE. WILY MUST HAVE TIME-CLONED HIM FROM BEFORE WE FOUGHT, BUT OUT-SIDE ARE ROBOT MASTERS FROM WELL AFTER THAT BATTLE. ARGH! I CAN'T COMPUTE ALL THIS TIME-TRAVEL STUFF! *
*MEGA MAN VOL. 5 GRAPHIC NOVEL!

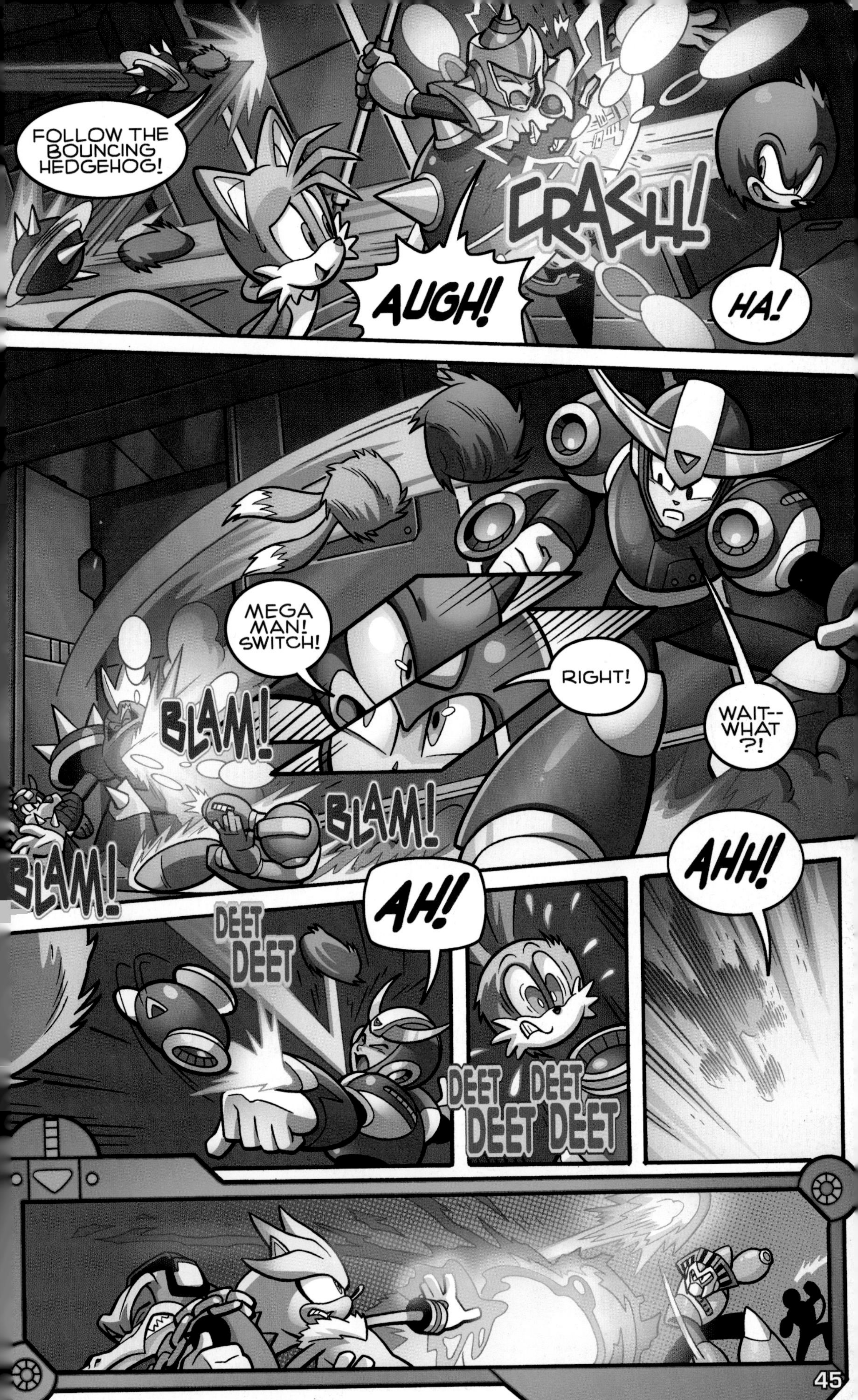
FOLLOW THE BOUNCING HEDGEHOG!
AUGH!
CRASH!
HA!
MEGA MAN! SWITCH!
RIGHT!
WAIT--WHAT?!
BLAM!
BLAM!
BLAM!
AH!
DEET DEET
AHH!
DEET DEET DEET DEET

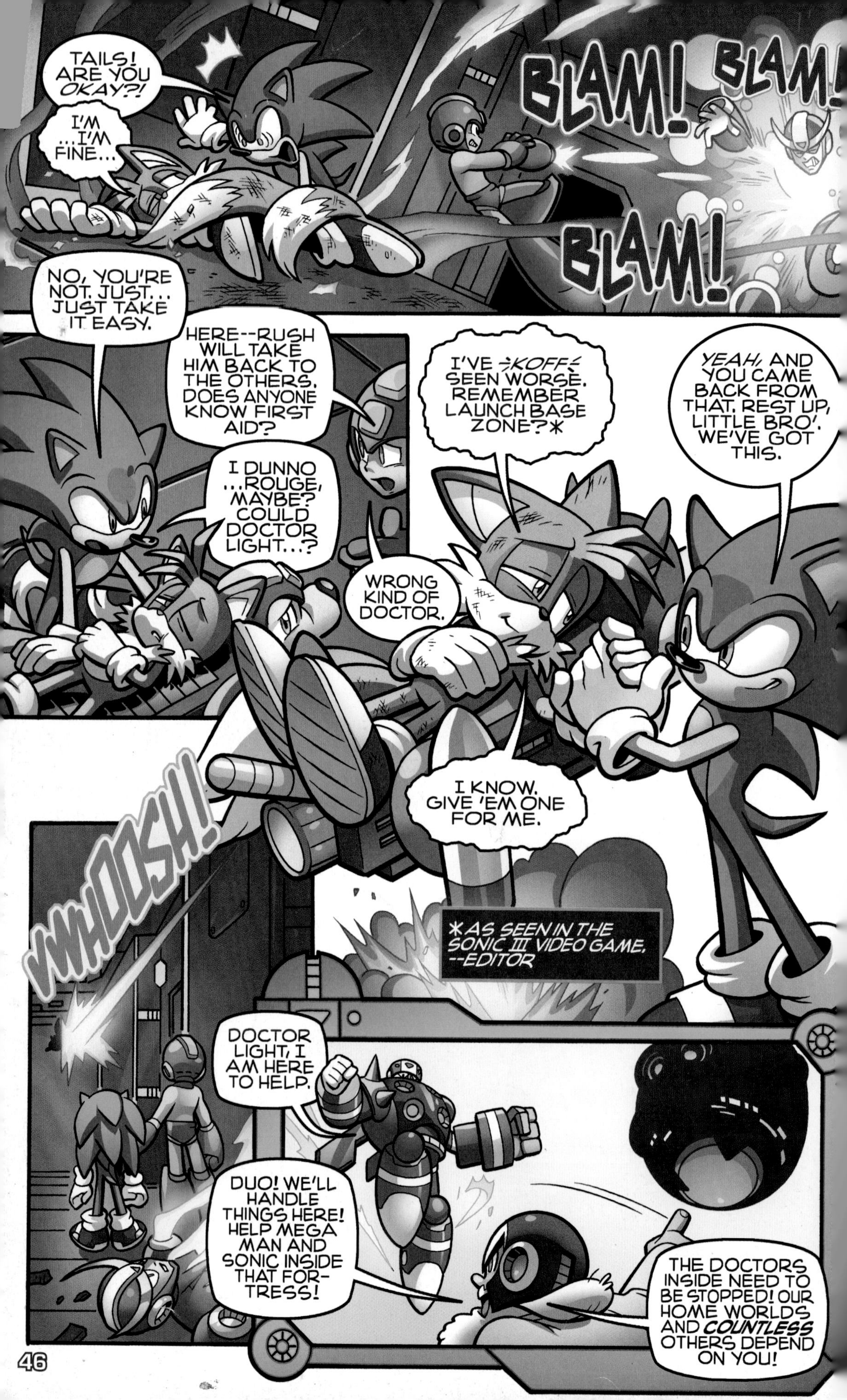
TAILS! ARE YOU *OKAY?!*
I'M ...I'M FINE...
BLAM! BLAM!
BLAM!
NO, YOU'RE NOT. JUST... JUST TAKE IT EASY.
HERE--RUSH WILL TAKE HIM BACK TO THE OTHERS. DOES ANYONE KNOW FIRST AID?
I DUNNO ...ROUGE, MAYBE? COULD DOCTOR LIGHT...?
WRONG KIND OF DOCTOR.
I'VE ~KOFF~ SEEN WORSE. REMEMBER LAUNCH BASE ZONE?*
*YEAH,* AND YOU CAME BACK FROM THAT. REST UP, LITTLE BRO'. WE'VE GOT THIS.
I KNOW. GIVE 'EM ONE FOR ME.
VWHOOSH!
*AS SEEN IN THE SONIC III VIDEO GAME. --EDITOR
DOCTOR LIGHT, I AM HERE TO HELP.
DUO! WE'LL HANDLE THINGS HERE! HELP MEGA MAN AND SONIC INSIDE THAT FOR-TRESS!
THE DOCTORS INSIDE NEED TO BE STOPPED! OUR HOME WORLDS AND *COUNTLESS* OTHERS DEPEND ON YOU!

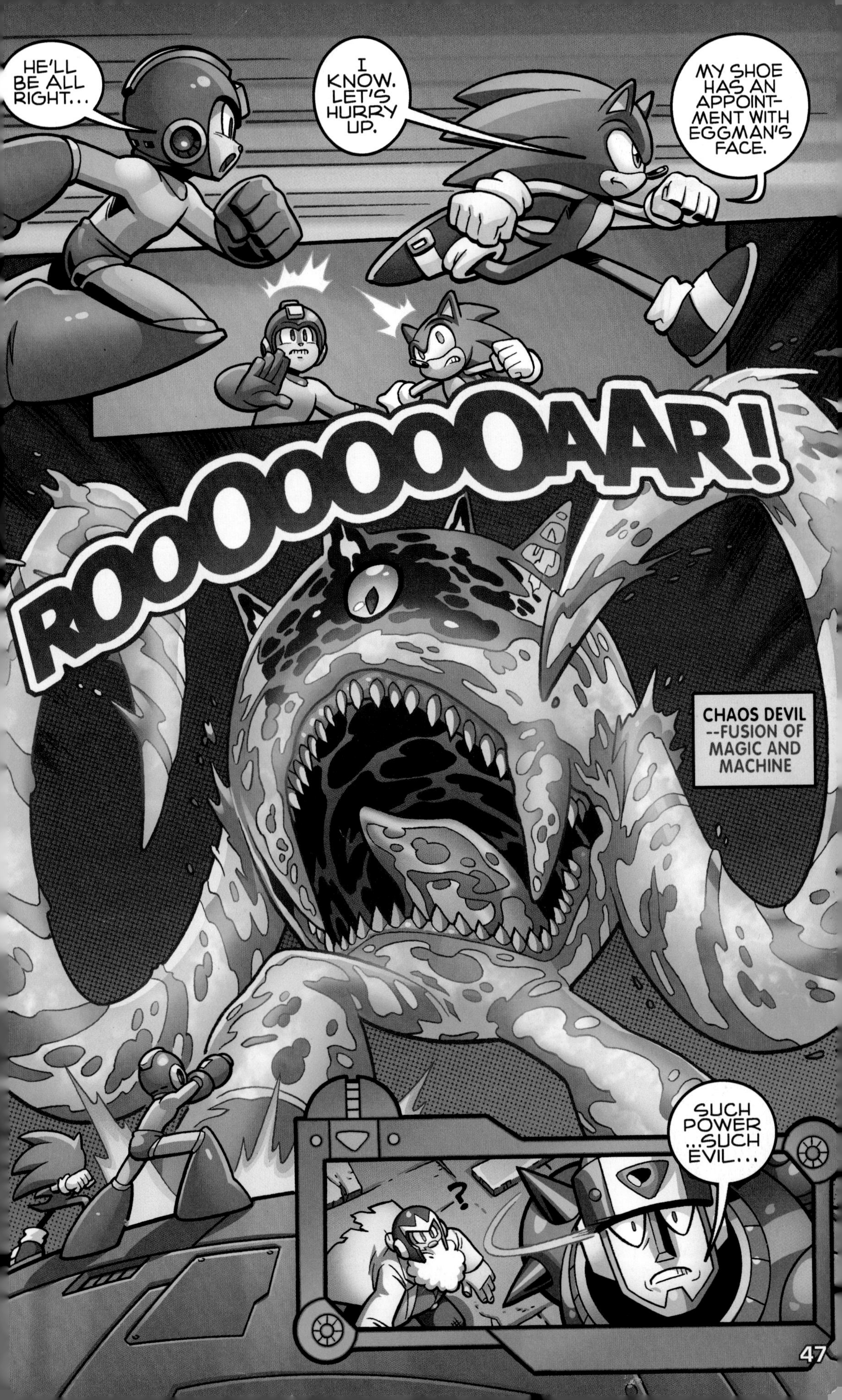
HE'LL BE ALL RIGHT...
I KNOW. LET'S HURRY UP.
MY SHOE HAS AN APPOINT-MENT WITH EGGMAN'S FACE.
ROOOOOOOAAR!
CHAOS DEVIL --FUSION OF MAGIC AND MACHINE
SUCH POWER ...SUCH EVIL...
?

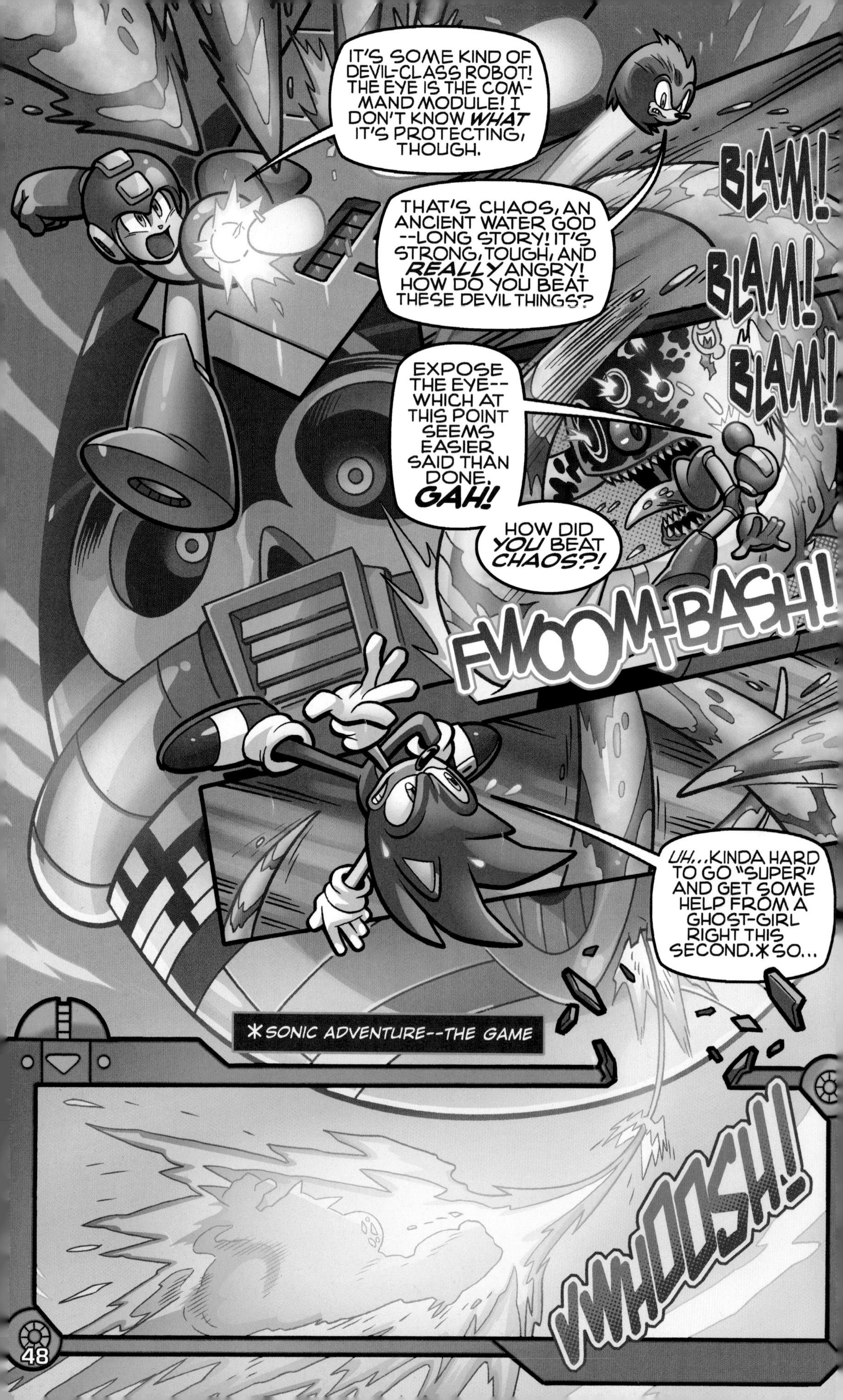
IT'S SOME KIND OF DEVIL-CLASS ROBOT! THE EYE IS THE COMMAND MODULE! I DON'T KNOW *WHAT* IT'S PROTECTING, THOUGH.
THAT'S CHAOS, AN ANCIENT WATER GOD --LONG STORY! IT'S STRONG, TOUGH, AND *REALLY* ANGRY! HOW DO YOU BEAT THESE DEVIL THINGS?
BLAM! BLAM! BLAM!
EXPOSE THE EYE-- WHICH AT THIS POINT SEEMS EASIER SAID THAN DONE. *GAH!*
HOW DID *YOU* BEAT CHAOS?!
FWOOM-BASH!
*UH*...KINDA HARD TO GO "SUPER" AND GET SOME HELP FROM A GHOST-GIRL RIGHT THIS SECOND.* SO...
*SONIC ADVENTURE--THE GAME
VWHOOSH!

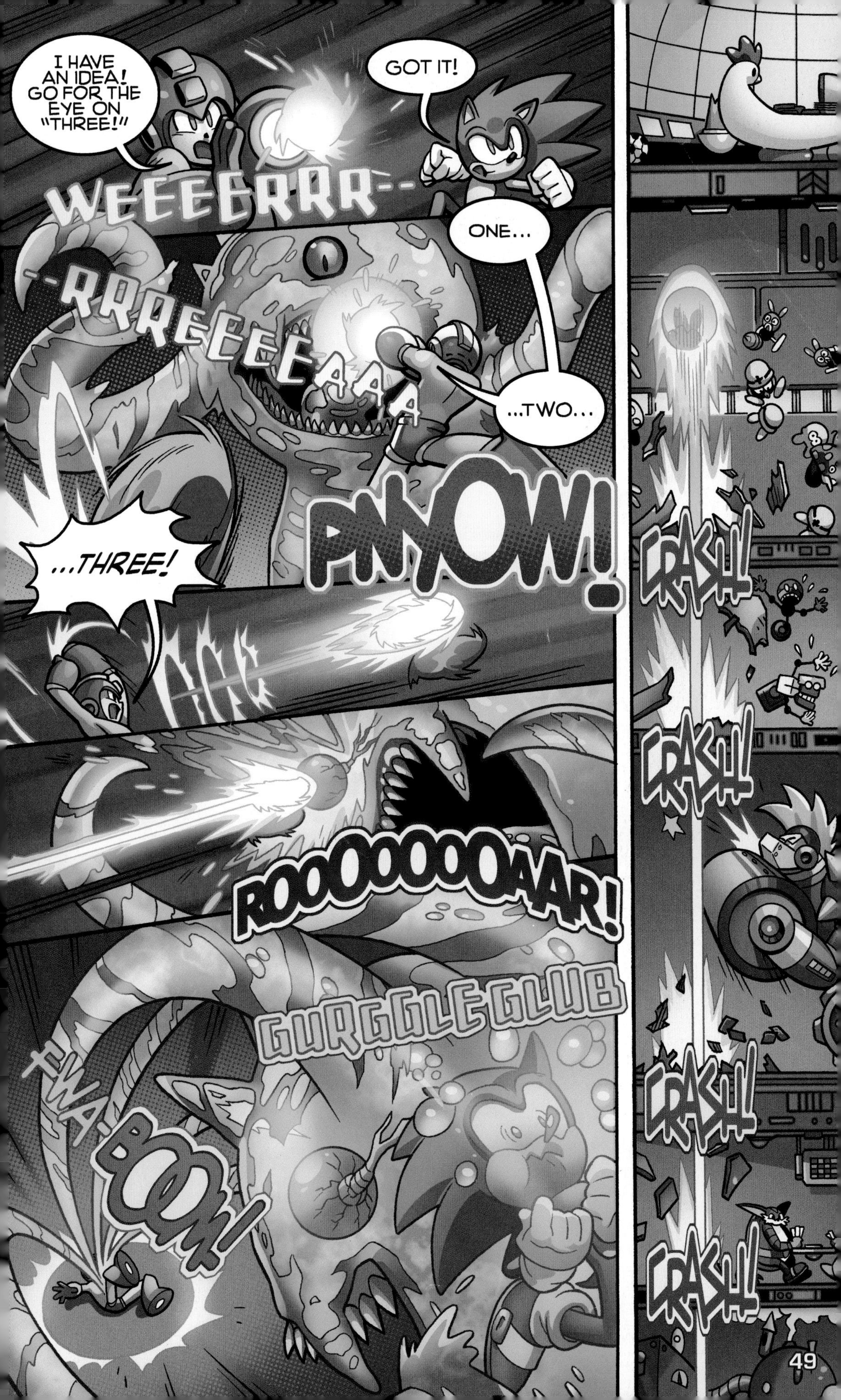

I HAVE AN IDEA! GO FOR THE EYE ON "THREE!"
GOT IT!
WEEEERRRR--
--RRREEEEEAAA
ONE...
...TWO...
...THREE!
PKYOW!
CRASH!
CRASH!
ROOOOOOOAAR!
GURGGLEGLUB
CRASH!
FWA-BOOM!
CRASH!

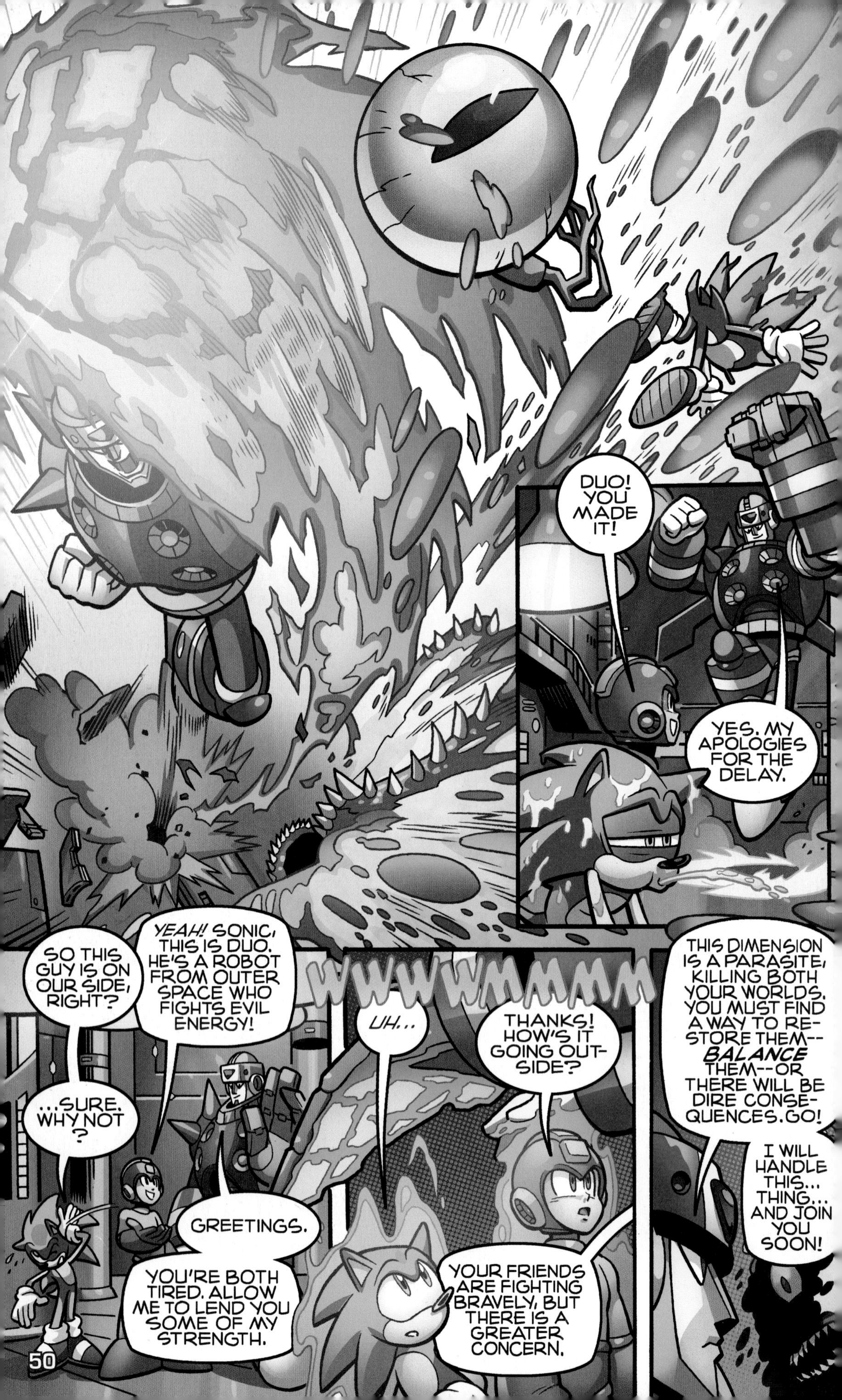
DUO! YOU MADE IT!
YES. MY APOLOGIES FOR THE DELAY.
SO THIS GUY IS ON OUR SIDE, RIGHT?
YEAH! SONIC, THIS IS DUO. HE'S A ROBOT FROM OUTER SPACE WHO FIGHTS EVIL ENERGY!
...SURE. WHY NOT?
GREETINGS.
YOU'RE BOTH TIRED. ALLOW ME TO LEND YOU SOME OF MY STRENGTH.
WWWWMMMM
UH...
THANKS! HOW'S IT GOING OUT-SIDE?
YOUR FRIENDS ARE FIGHTING BRAVELY, BUT THERE IS A GREATER CONCERN.
THIS DIMENSION IS A PARASITE, KILLING BOTH YOUR WORLDS. YOU MUST FIND A WAY TO RE-STORE THEM-- *BALANCE* THEM--OR THERE WILL BE DIRE CONSE-QUENCES. GO!
I WILL HANDLE THIS... THING... AND JOIN YOU SOON!

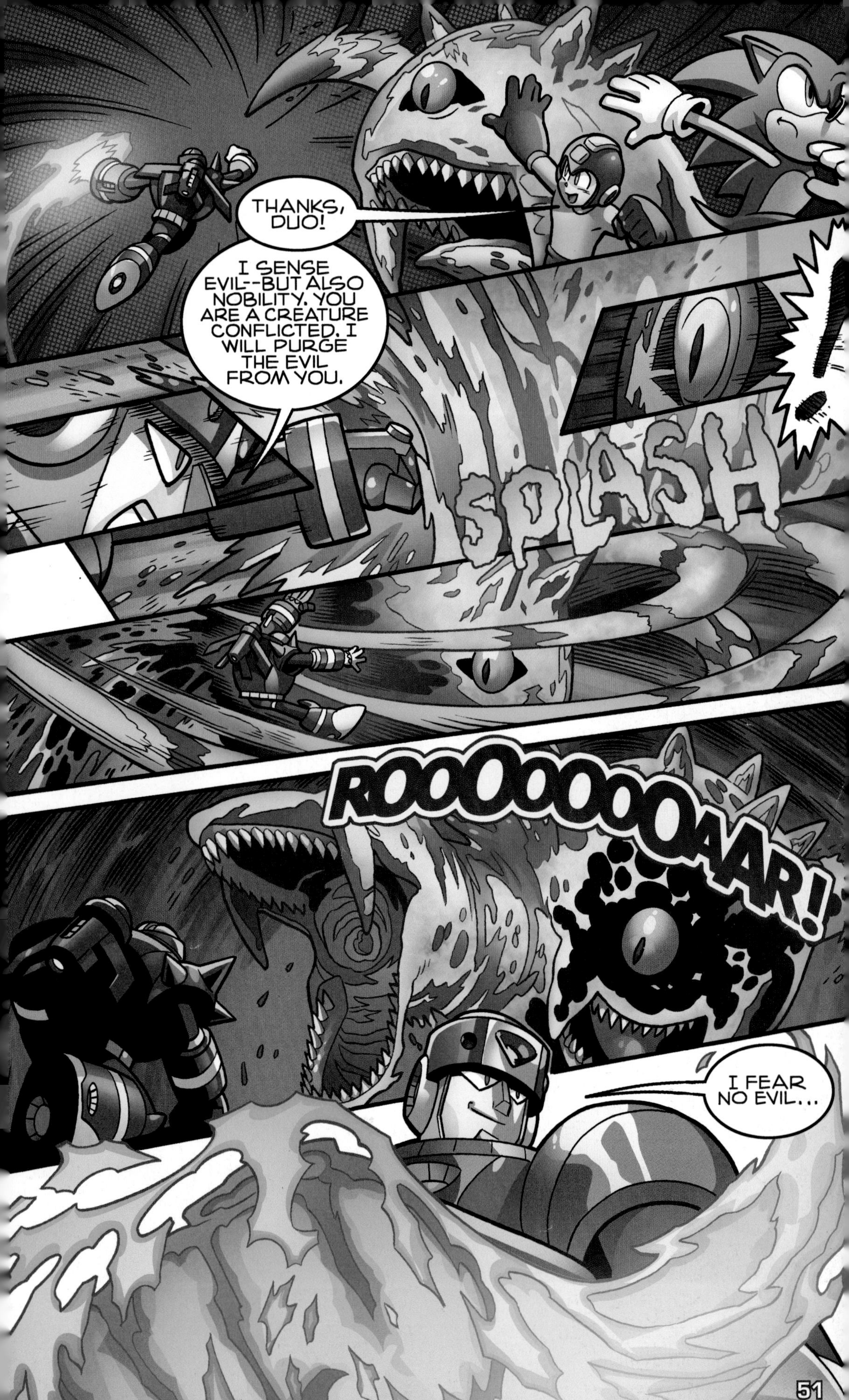
THANKS, DUO!
I SENSE EVIL--BUT ALSO NOBILITY. YOU ARE A CREATURE CONFLICTED. I WILL PURGE THE EVIL FROM YOU.
KO!
SPLASH
ROOOOOOOOAAR!
I FEAR NO EVIL...

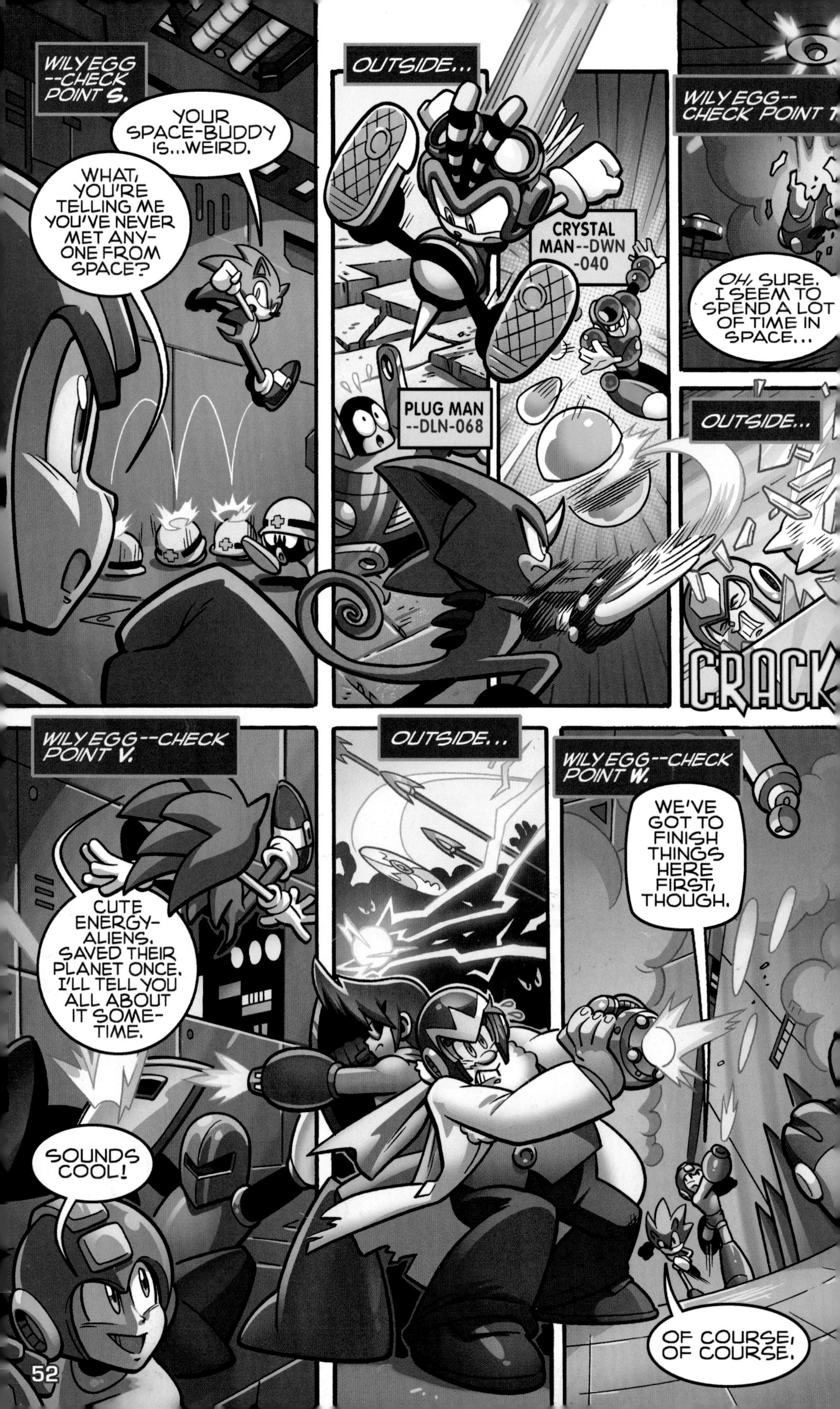
WILY EGG --CHECK POINT S.
YOUR SPACE-BUDDY IS...WEIRD.
WHAT, YOU'RE TELLING ME YOU'VE NEVER MET ANY-ONE FROM SPACE?
OUTSIDE...
CRYSTAL MAN--DWN -040
PLUG MAN --DLN-068
WILY EGG-- CHECK POINT T
OH, SURE. I SEEM TO SPEND A LOT OF TIME IN SPACE...
OUTSIDE...
CRACK
WILY EGG--CHECK POINT V.
CUTE ENERGY-ALIENS. SAVED THEIR PLANET ONCE. I'LL TELL YOU ALL ABOUT IT SOME-TIME.
SOUNDS COOL!
OUTSIDE...
WILY EGG--CHECK POINT W.
WE'VE GOT TO FINISH THINGS HERE FIRST, THOUGH.
OF COURSE! OF COURSE.

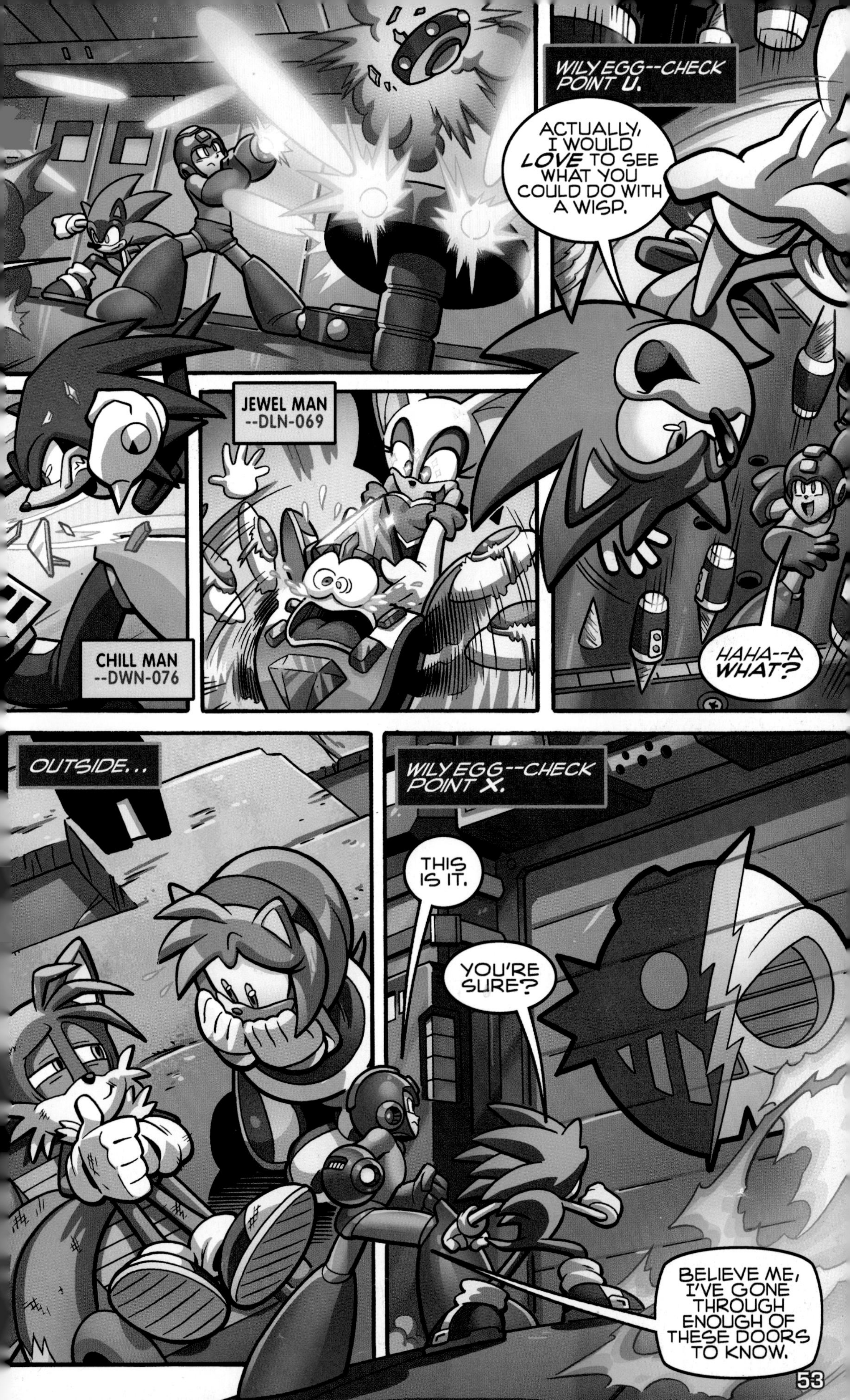
WILY EGG--CHECK POINT U.
ACTUALLY, I WOULD LOVE TO SEE WHAT YOU COULD DO WITH A WISP.
JEWEL MAN --DLN-069
CHILL MAN --DWN-076
HAHA--A WHAT?
OUTSIDE...
WILY EGG--CHECK POINT X.
THIS IS IT.
YOU'RE SURE?
BELIEVE ME, I'VE GONE THROUGH ENOUGH OF THESE DOORS TO KNOW.

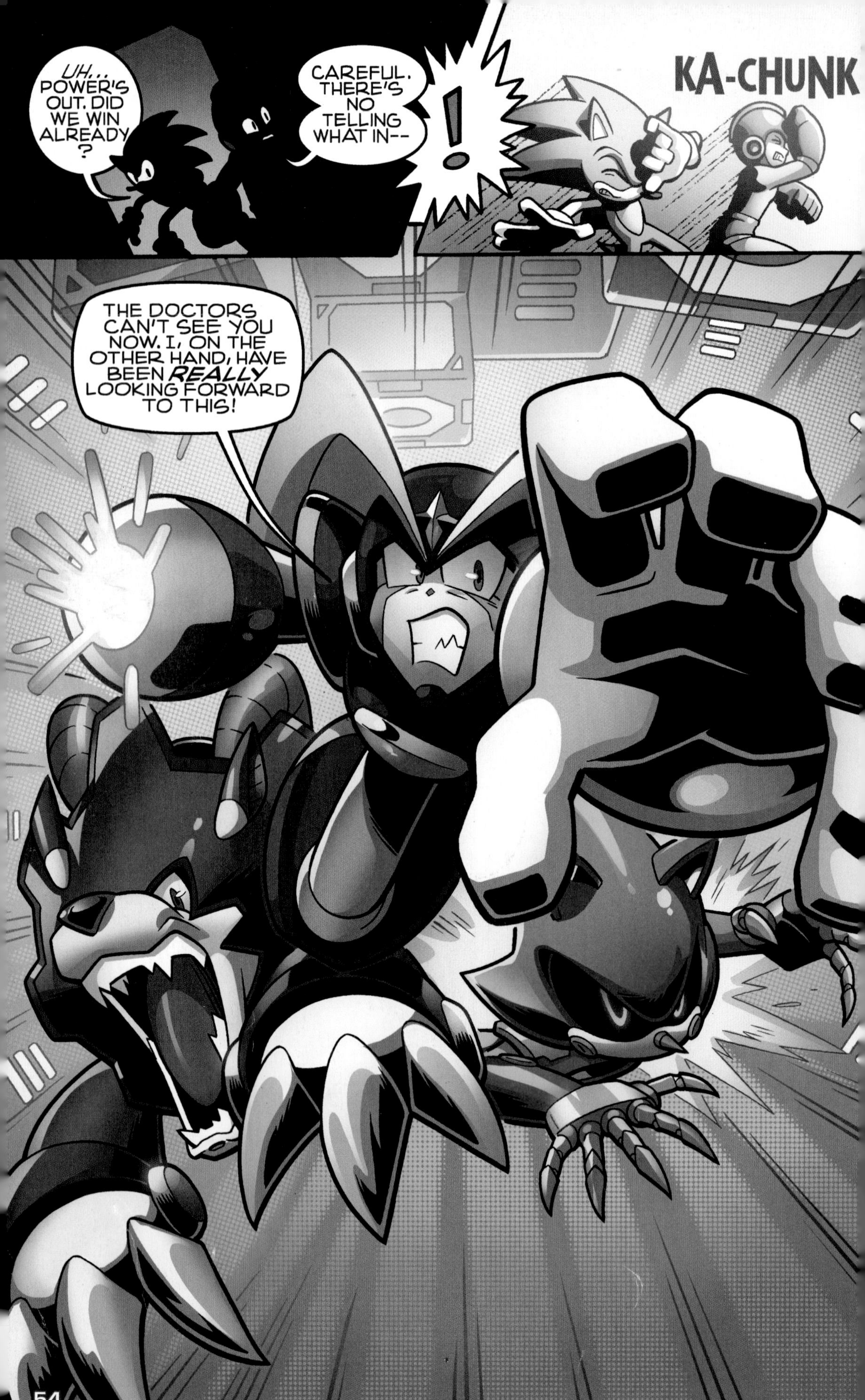
UH... POWER'S OUT. DID WE WIN ALREADY?
CAREFUL. THERE'S NO TELLING WHAT IN--
!
KA-CHUNK
THE DOCTORS CAN'T SEE YOU NOW. I, ON THE OTHER HAND, HAVE BEEN REALLY LOOKING FORWARD TO THIS!

# CHAPTER 3

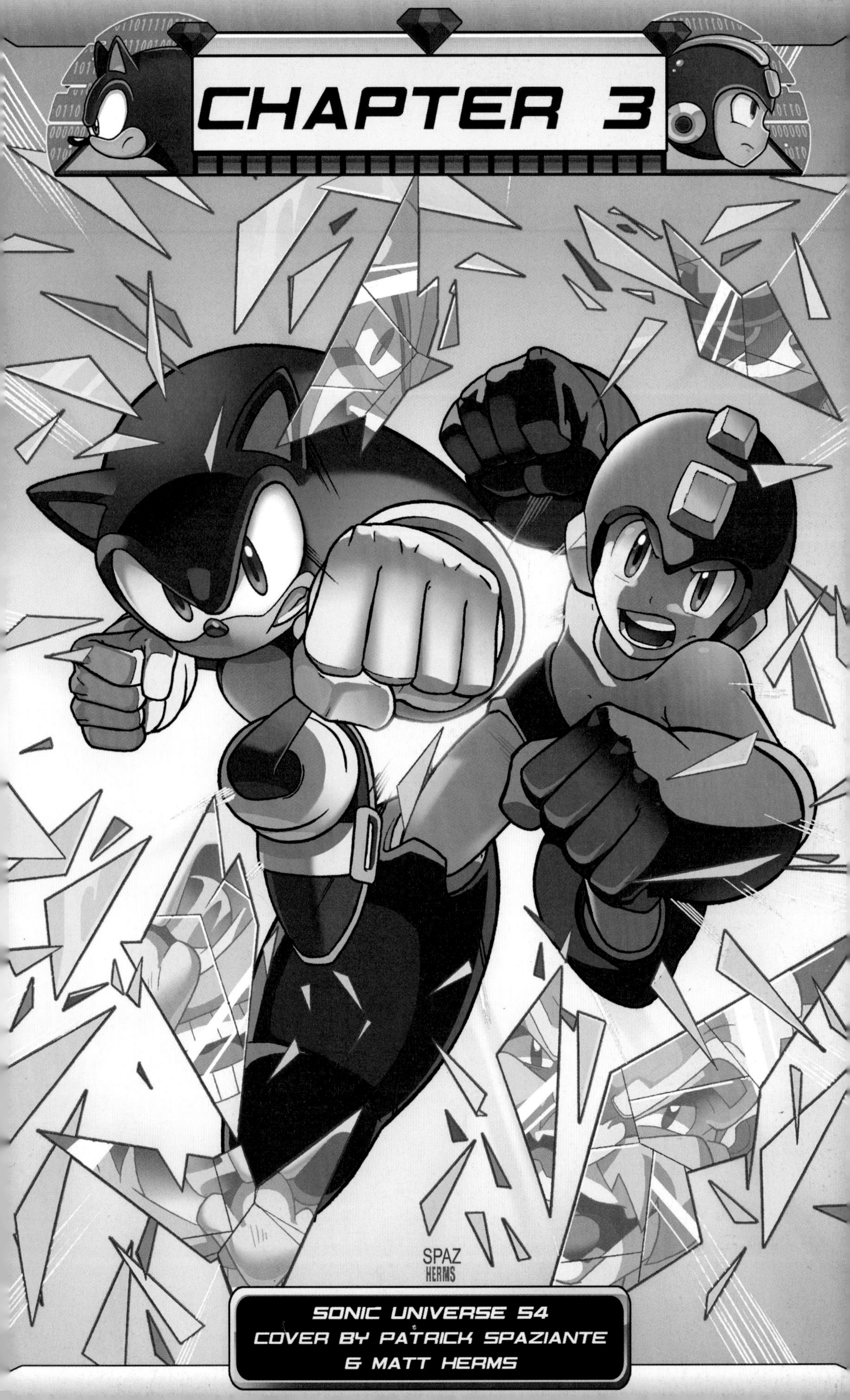
SPAZ
HERMS

SONIC UNIVERSE 54
COVER BY PATRICK SPAZIANTE
& MATT HERMS

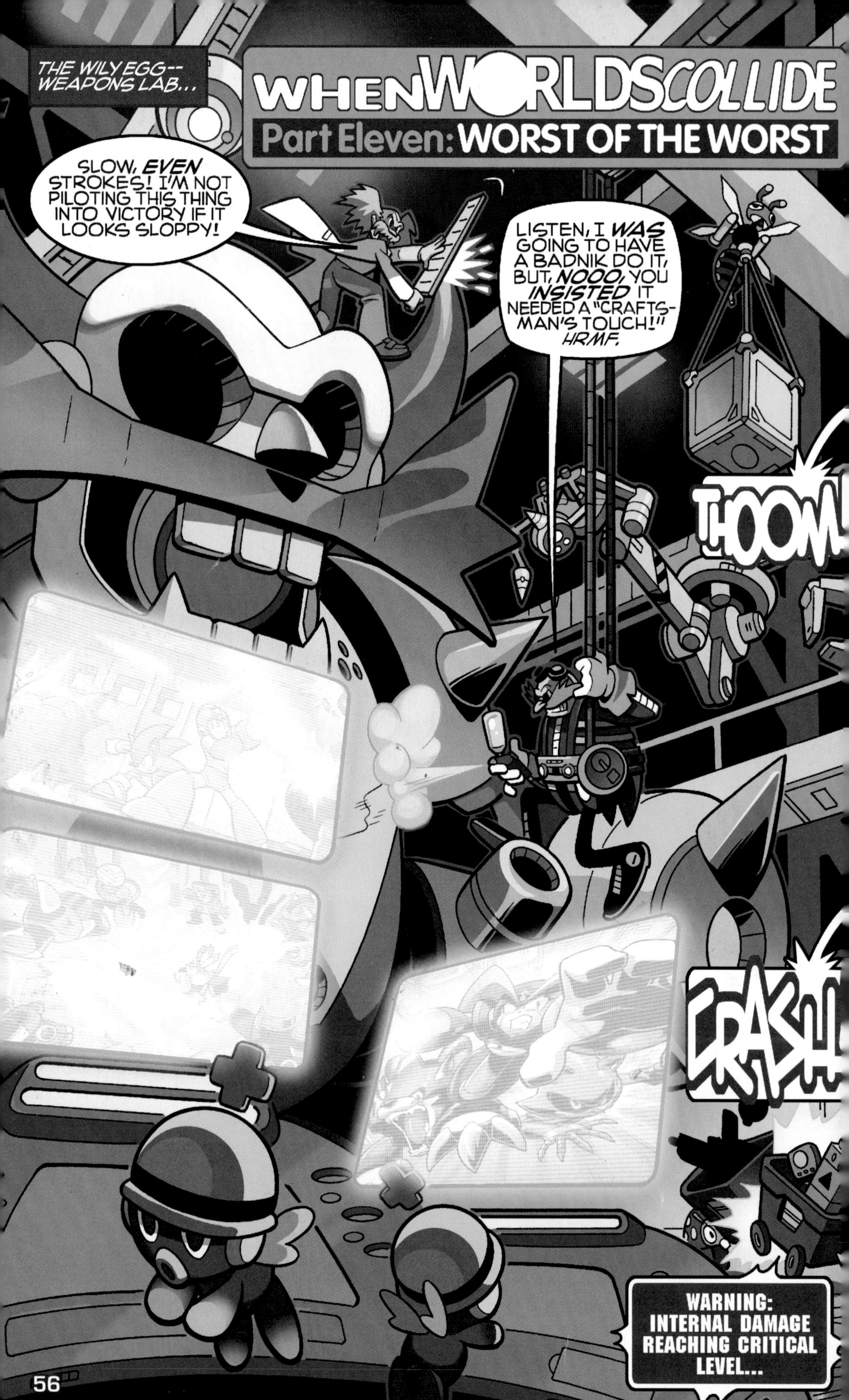
THE WILY EGG-- WEAPONS LAB...
WHEN WORLDS COLLIDE
Part Eleven: WORST OF THE WORST
SLOW, EVEN STROKES! I'M NOT PILOTING THIS THING INTO VICTORY IF IT LOOKS SLOPPY!
LISTEN, I WAS GOING TO HAVE A BADNIK DO IT, BUT, NOOO, YOU INSISTED IT NEEDED A "CRAFTS-MAN'S TOUCH!" HRMF.
THOOM
CRASH
WARNING: INTERNAL DAMAGE REACHING CRITICAL LEVEL...

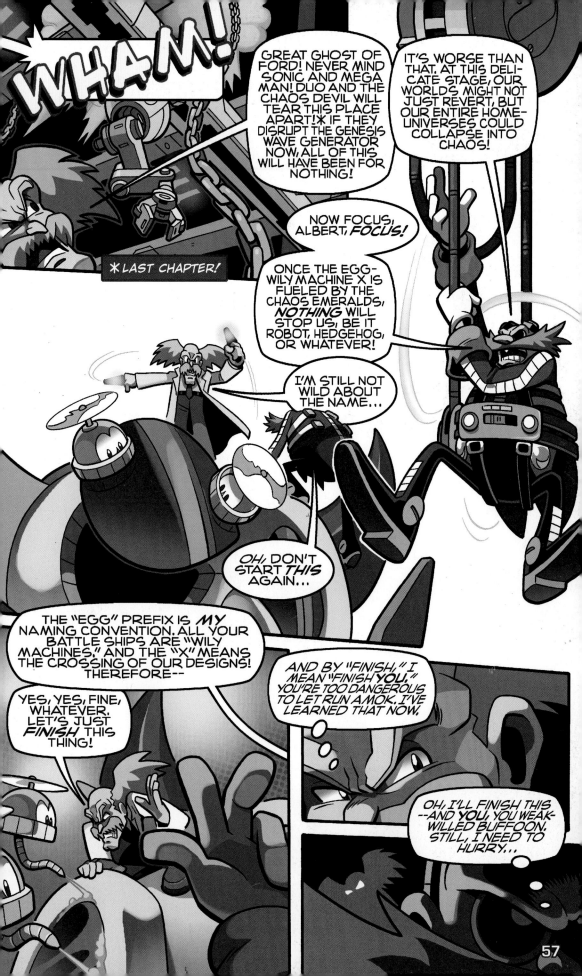

**WHAM!**

GREAT GHOST OF FORD! NEVER MIND SONIC AND MEGA MAN! DUO AND THE CHAOS DEVIL WILL TEAR THIS PLACE APART!* IF THEY DISRUPT THE GENESIS WAVE GENERATOR NOW, ALL OF THIS WILL HAVE BEEN FOR NOTHING!

IT'S WORSE THAN THAT. AT THIS DELICATE STAGE, OUR WORLDS MIGHT NOT JUST REVERT, BUT OUR ENTIRE HOME-UNIVERSES COULD COLLAPSE INTO CHAOS!

\* LAST CHAPTER!

NOW FOCUS, ALBERT, *FOCUS!*

ONCE THE EGG-WILY MACHINE X IS FUELED BY THE CHAOS EMERALDS, *NOTHING* WILL STOP US, BE IT ROBOT, HEDGEHOG, OR WHATEVER!

I'M STILL NOT WILD ABOUT THE NAME...

OH, DON'T START *THIS* AGAIN...

THE "EGG" PREFIX IS *MY* NAMING CONVENTION. ALL YOUR BATTLE SHIPS ARE "WILY MACHINES," AND THE "X" MEANS THE CROSSING OF OUR DESIGNS! THEREFORE--

YES, YES, FINE, WHATEVER. LET'S JUST *FINISH* THIS THING!

AND BY "FINISH," I MEAN "FINISH *YOU*." YOU'RE TOO DANGEROUS TO LET RUN AMOK. I'VE LEARNED THAT NOW.

OH, I'LL FINISH THIS --AND *YOU*, YOU WEAK-WILLED BUFFOON. STILL, I NEED TO HURRY...

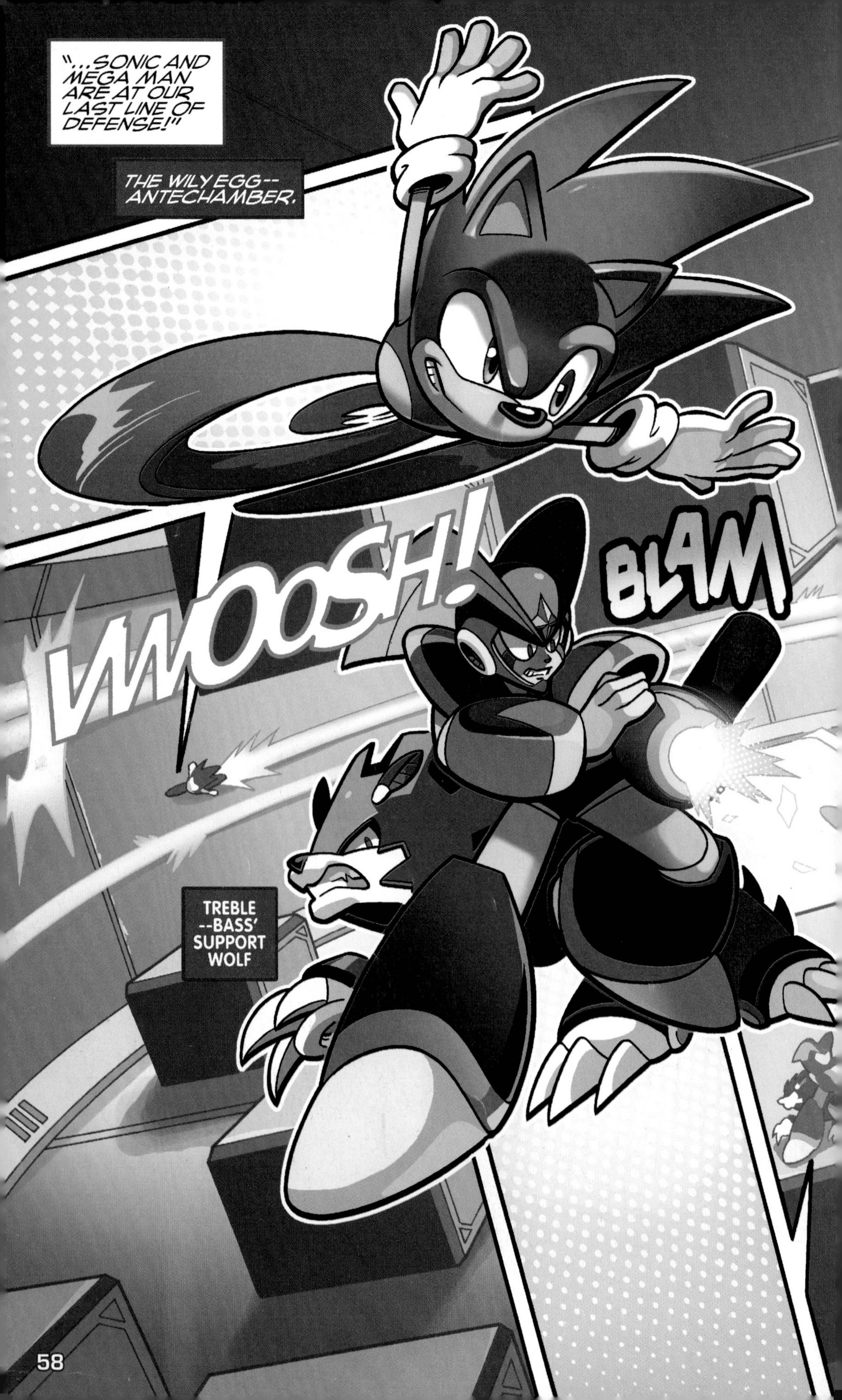
"...SONIC AND MEGA MAN ARE AT OUR LAST LINE OF DEFENSE!"
THE WILY EGG-- ANTECHAMBER.
WWOOSH!
BLAM
TREBLE --BASS' SUPPORT WOLF

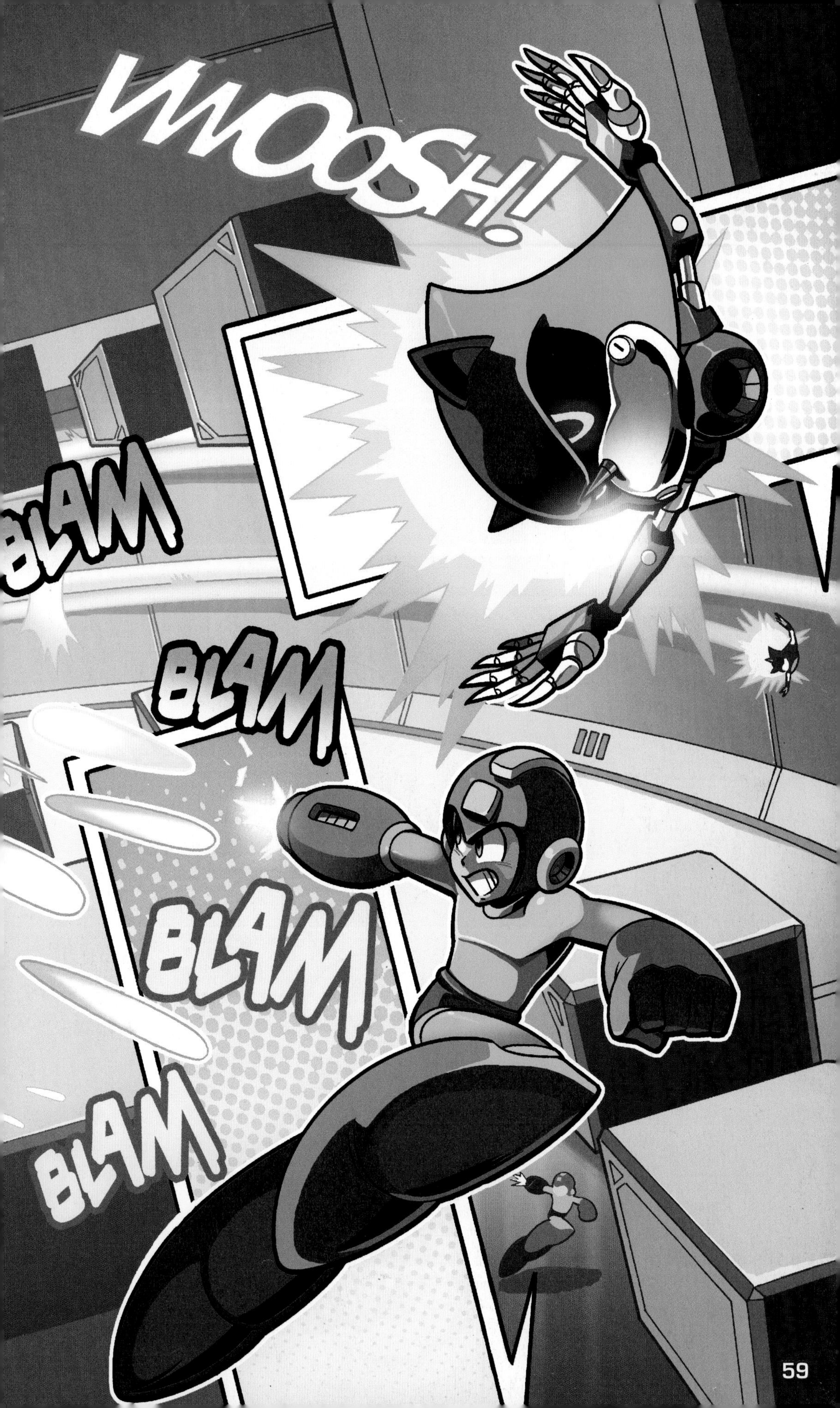
WHOOSH!
BLAM
BLAM
BLAM
BLAM

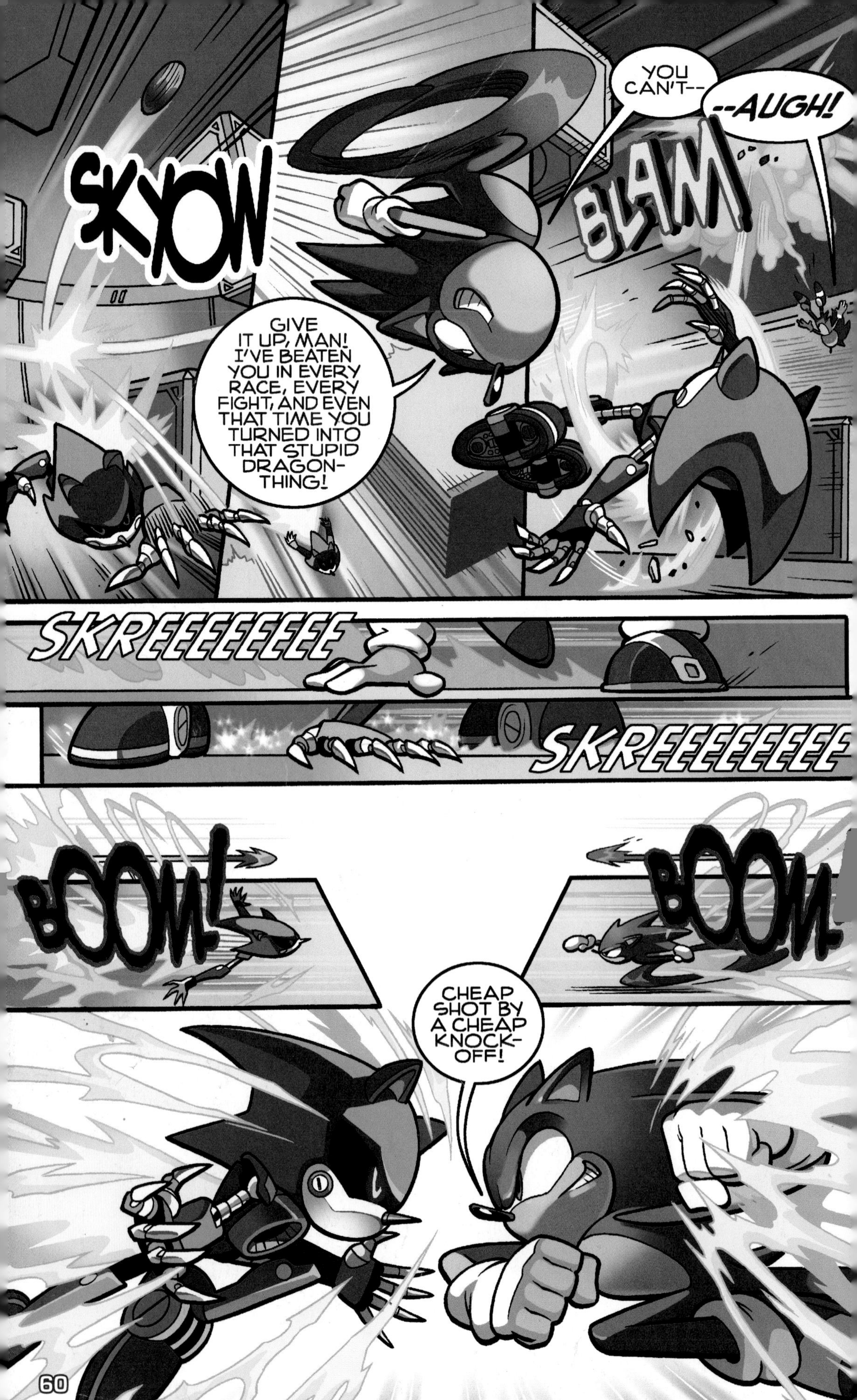
SKYOW
YOU CAN'T--
--AUGH!
BLAM
GIVE IT UP, MAN! I'VE BEATEN YOU IN EVERY RACE, EVERY FIGHT, AND EVEN THAT TIME YOU TURNED INTO THAT STUPID DRAGON-THING!
SKREEEEEEEEE
SKREEEEEEEEE
BOOM!
BOOM!
CHEAP SHOT BY A CHEAP KNOCK-OFF!

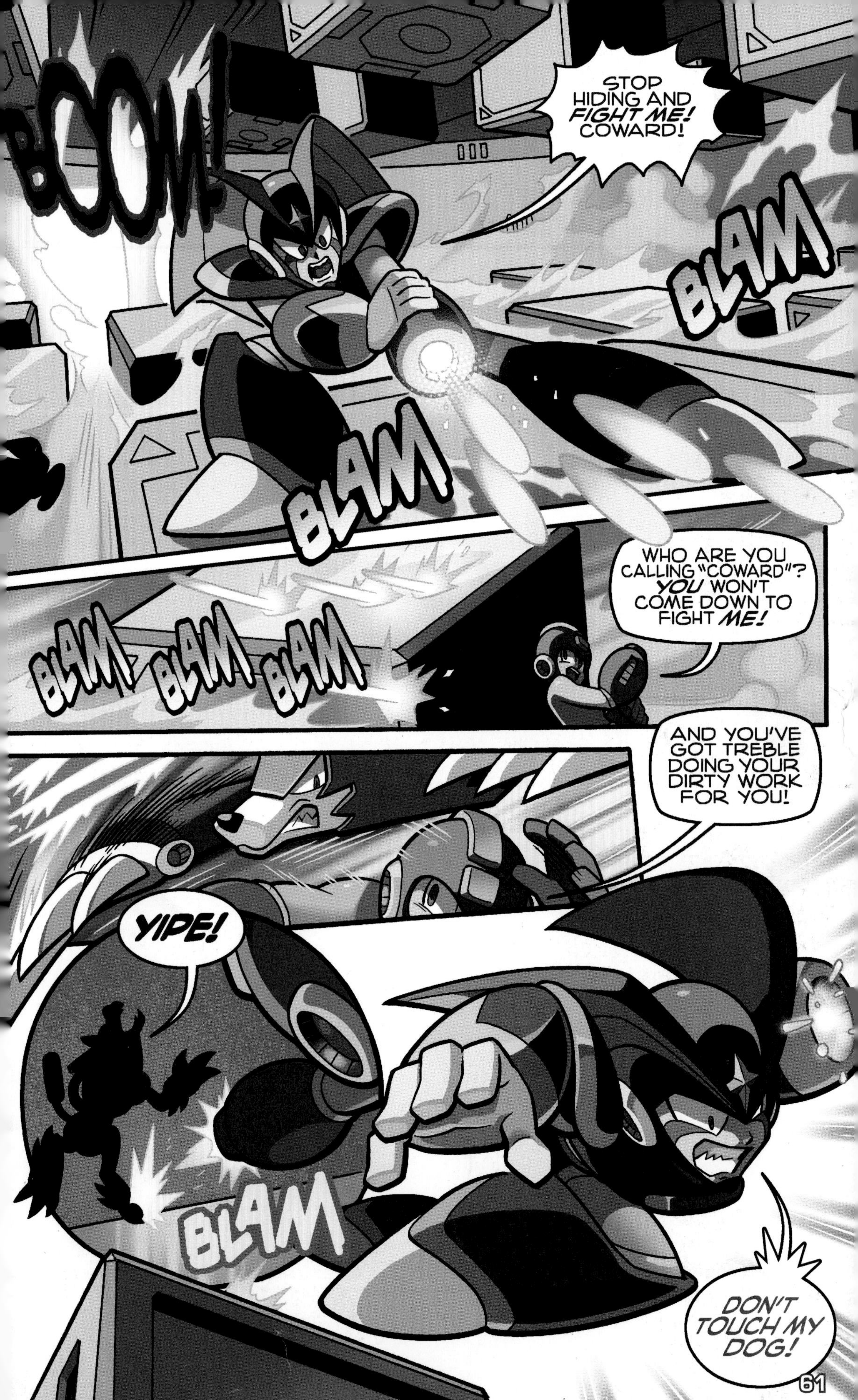
BOOM!
STOP HIDING AND FIGHT ME! COWARD!
BLAM
BLAM
WHO ARE YOU CALLING "COWARD"? YOU WON'T COME DOWN TO FIGHT ME!
BLAM BLAM BLAM
AND YOU'VE GOT TREBLE DOING YOUR DIRTY WORK FOR YOU!
YIPE!
BLAM
DON'T TOUCH MY DOG!

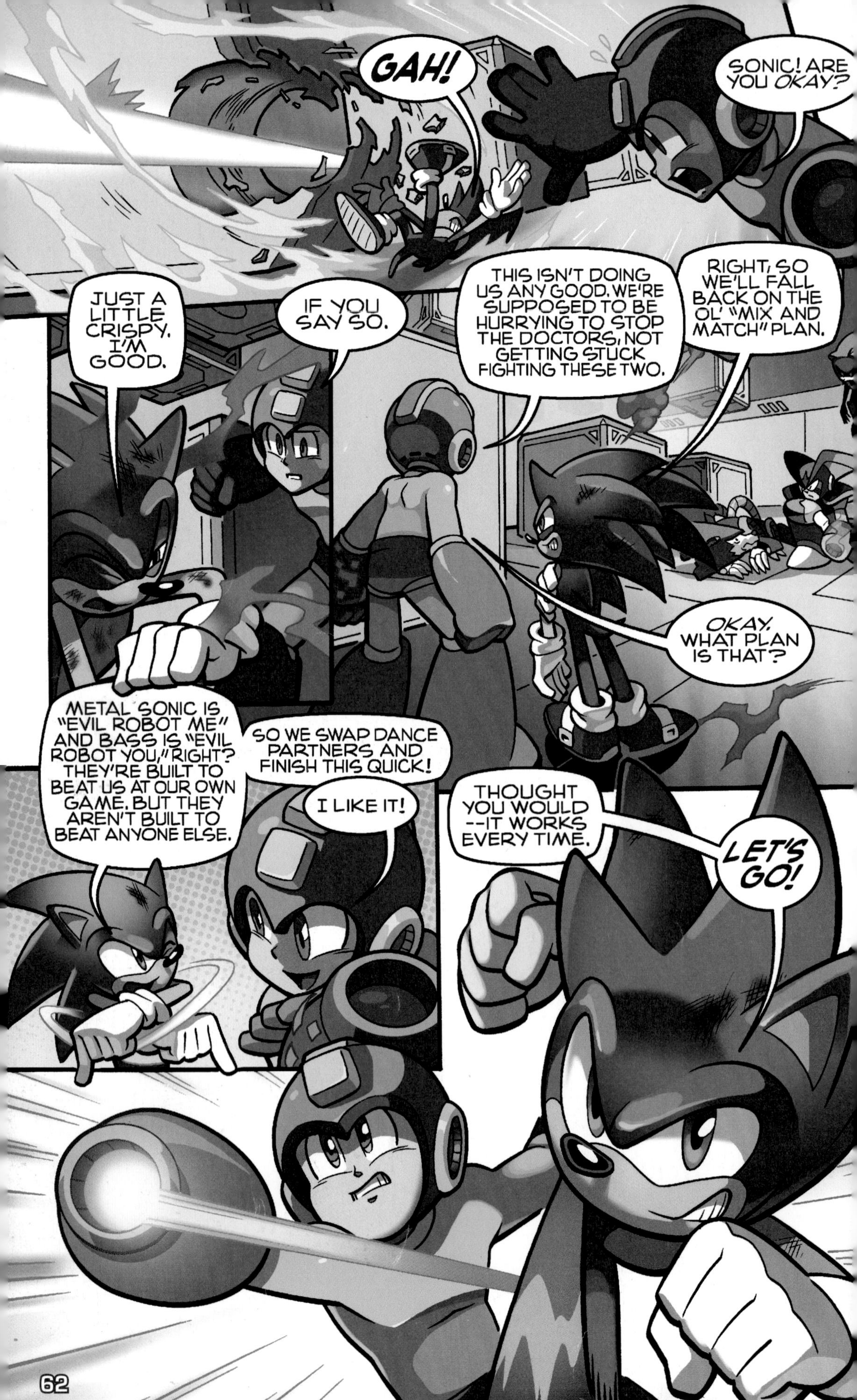
GAH!
SONIC! ARE YOU OKAY?
JUST A LITTLE CRISPY. I'M GOOD.
IF YOU SAY SO.
THIS ISN'T DOING US ANY GOOD. WE'RE SUPPOSED TO BE HURRYING TO STOP THE DOCTORS, NOT GETTING STUCK FIGHTING THESE TWO.
RIGHT, SO WE'LL FALL BACK ON THE OL' "MIX AND MATCH" PLAN.
OKAY. WHAT PLAN IS THAT?
METAL SONIC IS "EVIL ROBOT ME" AND BASS IS "EVIL ROBOT YOU," RIGHT? THEY'RE BUILT TO BEAT US AT OUR OWN GAME. BUT THEY AREN'T BUILT TO BEAT ANYONE ELSE.
SO WE SWAP DANCE PARTNERS AND FINISH THIS QUICK!
I LIKE IT!
THOUGHT YOU WOULD --IT WORKS EVERY TIME.
LET'S GO!

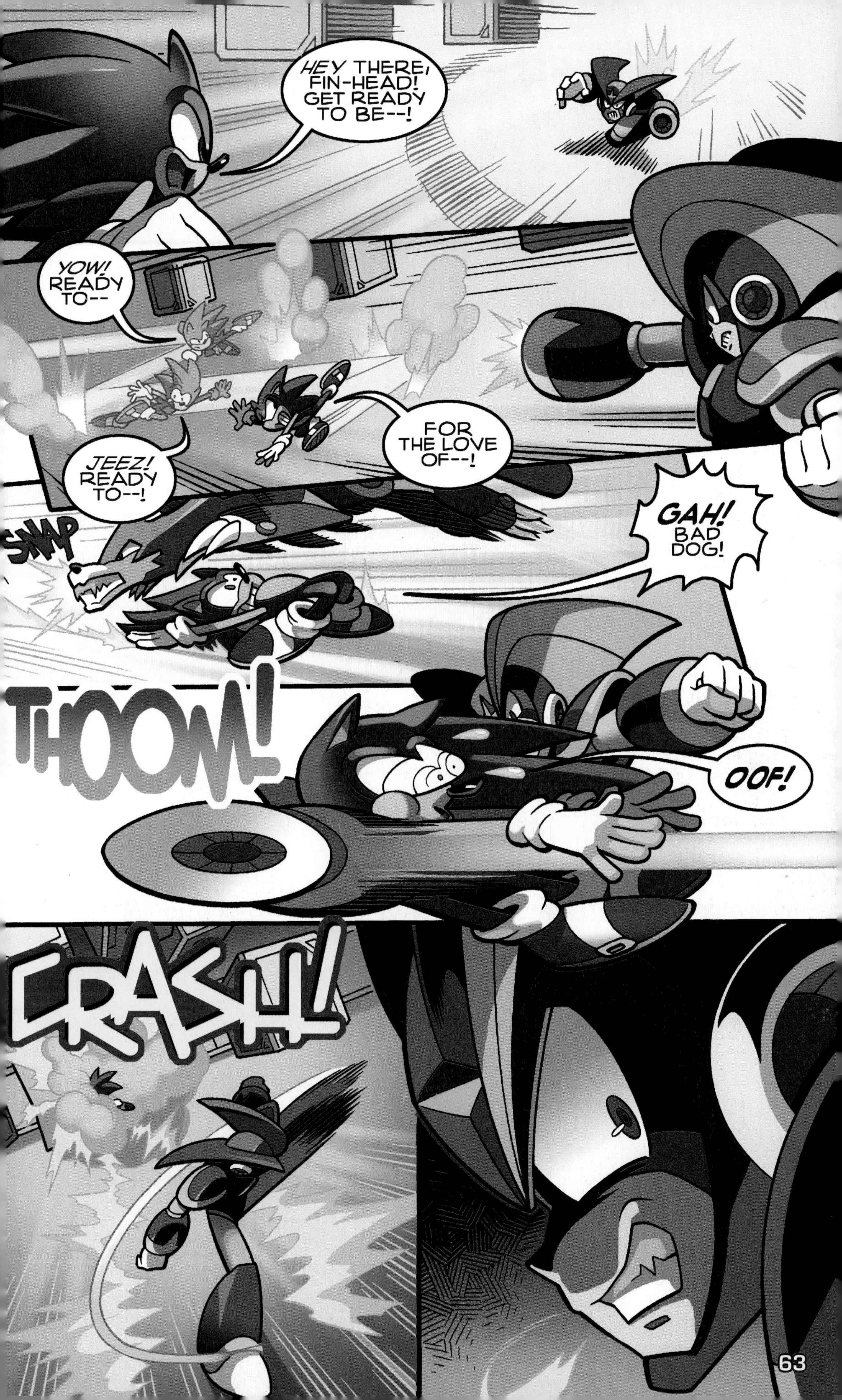
HEY THERE, FIN-HEAD! GET READY TO BE--!
YOW! READY TO--
JEEZ! READY TO--!
FOR THE LOVE OF--!
SNAP
GAH! BAD DOG!
THOOM!
OOF!
CRASH!

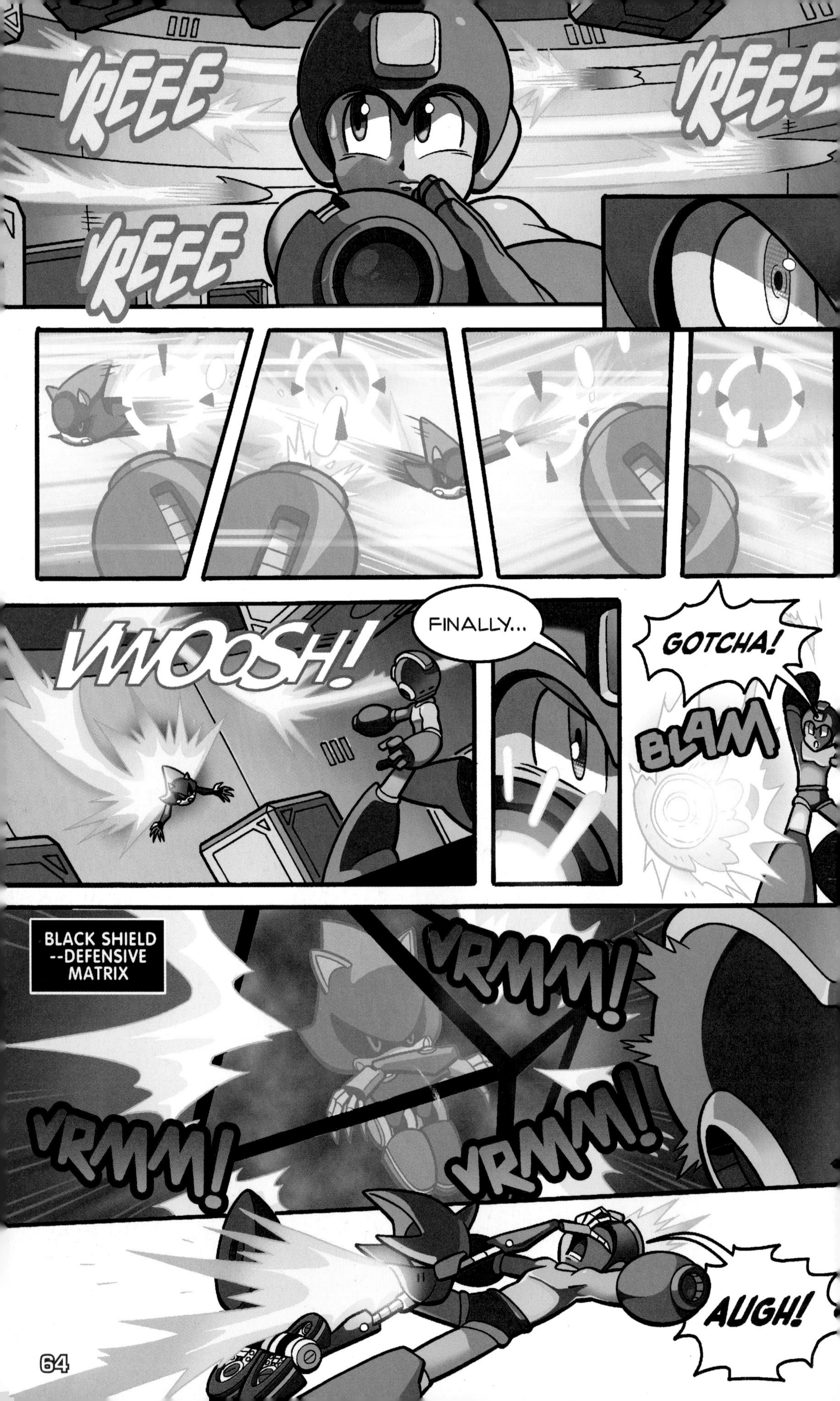
VREEE
VREEE
VREEE
VWOOSH!
FINALLY...
GOTCHA!
BLAM
BLACK SHIELD --DEFENSIVE MATRIX
VRMM!
VRMM!
VRMM!
AUGH!

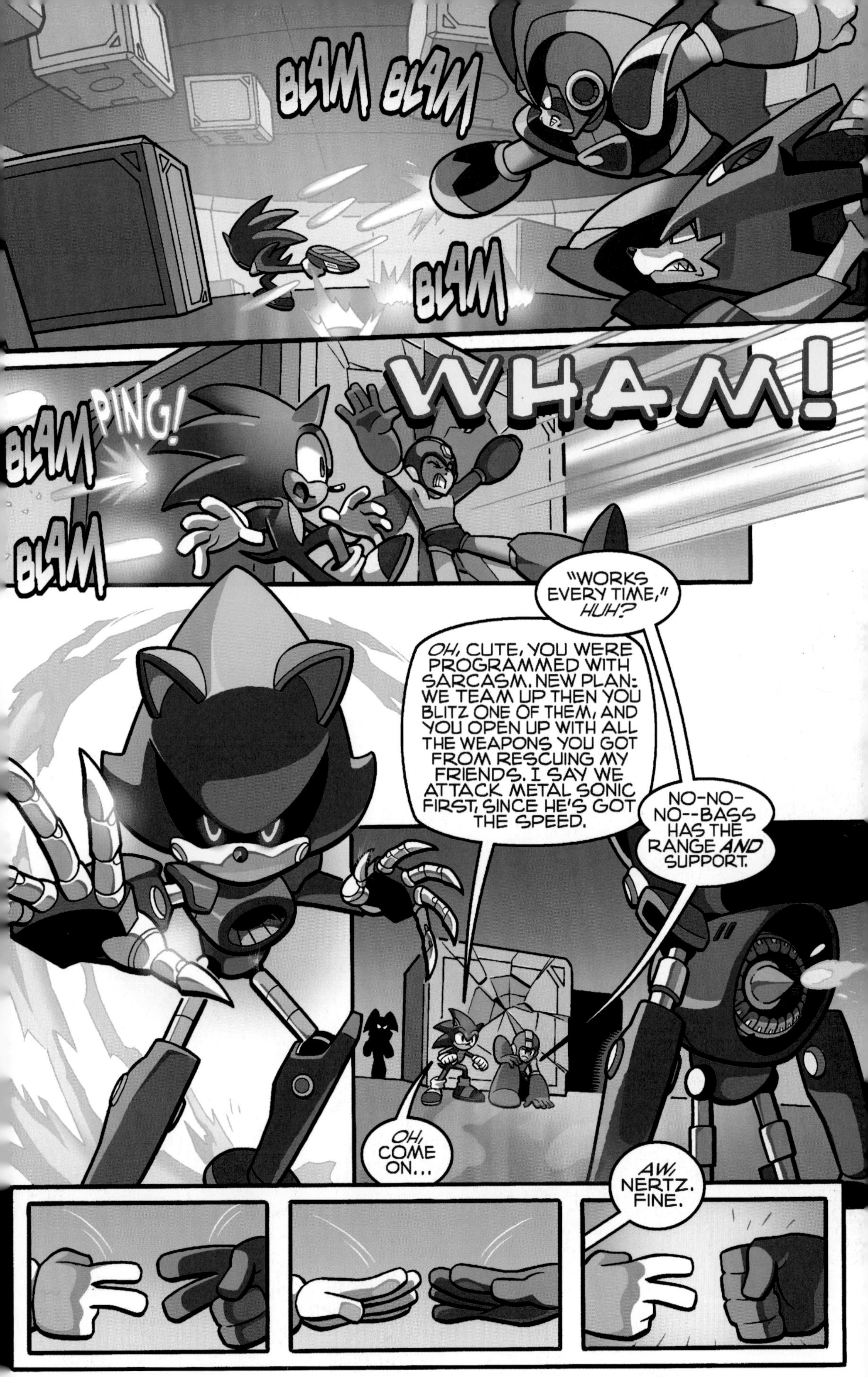
BLAM BLAM
BLAM
WHAM!
BLAM PING!
BLAM
"WORKS EVERY TIME," HUH?
OH, CUTE, YOU WERE PROGRAMMED WITH SARCASM. NEW PLAN: WE TEAM UP THEN YOU BLITZ ONE OF THEM, AND YOU OPEN UP WITH ALL THE WEAPONS YOU GOT FROM RESCUING MY FRIENDS. I SAY WE ATTACK METAL SONIC FIRST, SINCE HE'S GOT THE SPEED.
NO-NO-NO--BASS HAS THE RANGE *AND* SUPPORT.
OH, COME ON...
AW, NERTZ. FINE.

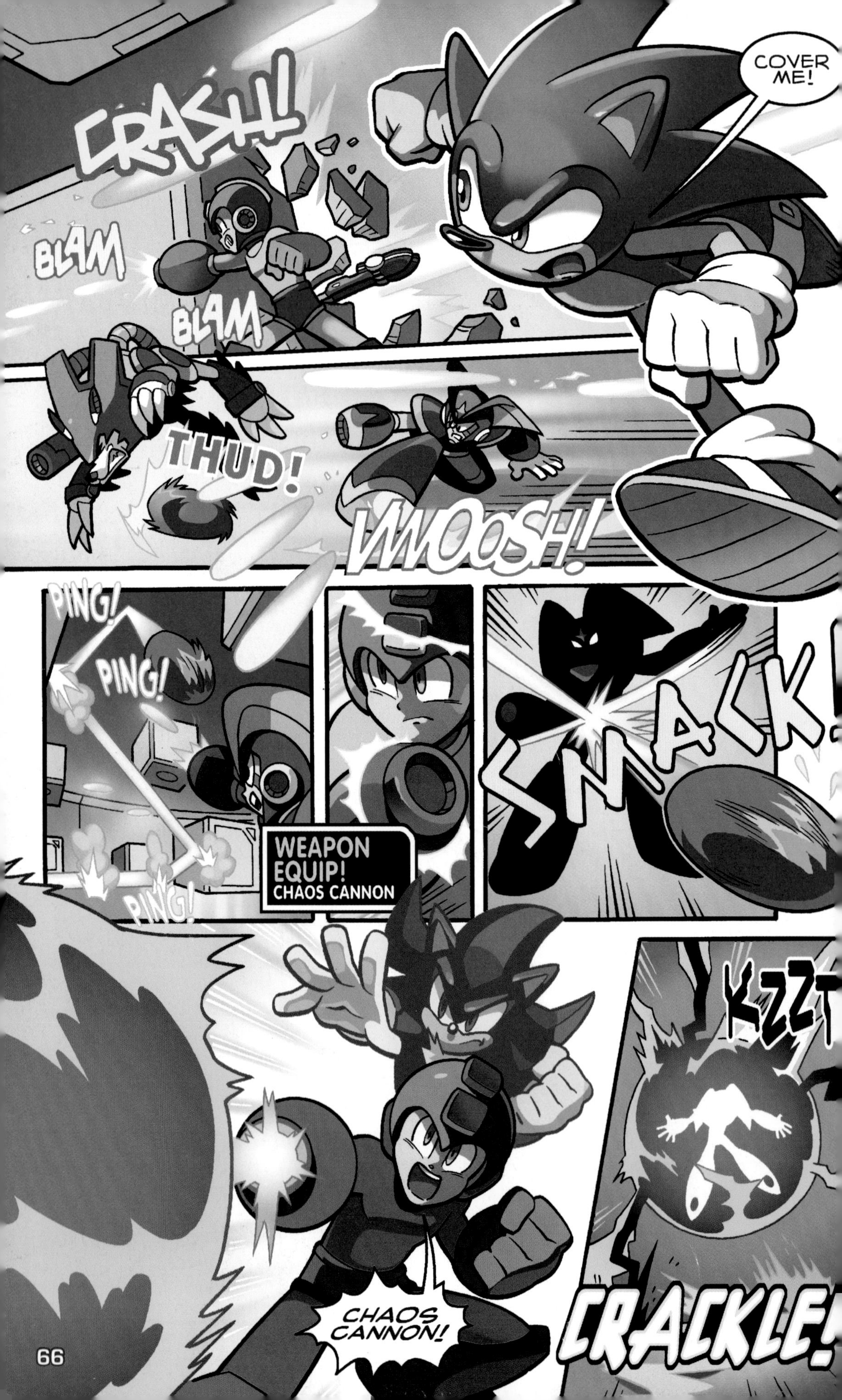
CRASH!
COVER ME!
BLAM
BLAM
THUD!
VWOOSH!
PING!
PING!
PING!
WEAPON EQUIP!
CHAOS CANNON
SMACK!
KZZT
CHAOS CANNON!
CRACKLE!

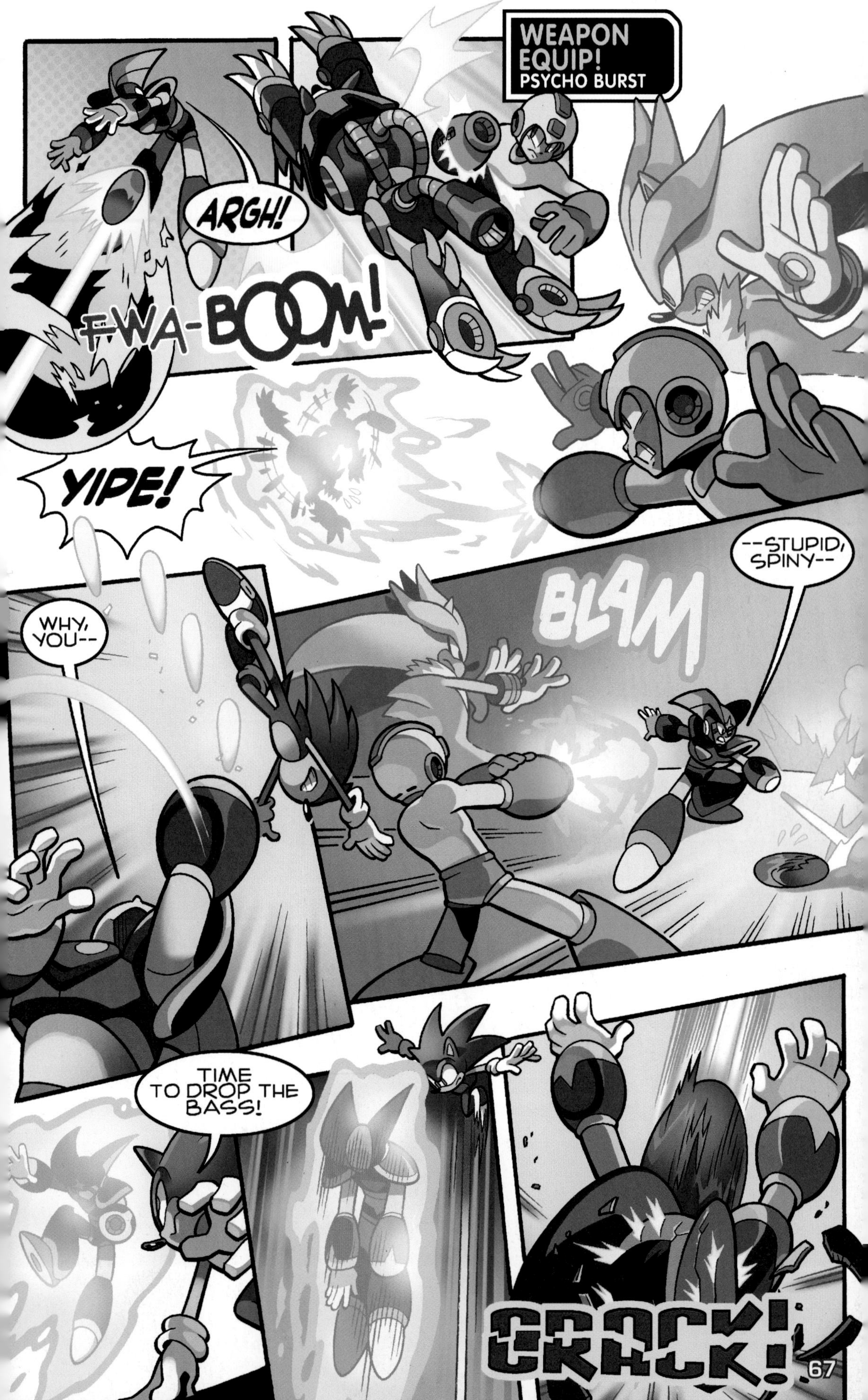
WEAPON EQUIP!
PSYCHO BURST
ARGH!
FWA-BOOM!
YIPE!
WHY, YOU--
BLAM
--STUPID, SPINY--
TIME TO DROP THE BASS!
CRACK! CRACK!

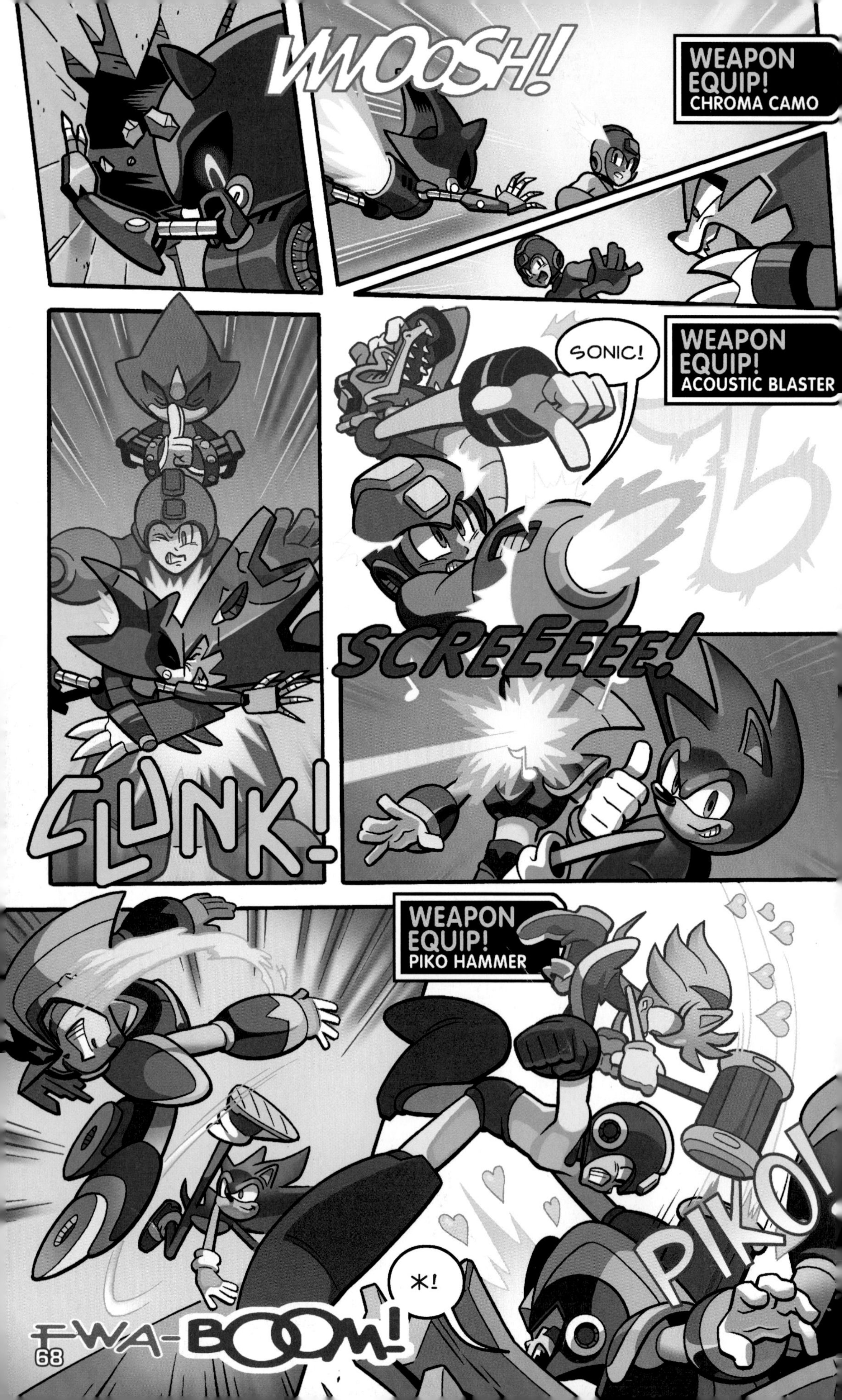

VWOOSH!
WEAPON EQUIP! CHROMA CAMO
SONIC!
WEAPON EQUIP! ACOUSTIC BLASTER
CLUNK!
SCREEEEEE!
WEAPON EQUIP! PIKO HAMMER
*!
PIKO!
FWA-BOOM!

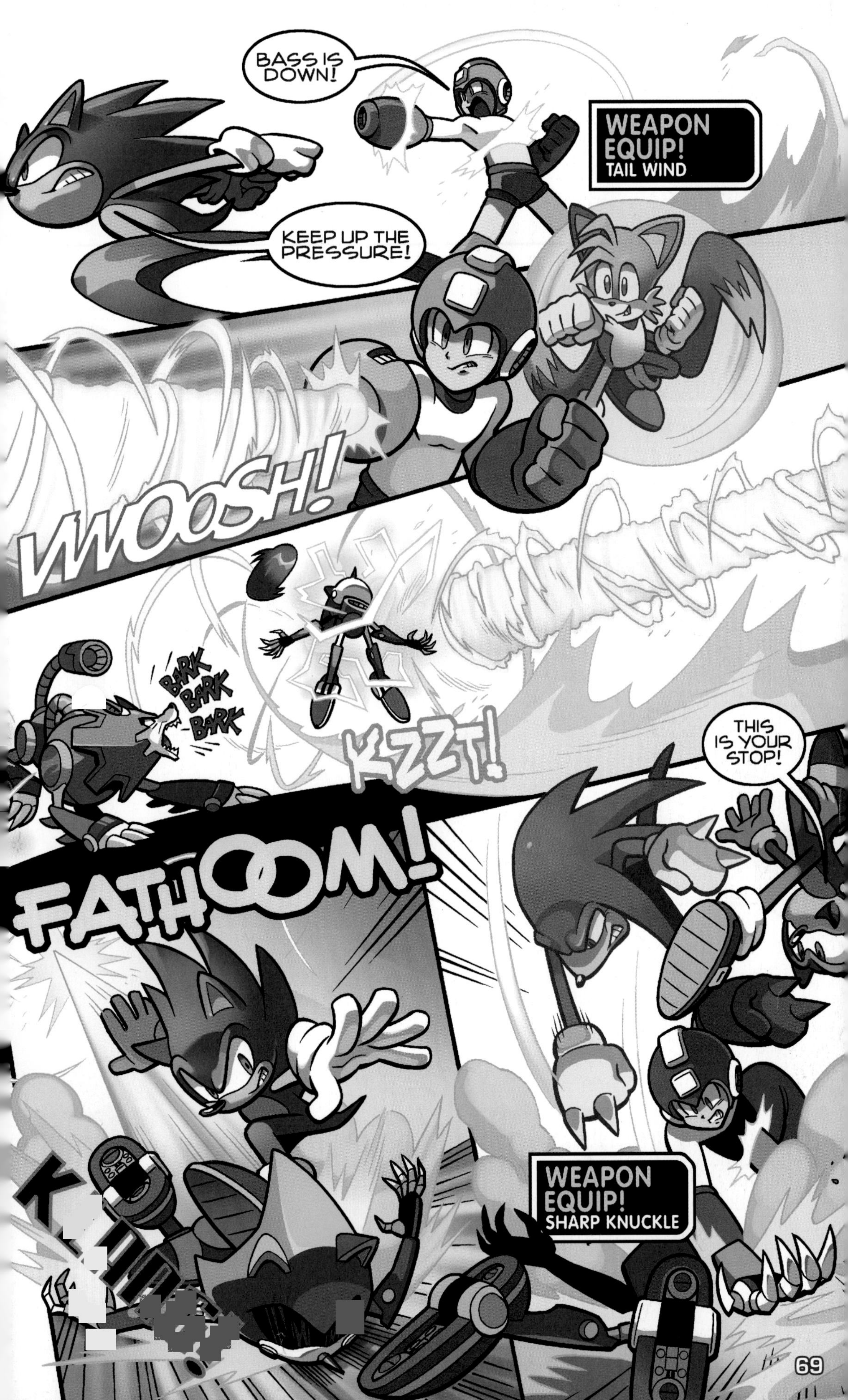
BASS IS DOWN!
WEAPON EQUIP! TAIL WIND
KEEP UP THE PRESSURE!
WWOOSH!
BARK BARK BARK
KZZT!
THIS IS YOUR STOP!
FATHOOM!
WEAPON EQUIP! SHARP KNUCKLE

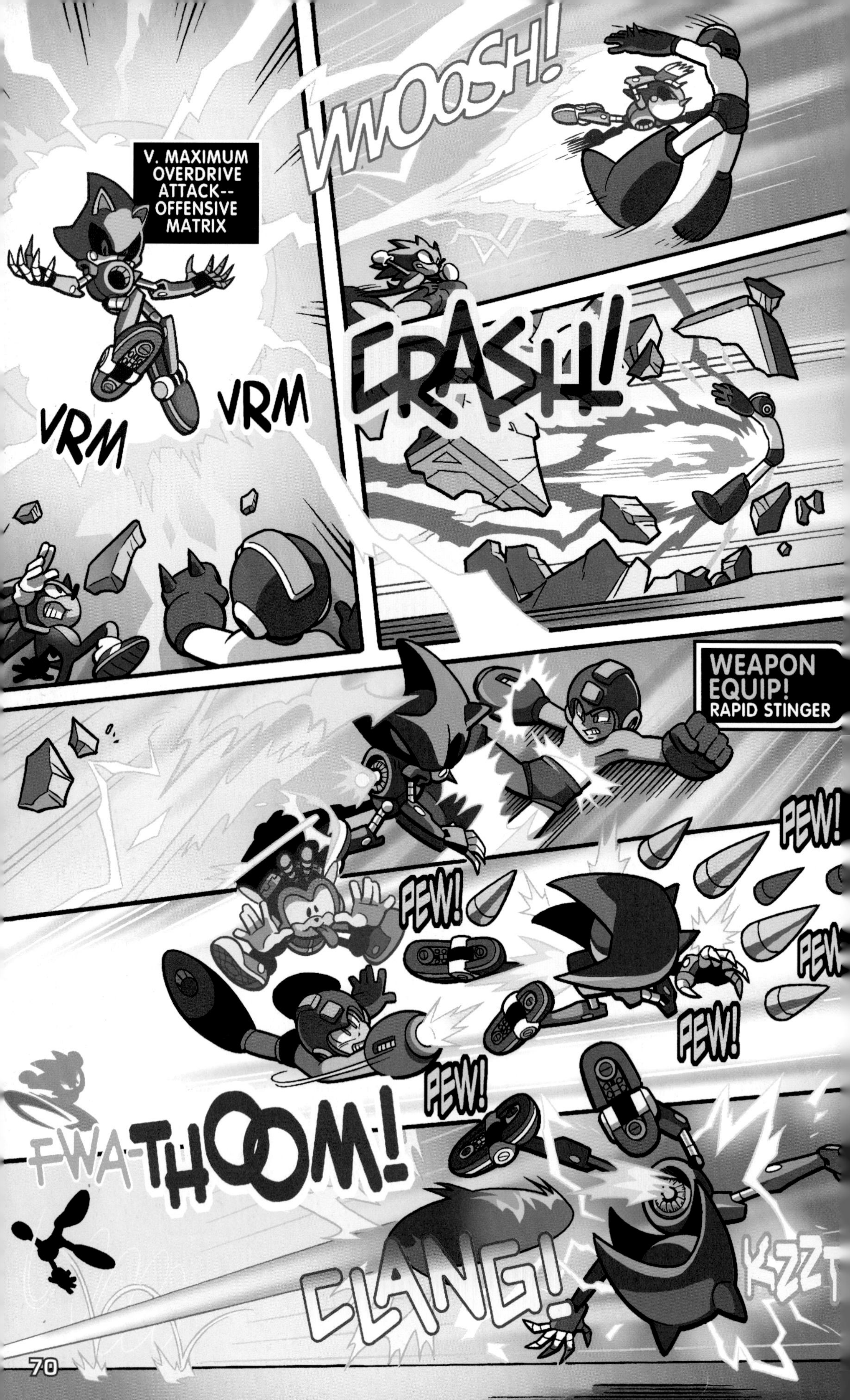

V. MAXIMUM OVERDRIVE ATTACK-- OFFENSIVE MATRIX
WWOOSH!
VRM
VRM
CRASH!
WEAPON EQUIP! RAPID STINGER
PEW!
PEW!
PEW!
PEW!
PEW!
FWA-THOOM!
CLANG!
KZZT

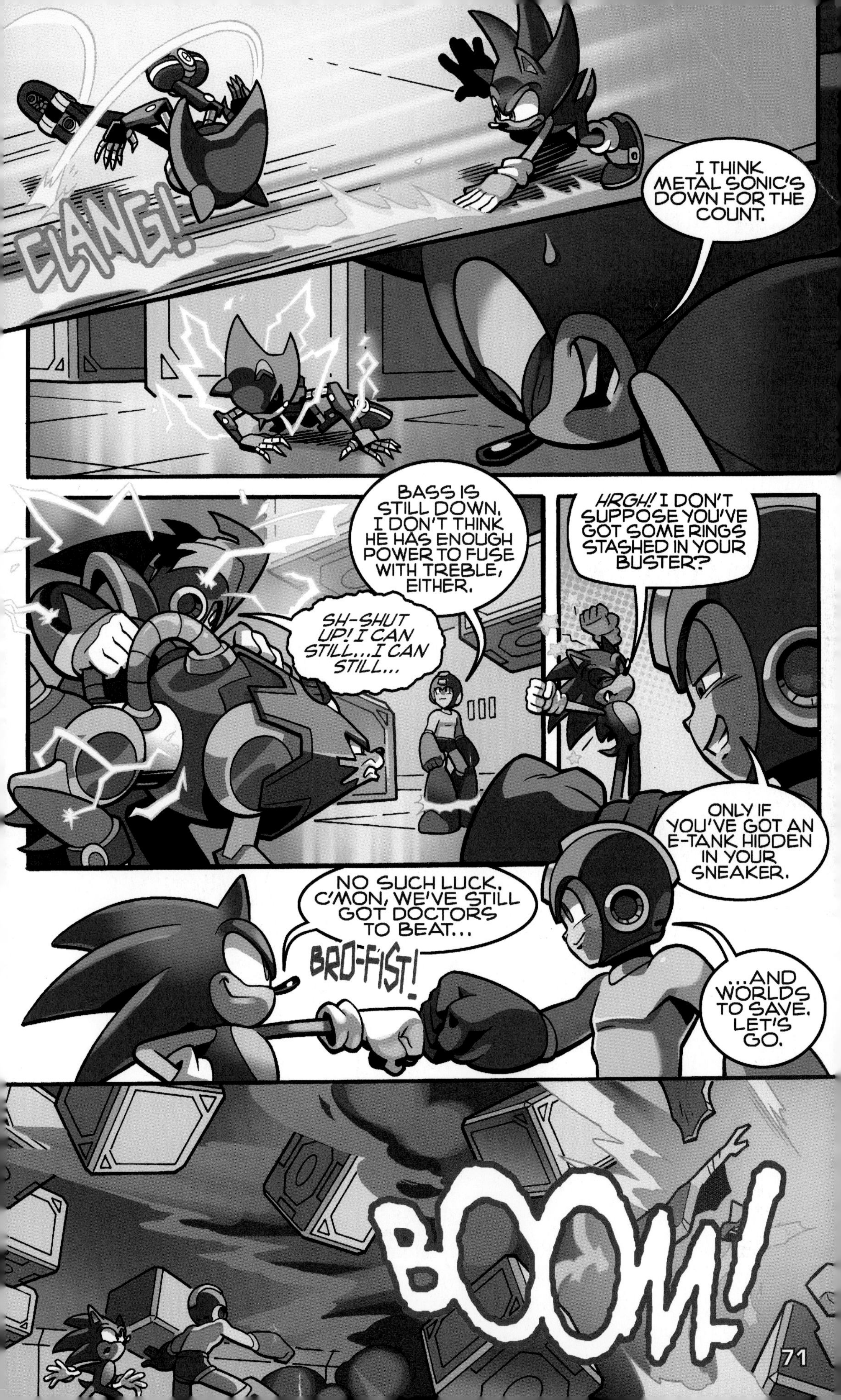
CLANG!
I THINK METAL SONIC'S DOWN FOR THE COUNT.
BASS IS STILL DOWN. I DON'T THINK HE HAS ENOUGH POWER TO FUSE WITH TREBLE, EITHER.
SH-SHUT UP! I CAN STILL...I CAN STILL...
HRGH! I DON'T SUPPOSE YOU'VE GOT SOME RINGS STASHED IN YOUR BUSTER?
ONLY IF YOU'VE GOT AN E-TANK HIDDEN IN YOUR SNEAKER.
NO SUCH LUCK. C'MON, WE'VE STILL GOT DOCTORS TO BEAT...
BRO-FIST!
...AND WORLDS TO SAVE. LET'S GO.
BOOM!

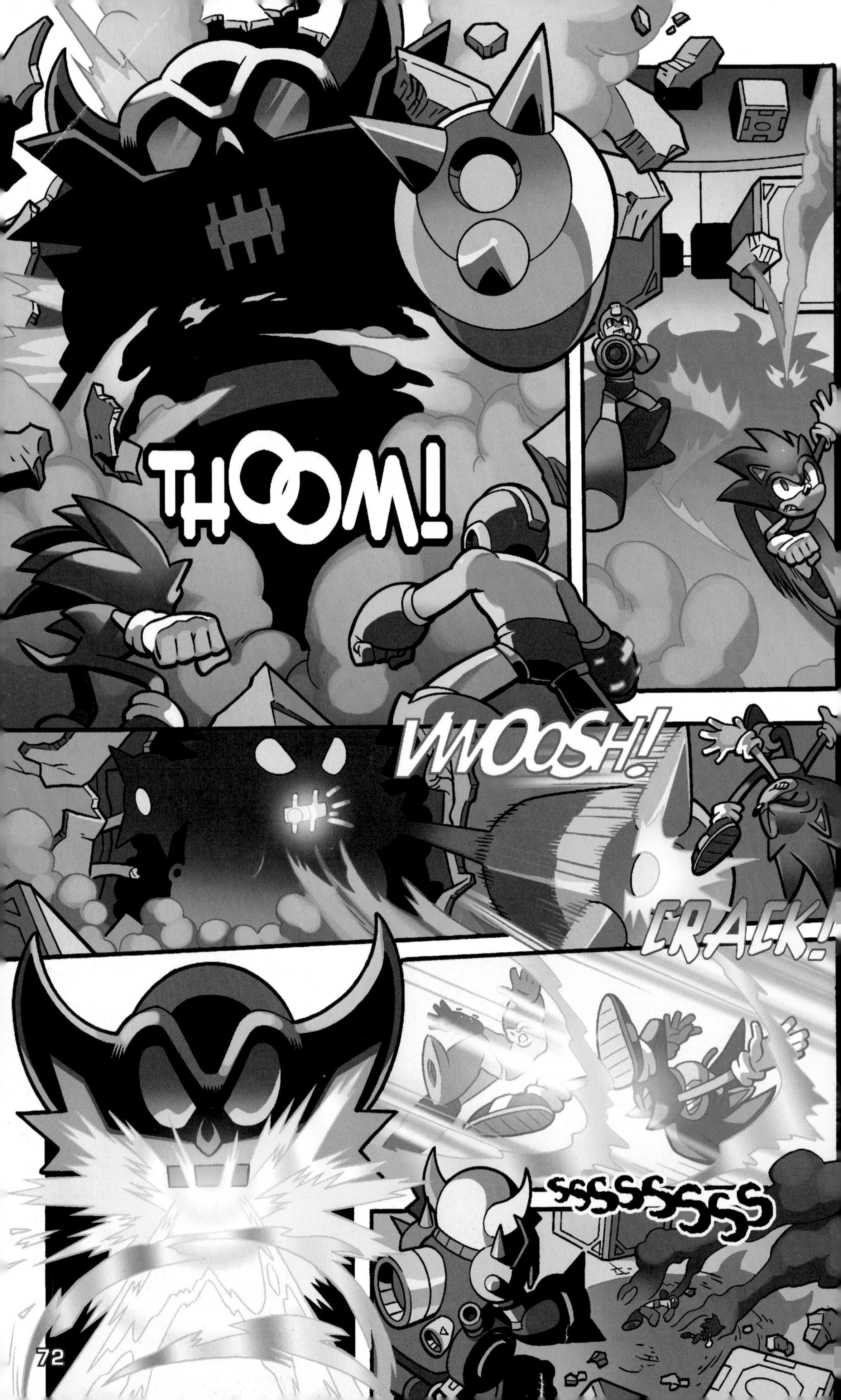
THOOM!
VWOOSH!
CRACK!
SSSSSSSSS

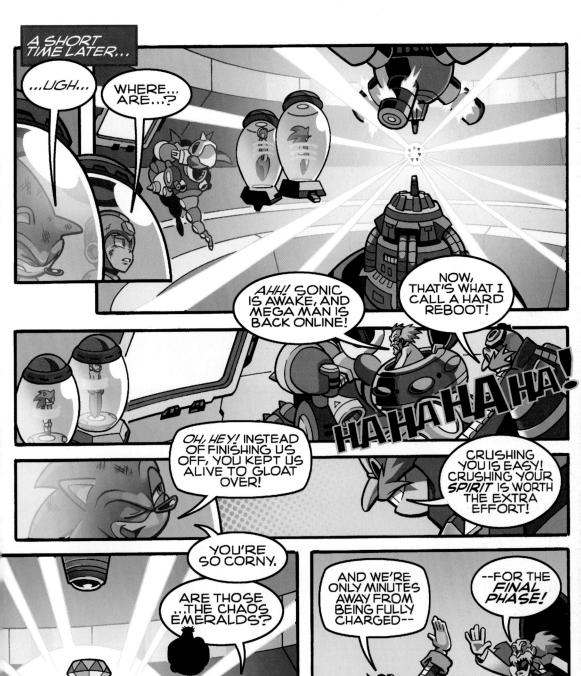

...UGH...

WHERE... ARE...?

*AHH!* SONIC IS AWAKE, AND MEGA MAN IS BACK ONLINE!

NOW, THAT'S WHAT I CALL A HARD REBOOT!

HA HA HA HA HA!

*OH, HEY!* INSTEAD OF FINISHING US OFF, YOU KEPT US ALIVE TO GLOAT OVER!

CRUSHING YOU IS EASY! CRUSHING YOUR *SPIRIT* IS WORTH THE EXTRA EFFORT!

YOU'RE SO CORNY.

ARE THOSE ...THE CHAOS EMERALDS?

AND WE'RE ONLY MINUTES AWAY FROM BEING FULLY CHARGED--

--FOR THE *FINAL PHASE!*

OF COURSE, YOU SIMPLE-TON! EACH ONE A VIRTUALLY LIMITLESS FOUNT OF ENERGY, AND *WE* HAVE *ALL SEVEN!*

SNEER!

73

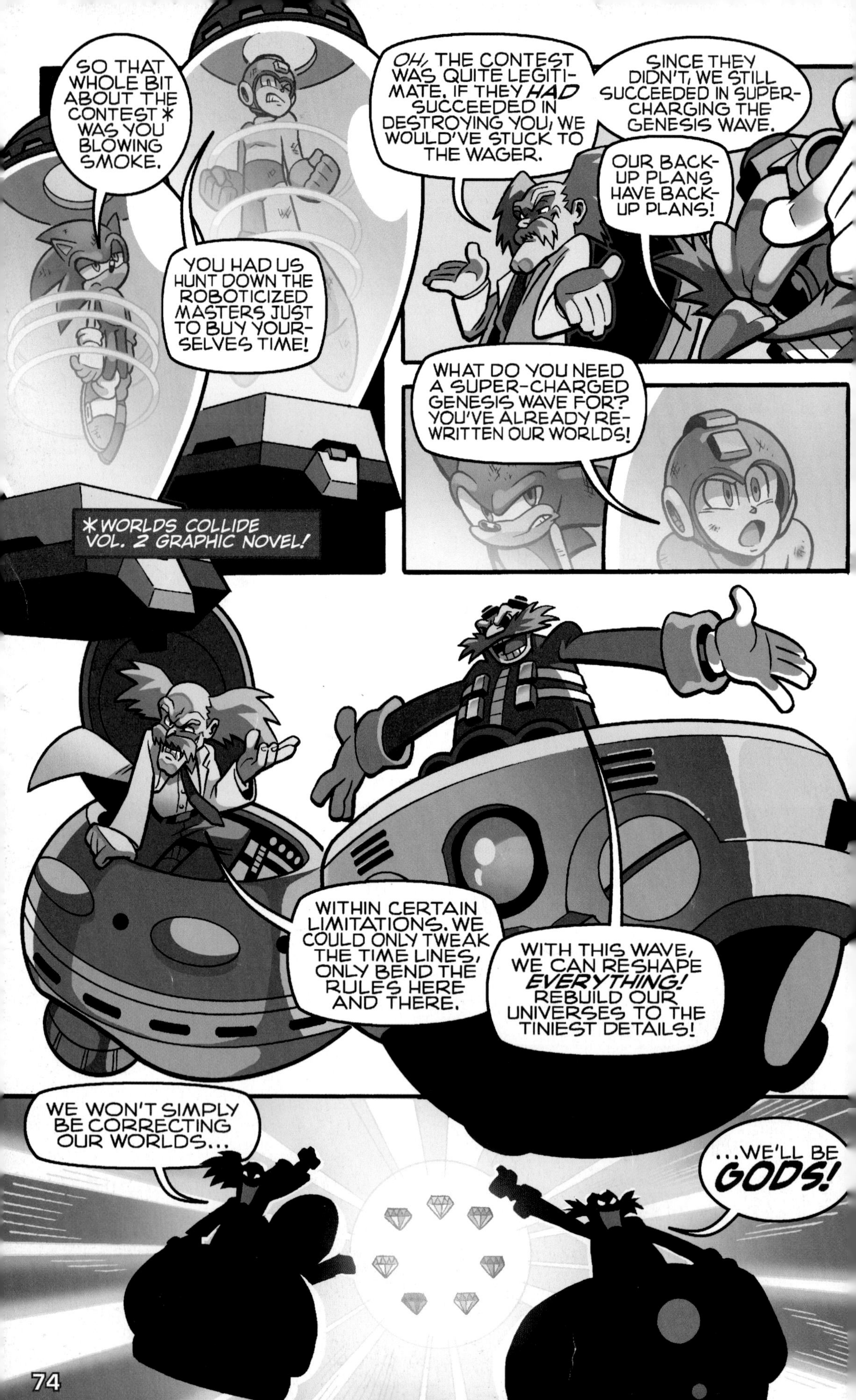
SO THAT WHOLE BIT ABOUT THE CONTEST * WAS YOU BLOWING SMOKE.
YOU HAD US HUNT DOWN THE ROBOTICIZED MASTERS JUST TO BUY YOURSELVES TIME!
*WORLDS COLLIDE VOL. 2 GRAPHIC NOVEL!
OH, THE CONTEST WAS QUITE LEGITIMATE. IF THEY HAD SUCCEEDED IN DESTROYING YOU, WE WOULD'VE STUCK TO THE WAGER.
SINCE THEY DIDN'T, WE STILL SUCCEEDED IN SUPER-CHARGING THE GENESIS WAVE.
OUR BACK-UP PLANS HAVE BACK-UP PLANS!
WHAT DO YOU NEED A SUPER-CHARGED GENESIS WAVE FOR? YOU'VE ALREADY RE-WRITTEN OUR WORLDS!
WITHIN CERTAIN LIMITATIONS. WE COULD ONLY TWEAK THE TIME LINES, ONLY BEND THE RULES HERE AND THERE.
WITH THIS WAVE, WE CAN RESHAPE EVERYTHING! REBUILD OUR UNIVERSES TO THE TINIEST DETAILS!
WE WON'T SIMPLY BE CORRECTING OUR WORLDS...
...WE'LL BE GODS!

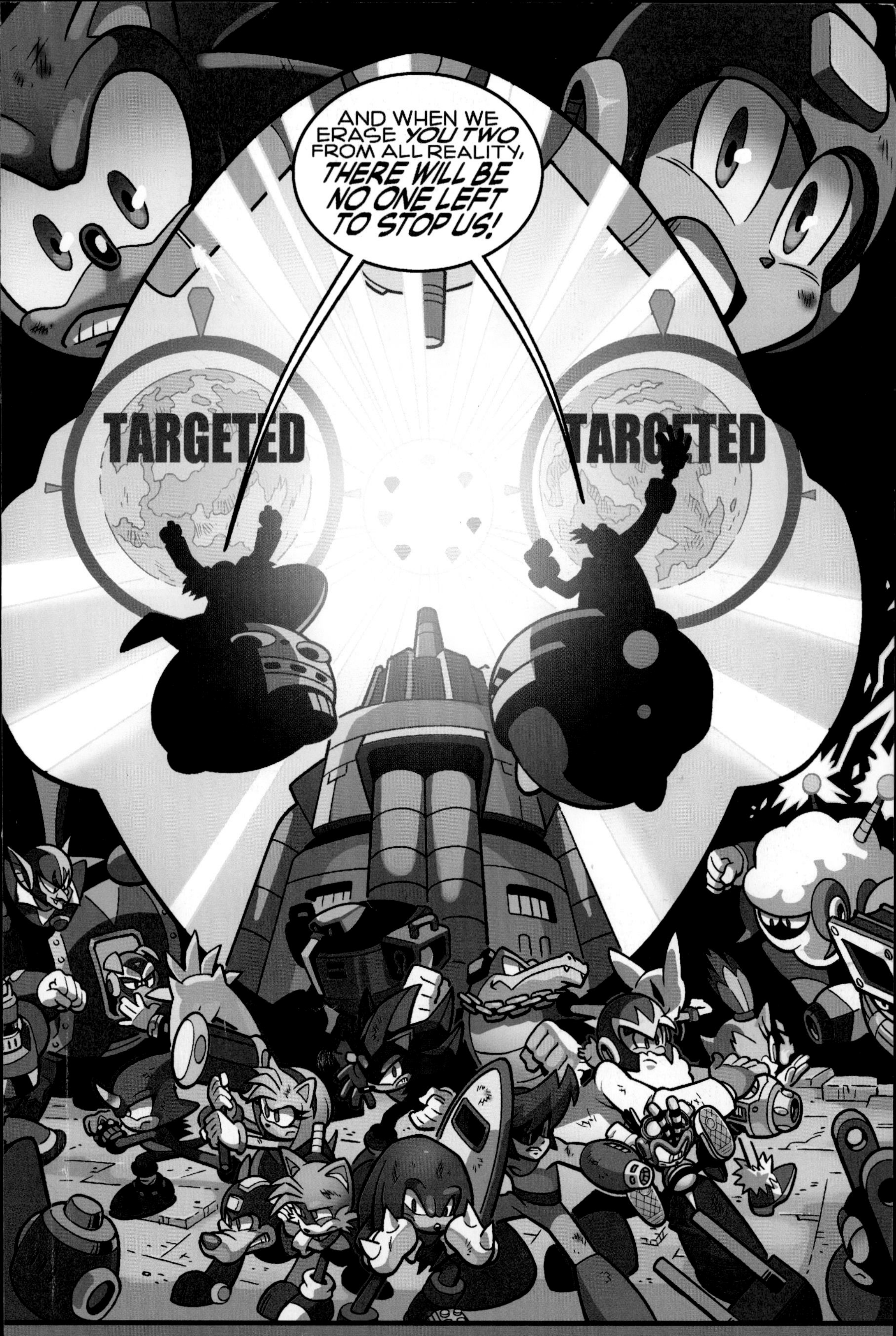

AND WHEN WE ERASE *YOU TWO* FROM ALL REALITY, *THERE WILL BE NO ONE LEFT TO STOP US!*
TARGETED
TARGETED

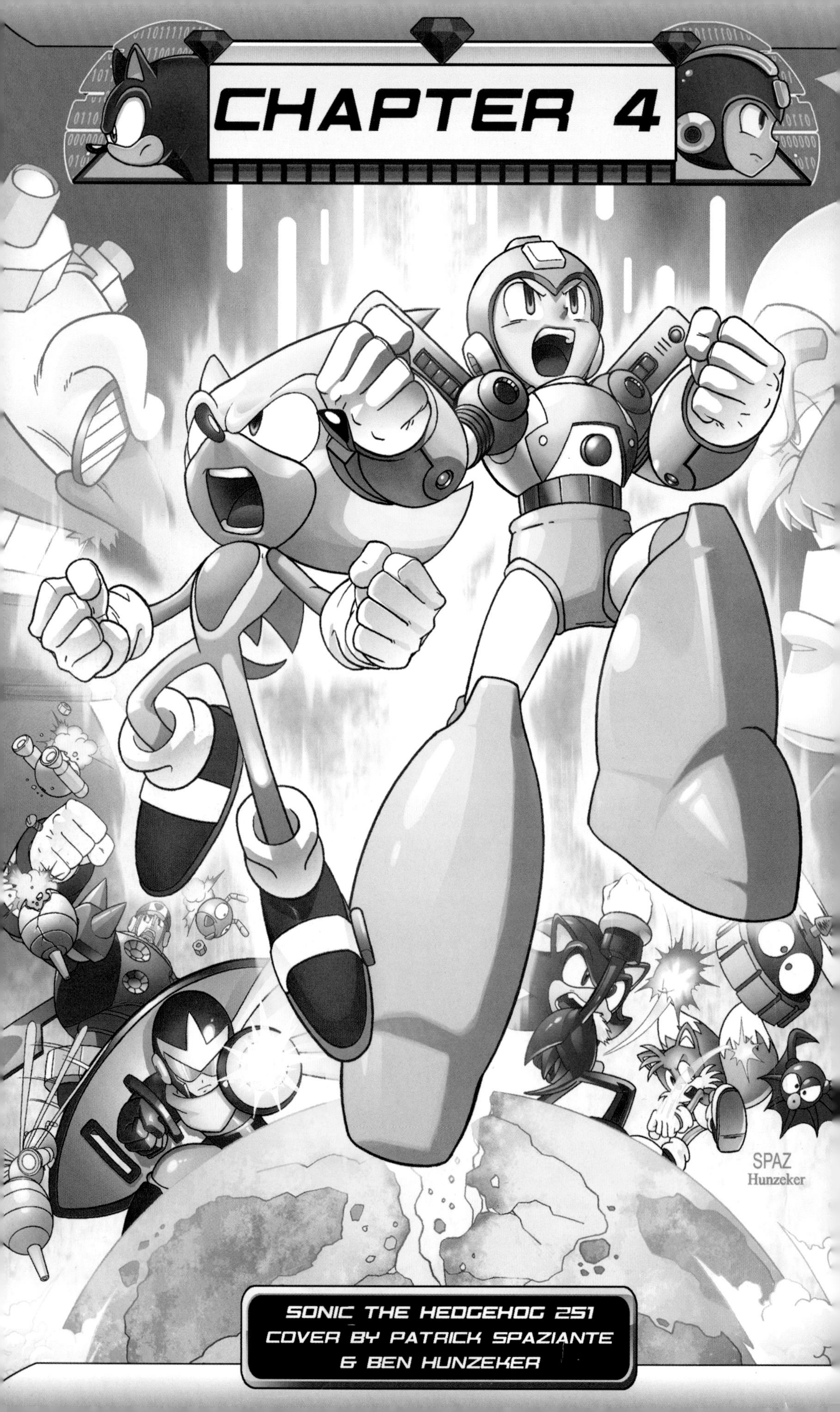
CHAPTER 4
SPAZ
Hunzeker
SONIC THE HEDGEHOG 251
COVER BY PATRICK SPAZIANTE
& BEN HUNZEKER

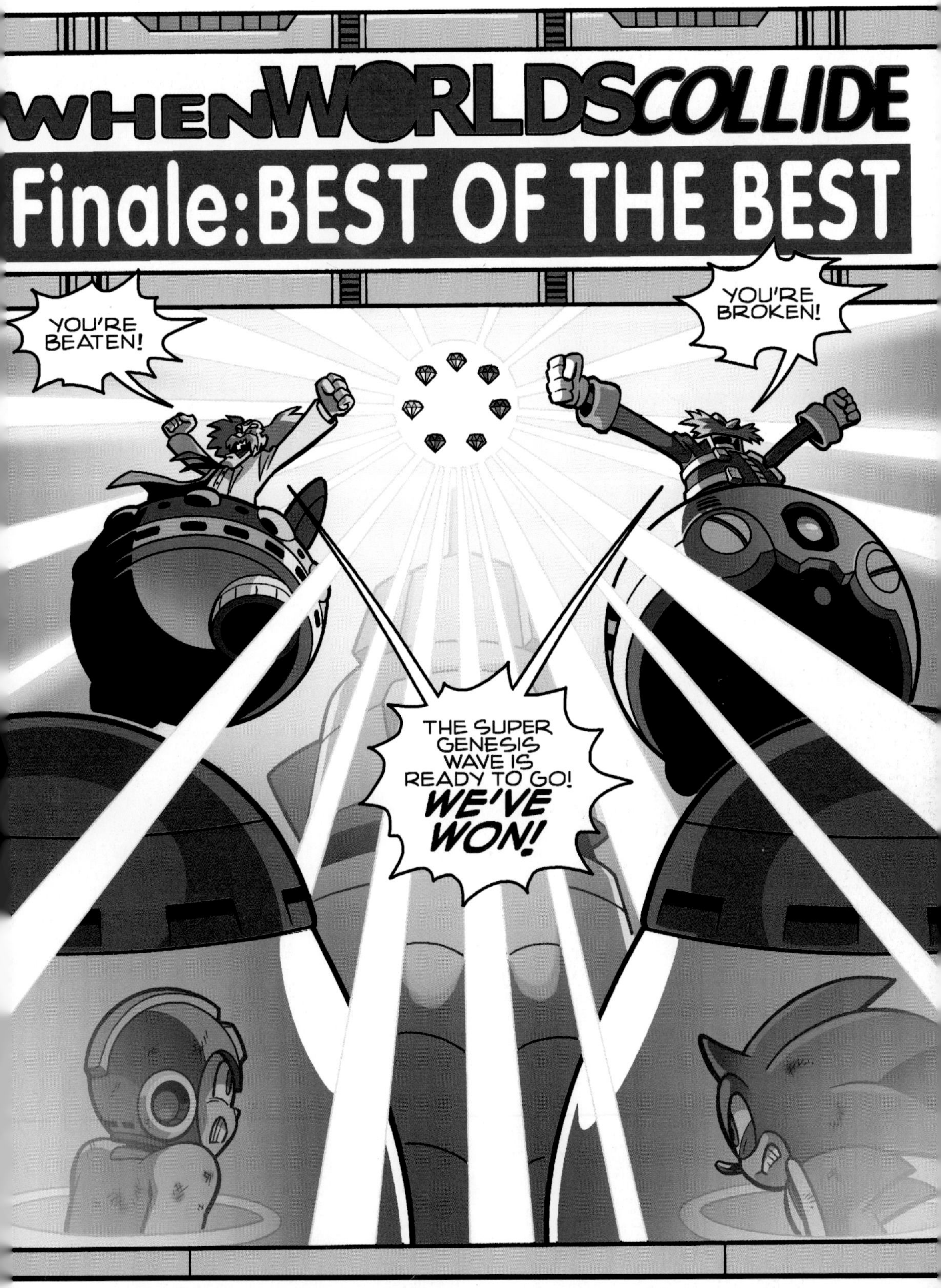
WHEN WORLDS COLLIDE
Finale: BEST OF THE BEST
YOU'RE BEATEN!
YOU'RE BROKEN!
THE SUPER GENESIS WAVE IS READY TO GO! WE'VE WON!

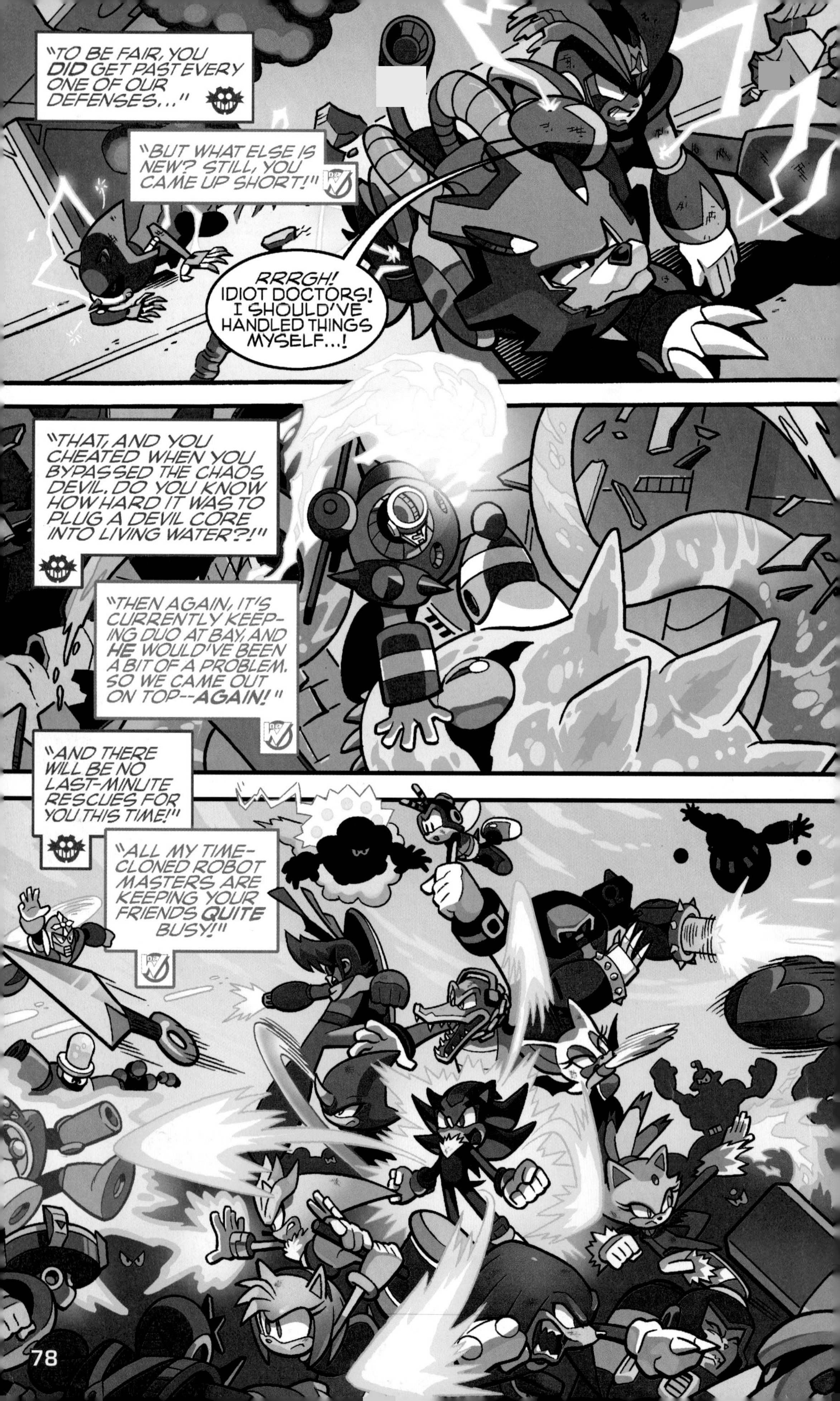
"TO BE FAIR, YOU DID GET PAST EVERY ONE OF OUR DEFENSES..."
"BUT WHAT ELSE IS NEW? STILL, YOU CAME UP SHORT!"
RRRGH! IDIOT DOCTORS! I SHOULD'VE HANDLED THINGS MYSELF...!
"THAT, AND YOU CHEATED WHEN YOU BYPASSED THE CHAOS DEVIL. DO YOU KNOW HOW HARD IT WAS TO PLUG A DEVIL CORE INTO LIVING WATER?!"
"THEN AGAIN, IT'S CURRENTLY KEEPING DUO AT BAY, AND HE WOULD'VE BEEN A BIT OF A PROBLEM. SO WE CAME OUT ON TOP--AGAIN!"
"AND THERE WILL BE NO LAST-MINUTE RESCUES FOR YOU THIS TIME!"
"ALL MY TIME-CLONED ROBOT MASTERS ARE KEEPING YOUR FRIENDS QUITE BUSY!"

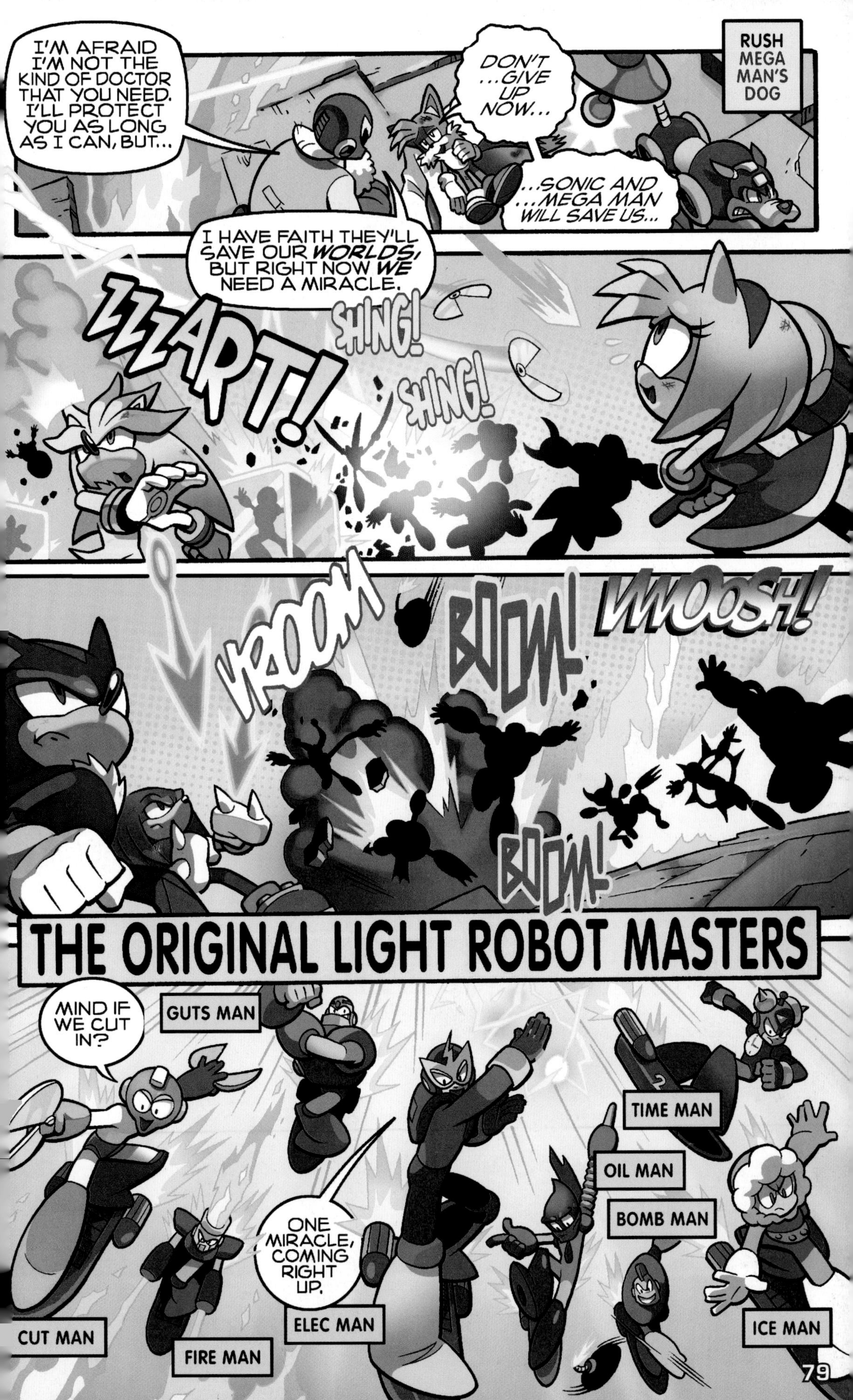
I'M AFRAID I'M NOT THE KIND OF DOCTOR THAT YOU NEED. I'LL PROTECT YOU AS LONG AS I CAN, BUT...
DON'T ...GIVE UP NOW...
RUSH MEGA MAN'S DOG
...SONIC AND ...MEGA MAN WILL SAVE US...
I HAVE FAITH THEY'LL SAVE OUR WORLDS, BUT RIGHT NOW WE NEED A MIRACLE.
ZZZART!
SHING!
SHING!
VROOM
BOOM!
VWOOSH!
BOOM!
THE ORIGINAL LIGHT ROBOT MASTERS
MIND IF WE CUT IN?
GUTS MAN
TIME MAN
OIL MAN
BOMB MAN
ONE MIRACLE, COMING RIGHT UP.
CUT MAN
FIRE MAN
ELEC MAN
ICE MAN

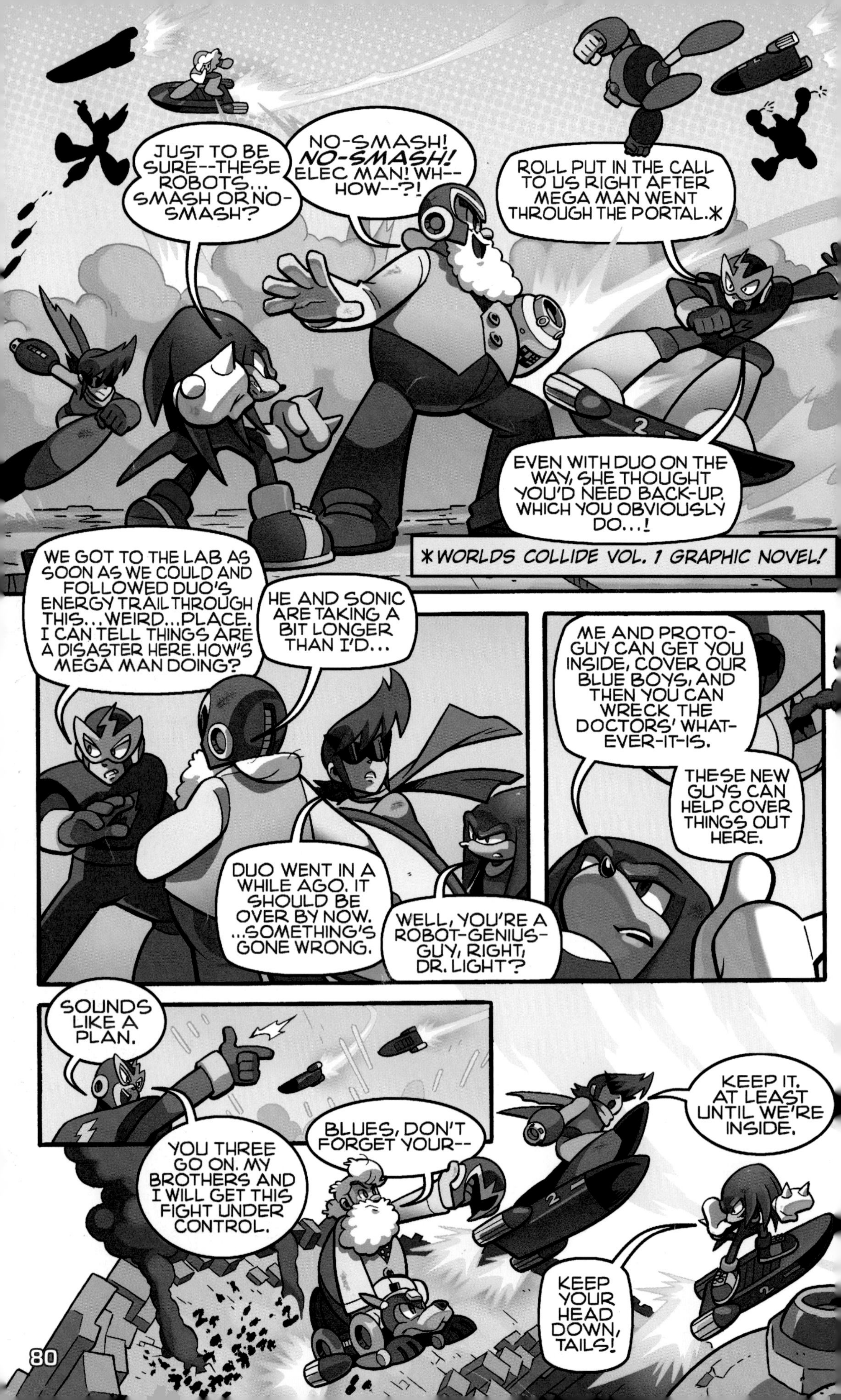

JUST TO BE SURE--THESE ROBOTS... SMASH OR NO-SMASH?
NO-SMASH! NO-SMASH! ELEC MAN! WH-- HOW--?!
ROLL PUT IN THE CALL TO US RIGHT AFTER MEGA MAN WENT THROUGH THE PORTAL.*
EVEN WITH DUO ON THE WAY, SHE THOUGHT YOU'D NEED BACK-UP. WHICH YOU OBVIOUSLY DO...!
*WORLDS COLLIDE VOL. 1 GRAPHIC NOVEL!
WE GOT TO THE LAB AS SOON AS WE COULD AND FOLLOWED DUO'S ENERGY TRAIL THROUGH THIS...WEIRD...PLACE. I CAN TELL THINGS ARE A DISASTER HERE. HOW'S MEGA MAN DOING?
HE AND SONIC ARE TAKING A BIT LONGER THAN I'D...
DUO WENT IN A WHILE AGO. IT SHOULD BE OVER BY NOW. ...SOMETHING'S GONE WRONG.
WELL, YOU'RE A ROBOT-GENIUS-GUY, RIGHT, DR. LIGHT?
ME AND PROTO-GUY CAN GET YOU INSIDE, COVER OUR BLUE BOYS, AND THEN YOU CAN WRECK THE DOCTORS' WHAT-EVER-IT-IS.
THESE NEW GUYS CAN HELP COVER THINGS OUT HERE.
SOUNDS LIKE A PLAN.
YOU THREE GO ON. MY BROTHERS AND I WILL GET THIS FIGHT UNDER CONTROL.
BLUES, DON'T FORGET YOUR--
KEEP IT. AT LEAST UNTIL WE'RE INSIDE.
KEEP YOUR HEAD DOWN, TAILS!

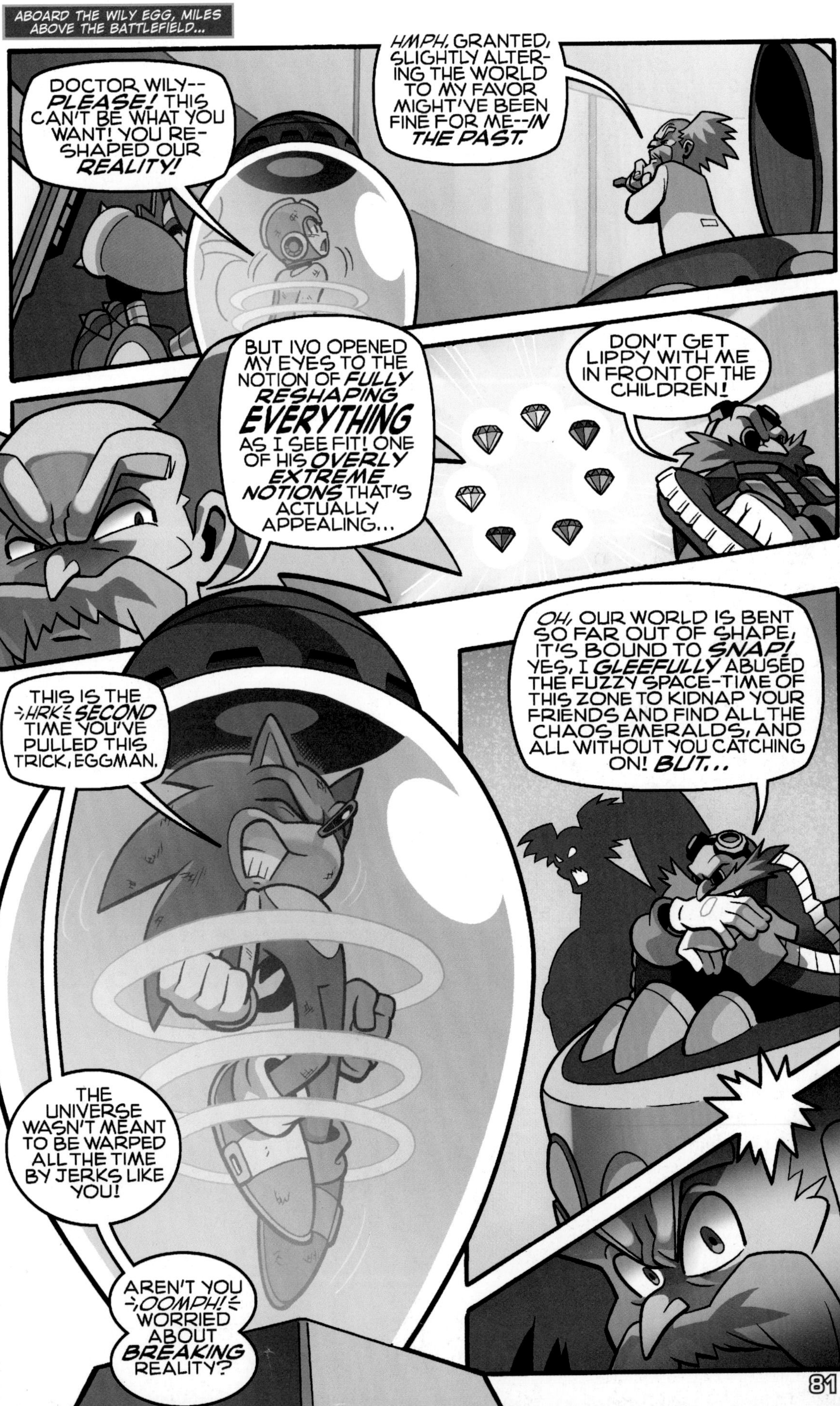
ABOARD THE WILY EGG, MILES ABOVE THE BATTLEFIELD...
DOCTOR WILY-- PLEASE! THIS CAN'T BE WHAT YOU WANT! YOU RESHAPED OUR REALITY!
HMPH, GRANTED, SLIGHTLY ALTERING THE WORLD TO MY FAVOR MIGHT'VE BEEN FINE FOR ME--IN THE PAST.
BUT IVO OPENED MY EYES TO THE NOTION OF FULLY RESHAPING EVERYTHING AS I SEE FIT! ONE OF HIS OVERLY EXTREME NOTIONS THAT'S ACTUALLY APPEALING...
DON'T GET LIPPY WITH ME IN FRONT OF THE CHILDREN!
THIS IS THE -HRK- SECOND TIME YOU'VE PULLED THIS TRICK, EGGMAN.
THE UNIVERSE WASN'T MEANT TO BE WARPED ALL THE TIME BY JERKS LIKE YOU!
ARE'NT YOU -OOMPH!- WORRIED ABOUT BREAKING REALITY?
OH, OUR WORLD IS BENT SO FAR OUT OF SHAPE, IT'S BOUND TO SNAP! YES, I GLEEFULLY ABUSED THE FUZZY SPACE-TIME OF THIS ZONE TO KIDNAP YOUR FRIENDS AND FIND ALL THE CHAOS EMERALDS, AND ALL WITHOUT YOU CATCHING ON! BUT...

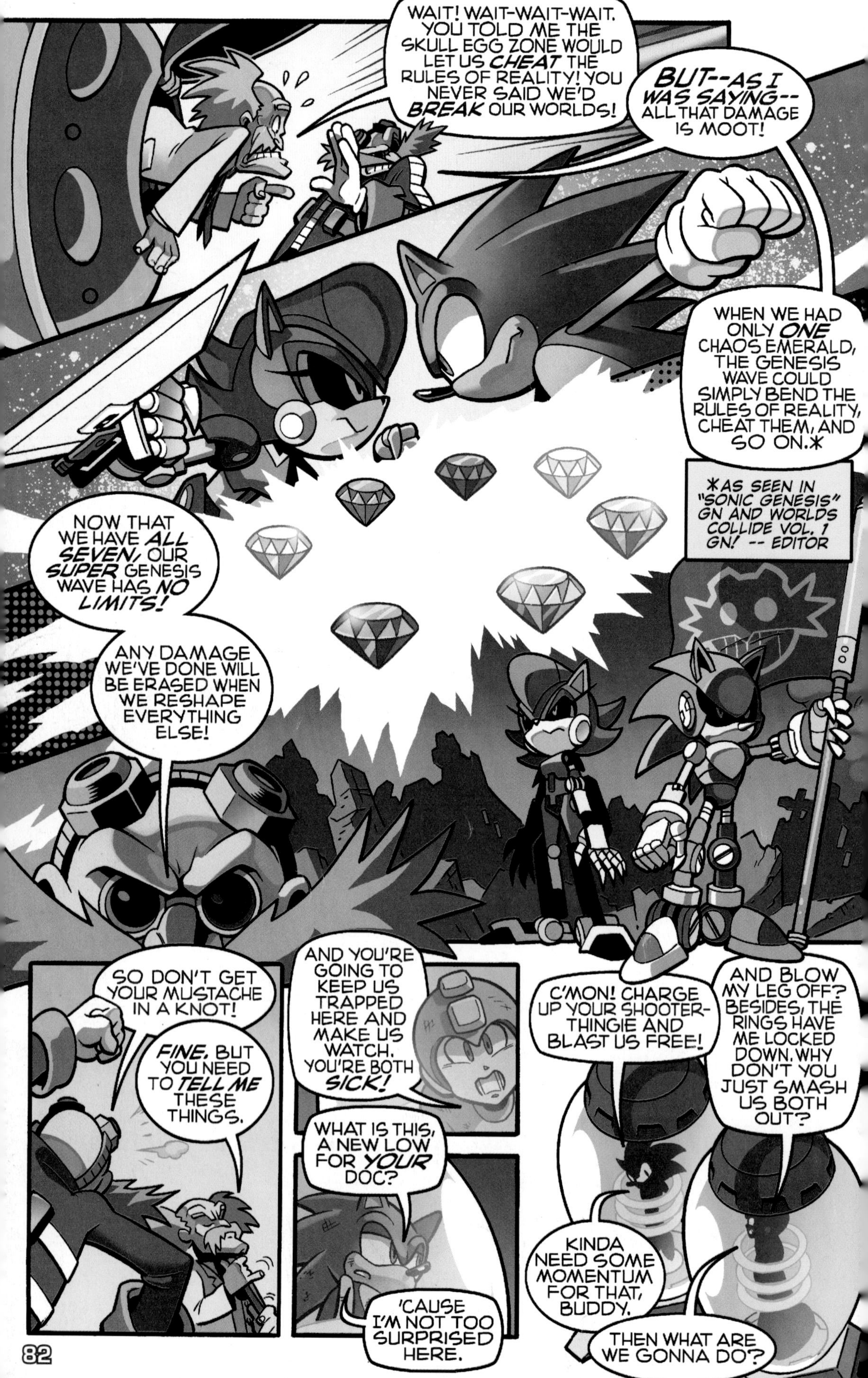

WAIT! WAIT-WAIT-WAIT. YOU TOLD ME THE SKULL EGG ZONE WOULD LET US CHEAT THE RULES OF REALITY! YOU NEVER SAID WE'D BREAK OUR WORLDS!
BUT--AS I WAS SAYING-- ALL THAT DAMAGE IS MOOT!
WHEN WE HAD ONLY ONE CHAOS EMERALD, THE GENESIS WAVE COULD SIMPLY BEND THE RULES OF REALITY, CHEAT THEM, AND SO ON.*
*AS SEEN IN "SONIC GENESIS" GN AND WORLDS COLLIDE VOL. 1 GN! -- EDITOR
NOW THAT WE HAVE ALL SEVEN, OUR SUPER GENESIS WAVE HAS NO LIMITS!
ANY DAMAGE WE'VE DONE WILL BE ERASED WHEN WE RESHAPE EVERYTHING ELSE!
SO DON'T GET YOUR MUSTACHE IN A KNOT!
FINE, BUT YOU NEED TO TELL ME THESE THINGS.
AND YOU'RE GOING TO KEEP US TRAPPED HERE AND MAKE US WATCH. YOU'RE BOTH SICK!
WHAT IS THIS, A NEW LOW FOR YOUR DOC?
'CAUSE I'M NOT TOO SURPRISED HERE.
C'MON! CHARGE UP YOUR SHOOTER-THINGIE AND BLAST US FREE!
AND BLOW MY LEG OFF? BESIDES, THE RINGS HAVE ME LOCKED DOWN. WHY DON'T YOU JUST SMASH US BOTH OUT?
KINDA NEED SOME MOMENTUM FOR THAT, BUDDY.
THEN WHAT ARE WE GONNA DO?

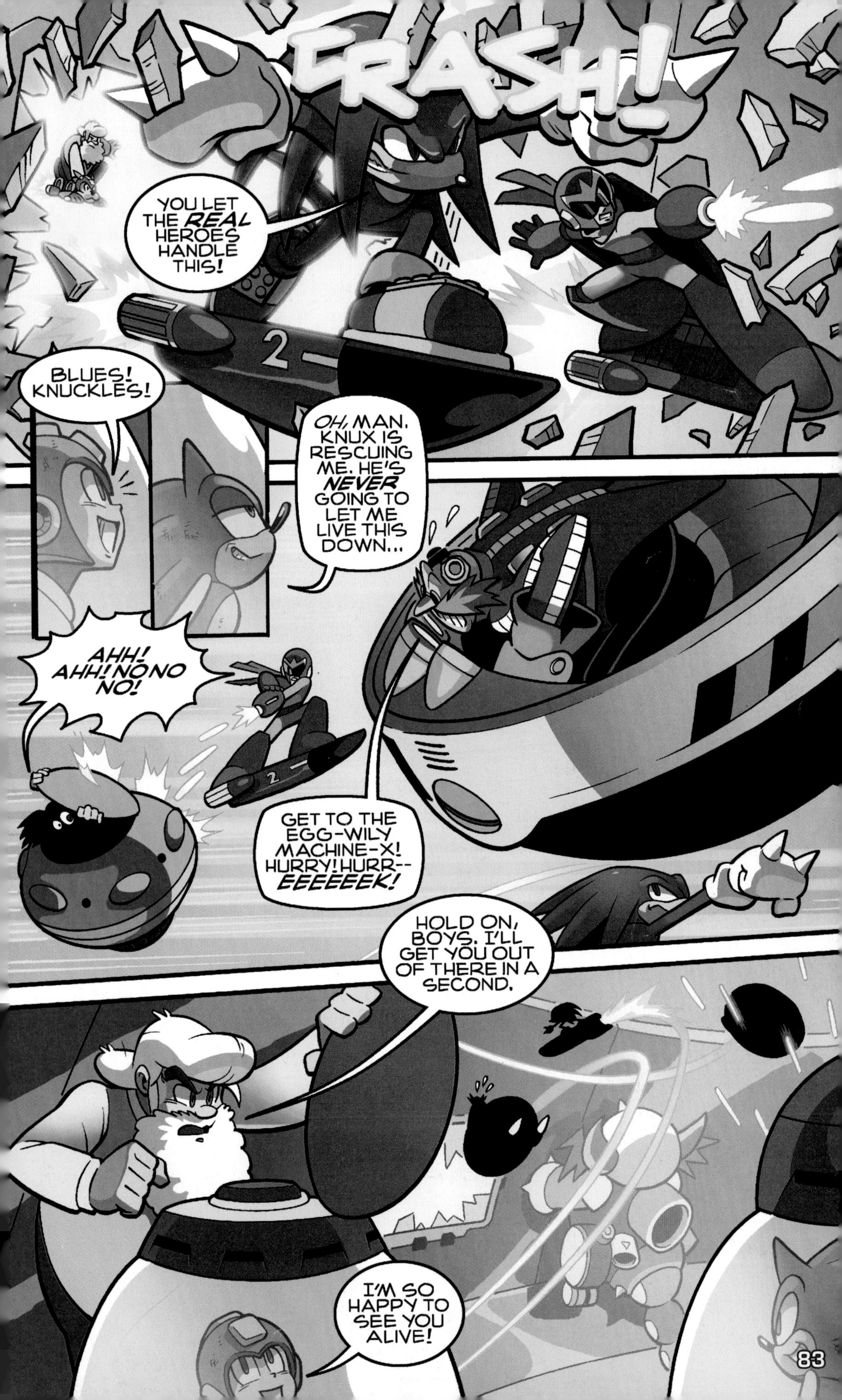
CRASH!
YOU LET THE REAL HEROES HANDLE THIS!
BLUES! KNUCKLES!
OH, MAN. KNUX IS RESCUING ME. HE'S NEVER GOING TO LET ME LIVE THIS DOWN...
AHH! AHH! NO NO NO!
GET TO THE EGG-WILY MACHINE-X! HURRY! HURR-- EEEEEEK!
HOLD ON, BOYS. I'LL GET YOU OUT OF THERE IN A SECOND.
I'M SO HAPPY TO SEE YOU ALIVE!

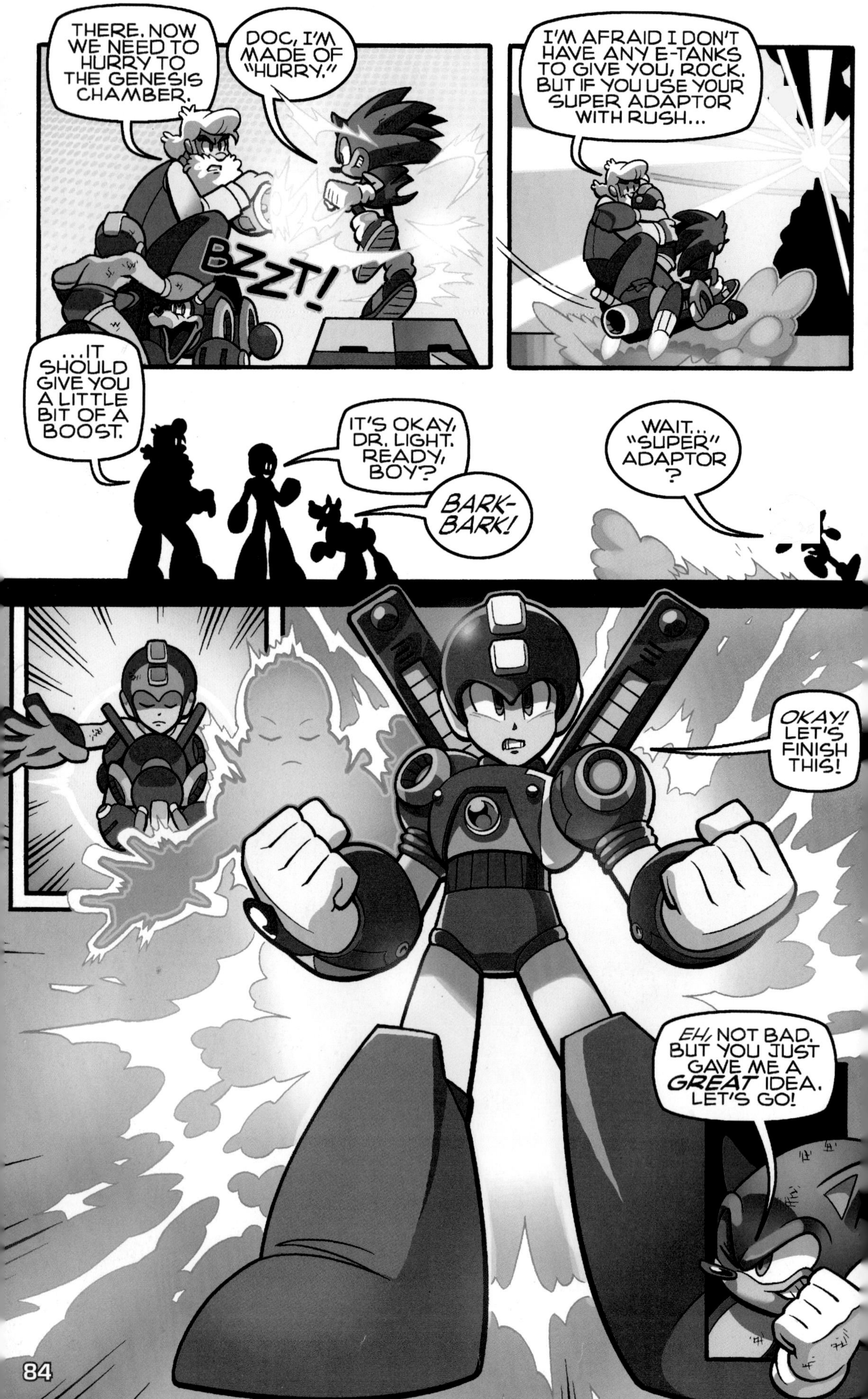

THERE. NOW WE NEED TO HURRY TO THE GENESIS CHAMBER.
DOC, I'M MADE OF "HURRY."
BZZT!
I'M AFRAID I DON'T HAVE ANY E-TANKS TO GIVE YOU, ROCK. BUT IF YOU USE YOUR SUPER ADAPTOR WITH RUSH...
...IT SHOULD GIVE YOU A LITTLE BIT OF A BOOST.
IT'S OKAY, DR. LIGHT. READY, BOY?
BARK-BARK!
WAIT... "SUPER" ADAPTOR?
OKAY! LET'S FINISH THIS!
EH, NOT BAD. BUT YOU JUST GAVE ME A *GREAT* IDEA. LET'S GO!

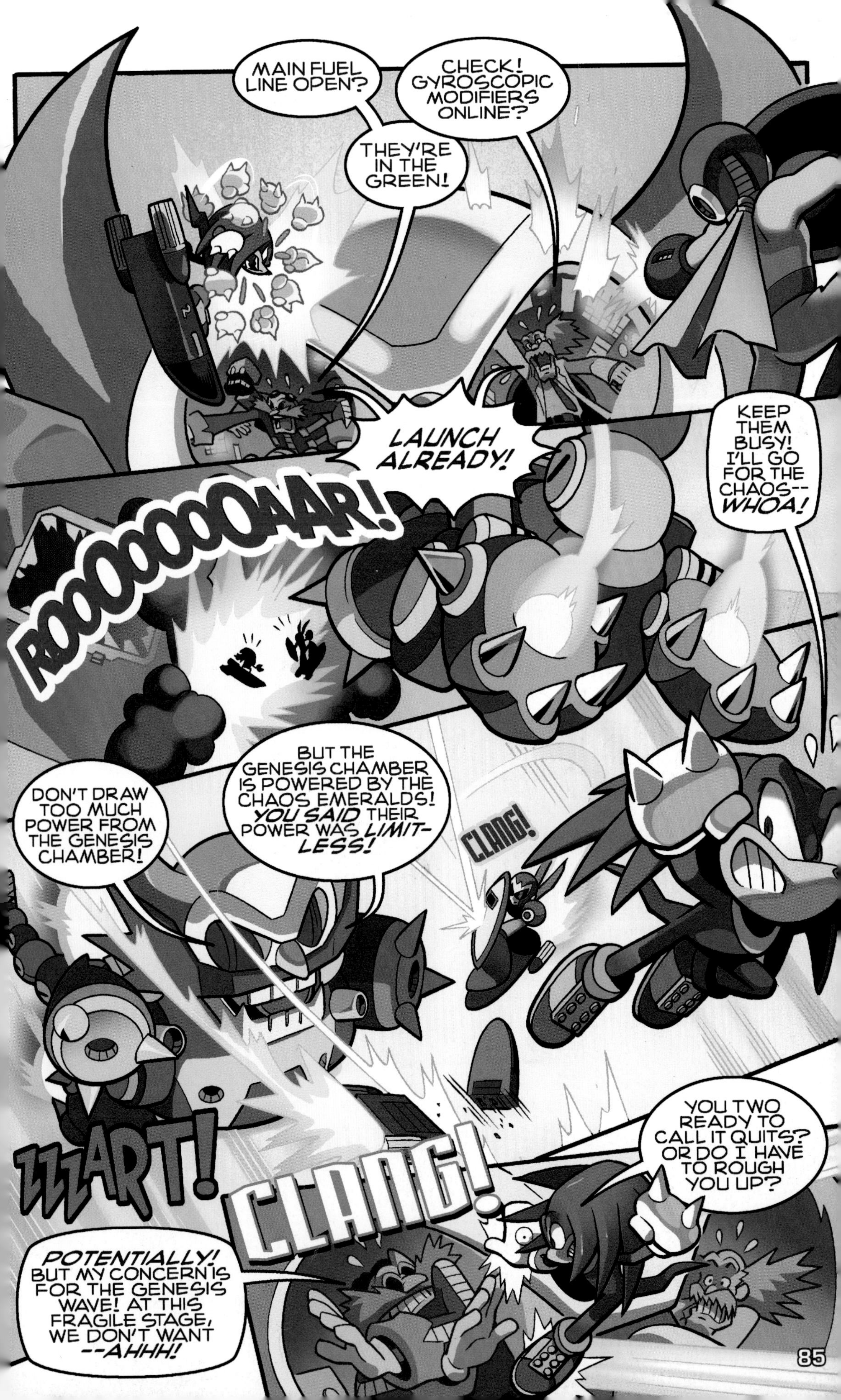
MAIN FUEL LINE OPEN?
CHECK! GYROSCOPIC MODIFIERS ONLINE?
THEY'RE IN THE GREEN!
LAUNCH ALREADY!
KEEP THEM BUSY! I'LL GO FOR THE CHAOS-- WHOA!
ROOOOOOOAAR!
DON'T DRAW TOO MUCH POWER FROM THE GENESIS CHAMBER!
BUT THE GENESIS CHAMBER IS POWERED BY THE CHAOS EMERALDS! YOU SAID THEIR POWER WAS LIMIT-LESS!
CLANG!
ZZZART!
CLANG!
YOU TWO READY TO CALL IT QUITS? OR DO I HAVE TO ROUGH YOU UP?
POTENTIALLY! BUT MY CONCERN IS FOR THE GENESIS WAVE! AT THIS FRAGILE STAGE, WE DON'T WANT --AHHH!

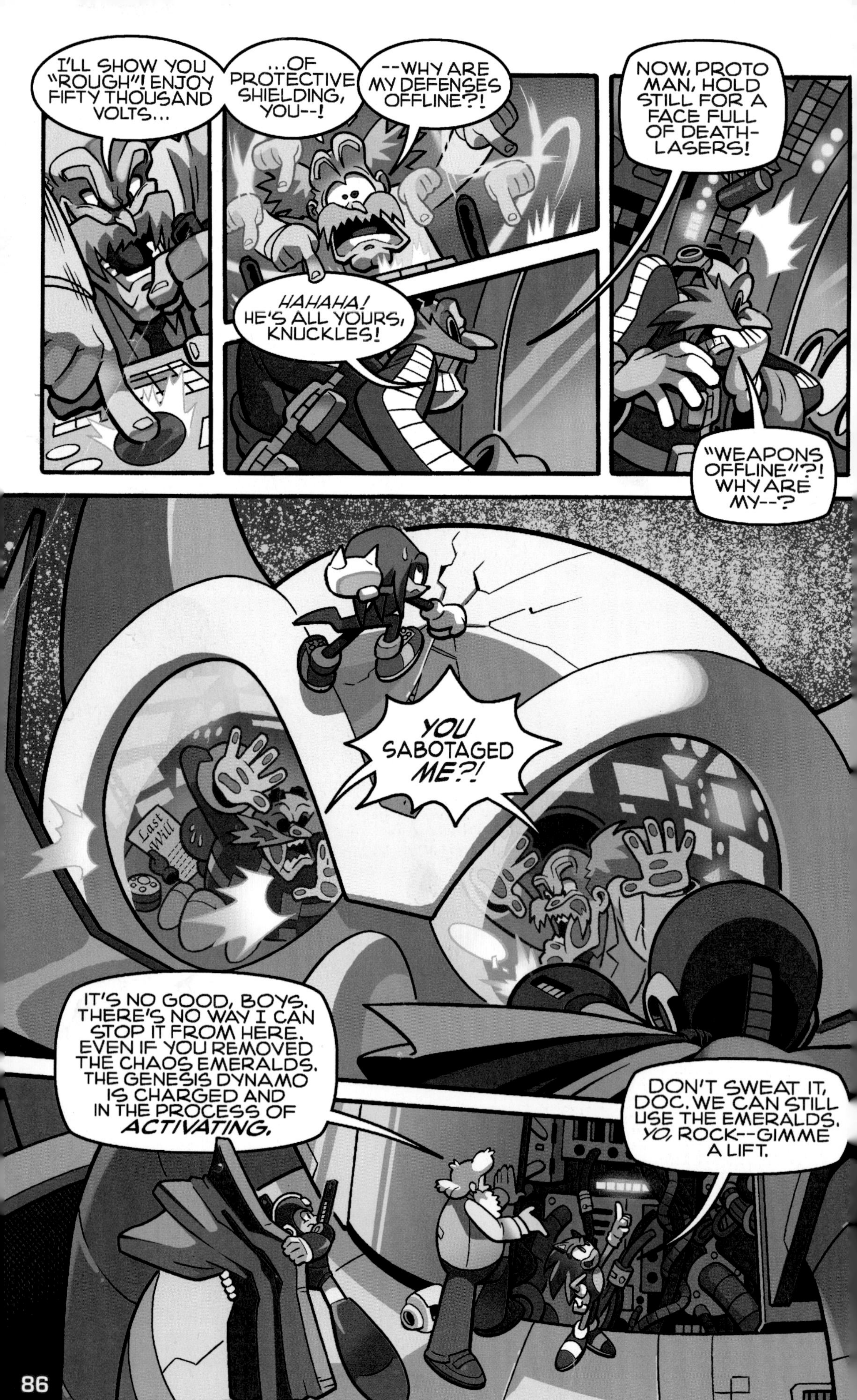

I'LL SHOW YOU "ROUGH"! ENJOY FIFTY THOUSAND VOLTS...
...OF PROTECTIVE SHIELDING, YOU--!
--WHY ARE MY DEFENSES OFFLINE?!
HAHAHA! HE'S ALL YOURS, KNUCKLES!
NOW, PROTO MAN, HOLD STILL FOR A FACE FULL OF DEATH-LASERS!
"WEAPONS OFFLINE"?! WHY ARE MY--?
YOU SABOTAGED ME?!
Last Will
IT'S NO GOOD, BOYS. THERE'S NO WAY I CAN STOP IT FROM HERE. EVEN IF YOU REMOVED THE CHAOS EMERALDS, THE GENESIS DYNAMO IS CHARGED AND IN THE PROCESS OF ACTIVATING.
DON'T SWEAT IT, DOC. WE CAN STILL USE THE EMERALDS. YO, ROCK--GIMME A LIFT.

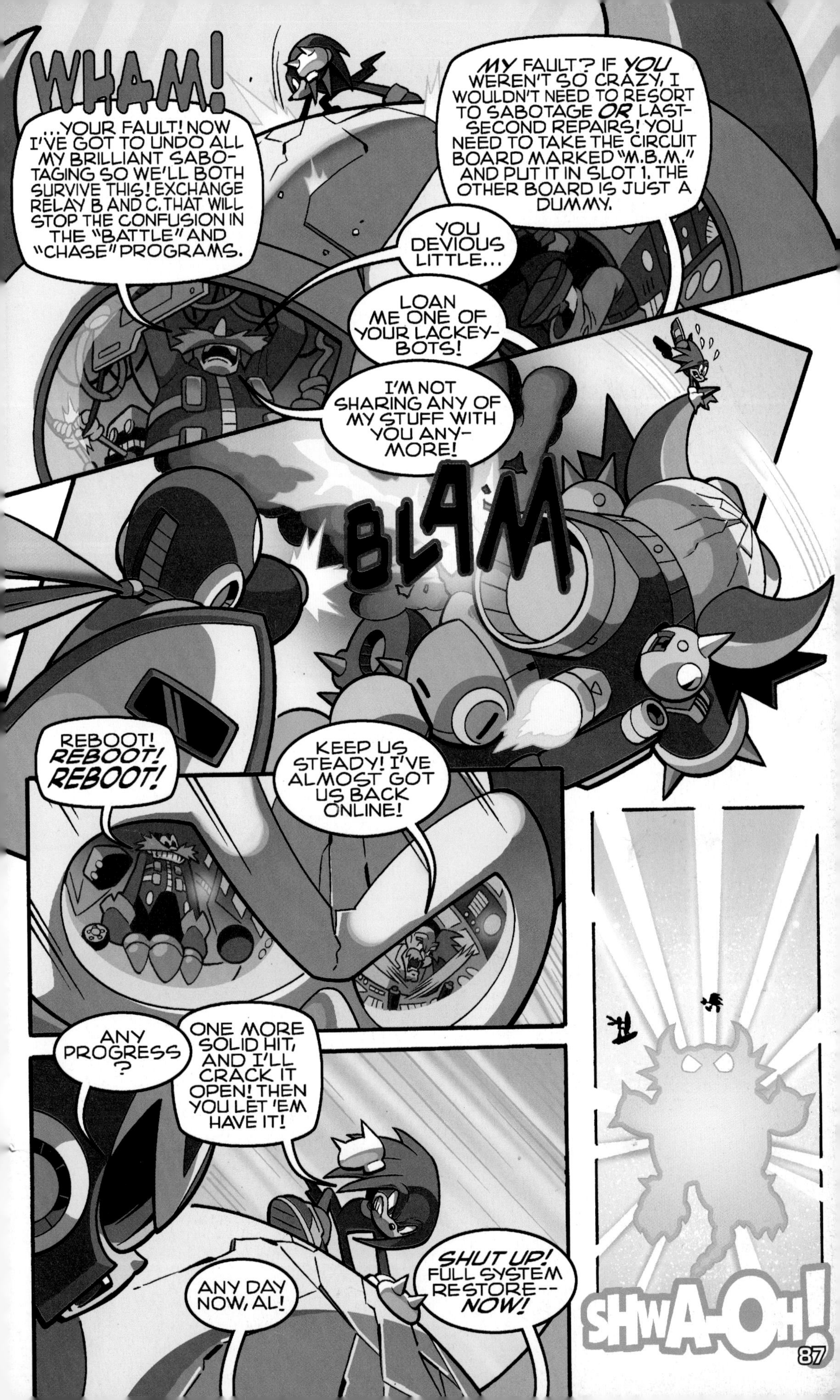
WHAM!
...YOUR FAULT! NOW I'VE GOT TO UNDO ALL MY BRILLIANT SABO-TAGING SO WE'LL BOTH SURVIVE THIS! EXCHANGE RELAY B AND C. THAT WILL STOP THE CONFUSION IN THE "BATTLE" AND "CHASE" PROGRAMS.
MY FAULT? IF YOU WEREN'T SO CRAZY, I WOULDN'T NEED TO RESORT TO SABOTAGE OR LAST-SECOND REPAIRS! YOU NEED TO TAKE THE CIRCUIT BOARD MARKED "M.B.M." AND PUT IT IN SLOT 1. THE OTHER BOARD IS JUST A DUMMY.
YOU DEVIOUS LITTLE...
LOAN ME ONE OF YOUR LACKEY-BOTS!
I'M NOT SHARING ANY OF MY STUFF WITH YOU ANY-MORE!
BLAM
REBOOT! REBOOT! REBOOT!
KEEP US STEADY! I'VE ALMOST GOT US BACK ONLINE!
ANY PROGRESS?
ONE MORE SOLID HIT, AND I'LL CRACK IT OPEN! THEN YOU LET 'EM HAVE IT!
ANY DAY NOW, AL!
SHUT UP! FULL SYSTEM RESTORE-- NOW!
SHWA-OH!

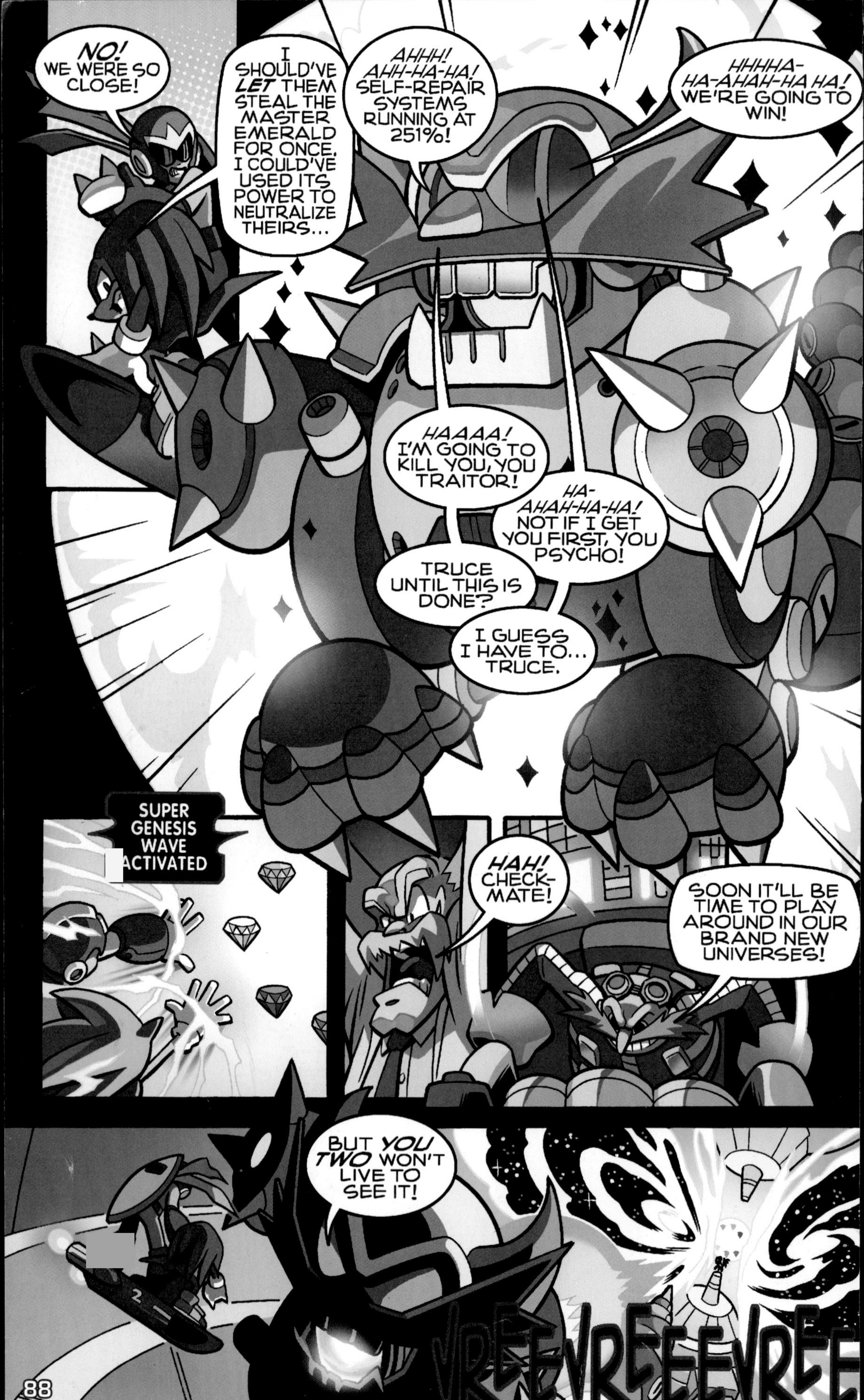
NO! WE WERE SO CLOSE!
I SHOULD'VE LET THEM STEAL THE MASTER EMERALD FOR ONCE. I COULD'VE USED ITS POWER TO NEUTRALIZE THEIRS...
AHHH! AHH-HA-HA! SELF-REPAIR SYSTEMS RUNNING AT 251%!
HHHHA-HA-AHAH-HA HA! WE'RE GOING TO WIN!
HAAAAA! I'M GOING TO KILL YOU, YOU TRAITOR!
HA-AHAH-HA-HA! NOT IF I GET YOU FIRST, YOU PSYCHO!
TRUCE UNTIL THIS IS DONE?
I GUESS I HAVE TO... TRUCE.
SUPER GENESIS WAVE ACTIVATED
HAH! CHECKMATE!
SOON IT'LL BE TIME TO PLAY AROUND IN OUR BRAND NEW UNIVERSES!
BUT YOU TWO WON'T LIVE TO SEE IT!
VREEVREEEVREE

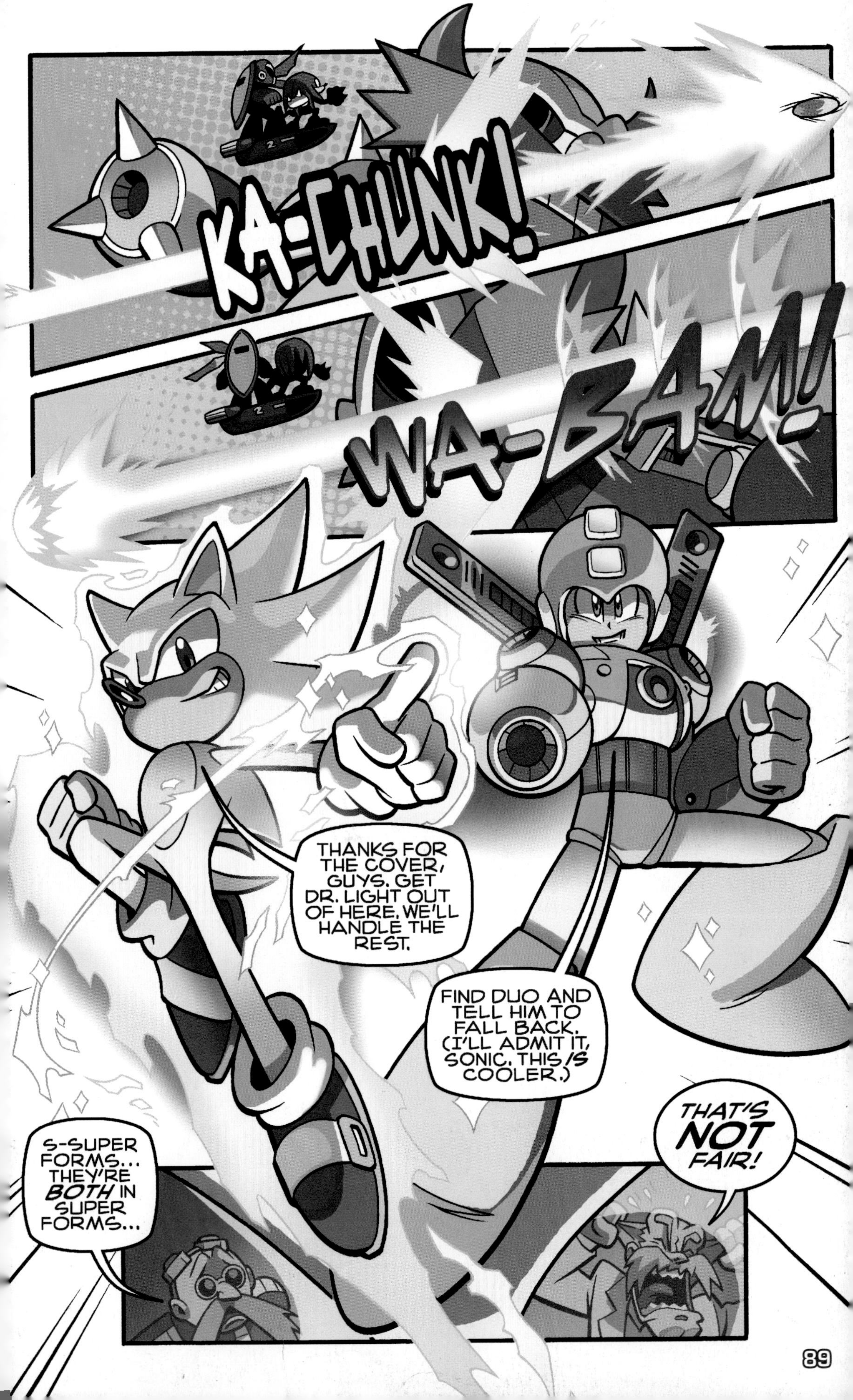

KA-CHUNK!
WA-BAM!
THANKS FOR THE COVER, GUYS. GET DR. LIGHT OUT OF HERE, WE'LL HANDLE THE REST.
FIND DUO AND TELL HIM TO FALL BACK. (I'LL ADMIT IT, SONIC. THIS *IS* COOLER.)
S-SUPER FORMS... THEY'RE *BOTH* IN SUPER FORMS...
THAT'S **NOT** FAIR!

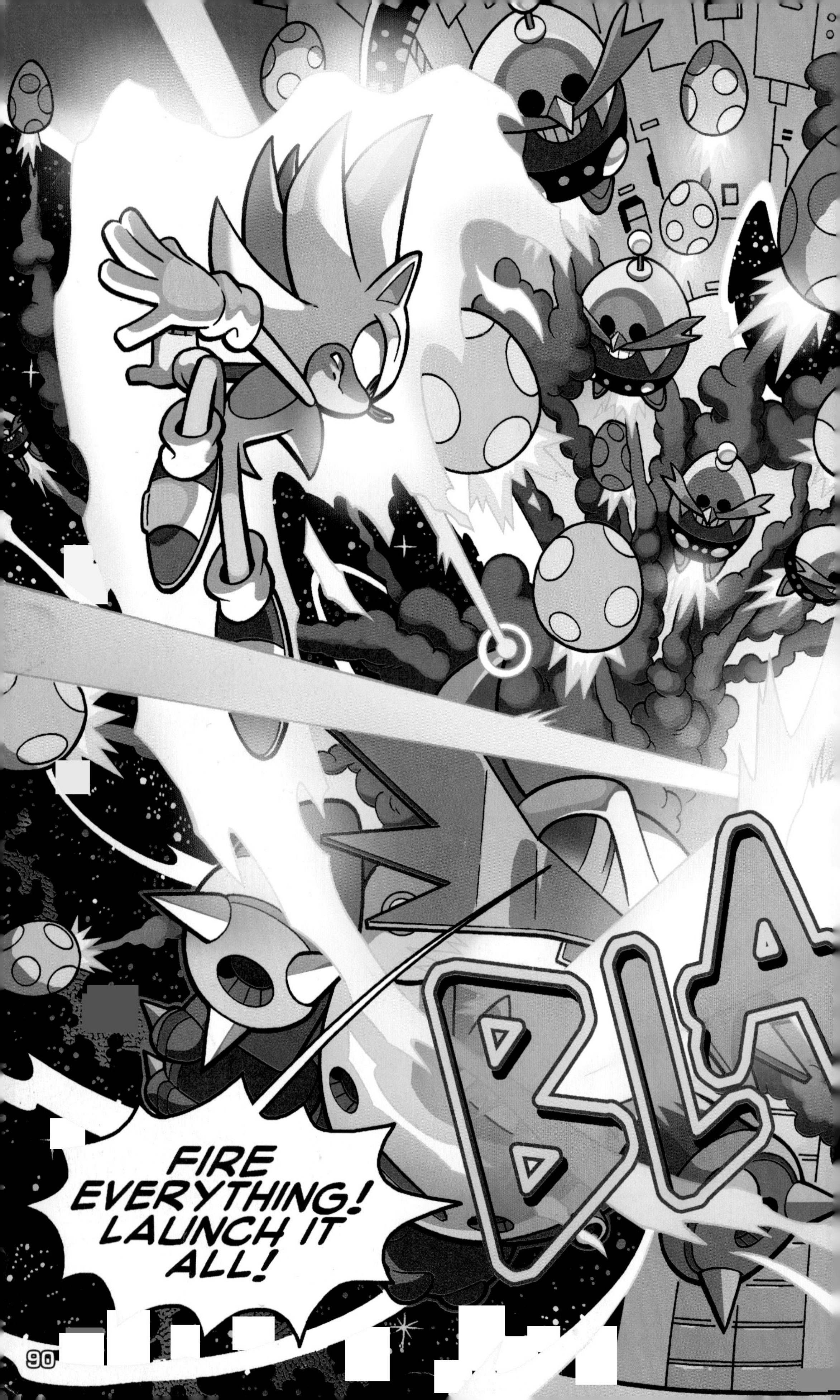
FIRE EVERYTHING! LAUNCH IT ALL!
BLA

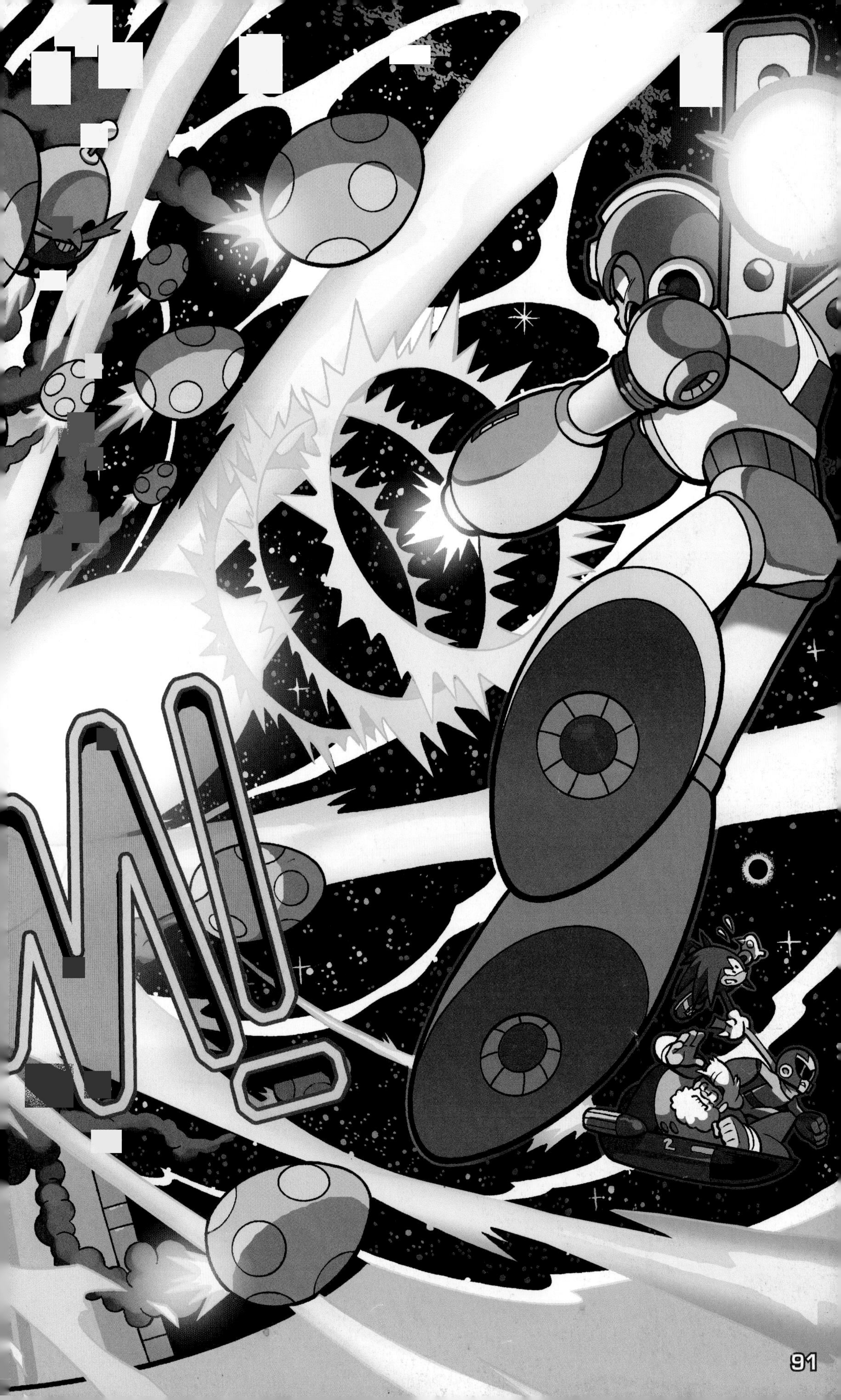

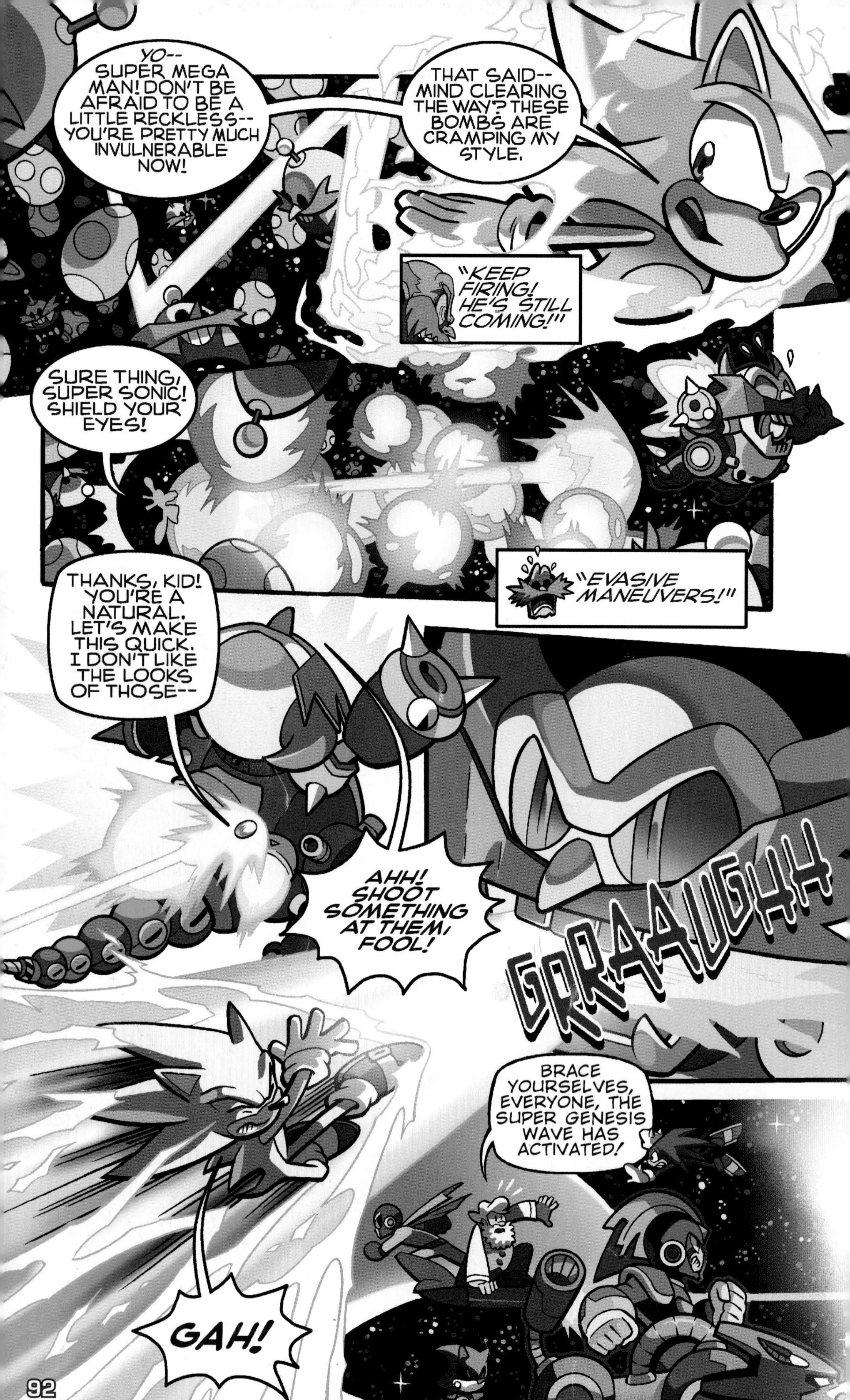
YO-- SUPER MEGA MAN! DON'T BE AFRAID TO BE A LITTLE RECKLESS-- YOU'RE PRETTY MUCH INVULNERABLE NOW!
THAT SAID-- MIND CLEARING THE WAY? THESE BOMBS ARE CRAMPING MY STYLE.
"KEEP FIRING! HE'S STILL COMING!"
SURE THING, SUPER SONIC! SHIELD YOUR EYES!
"EVASIVE MANEUVERS!"
THANKS, KID! YOU'RE A NATURAL. LET'S MAKE THIS QUICK. I DON'T LIKE THE LOOKS OF THOSE--
AHH! SHOOT SOMETHING AT THEM, FOOL!
GRRAAUGHH
BRACE YOURSELVES, EVERYONE, THE SUPER GENESIS WAVE HAS ACTIVATED!
GAH!

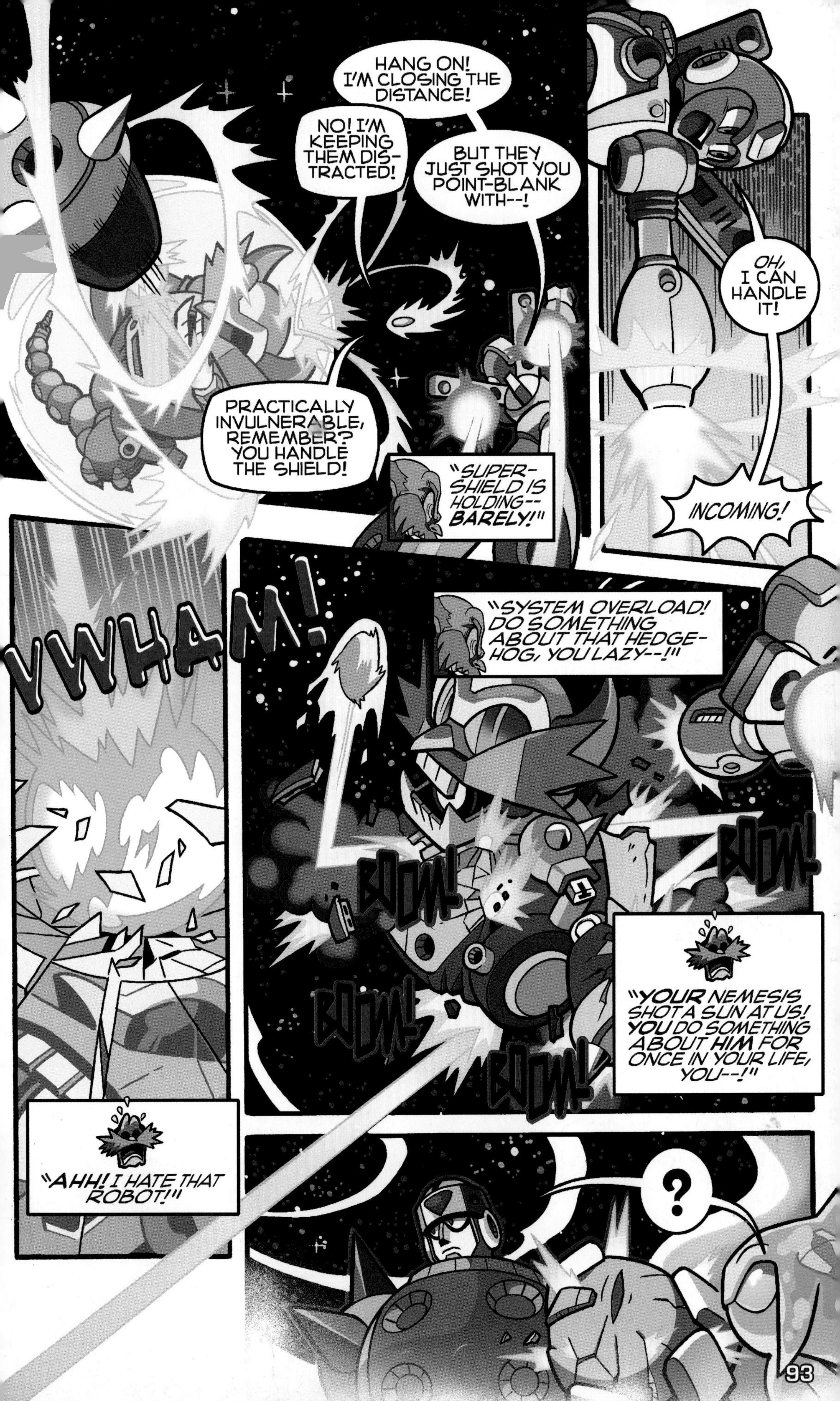
HANG ON! I'M CLOSING THE DISTANCE!
NO! I'M KEEPING THEM DIS-TRACTED!
BUT THEY JUST SHOT YOU POINT-BLANK WITH--!
PRACTICALLY INVULNERABLE, REMEMBER? YOU HANDLE THE SHIELD!
"SUPER-SHIELD IS HOLDING--BARELY!"
OH, I CAN HANDLE IT!
INCOMING!
VWHAM!
"SYSTEM OVERLOAD! DO SOMETHING ABOUT THAT HEDGE-HOG, YOU LAZY--!"
BOOM!
BOOM!
BOOM!
BOOM!
"YOUR NEMESIS SHOT A SUN AT US! YOU DO SOMETHING ABOUT HIM FOR ONCE IN YOUR LIFE, YOU--!"
"AHH! I HATE THAT ROBOT!"
?

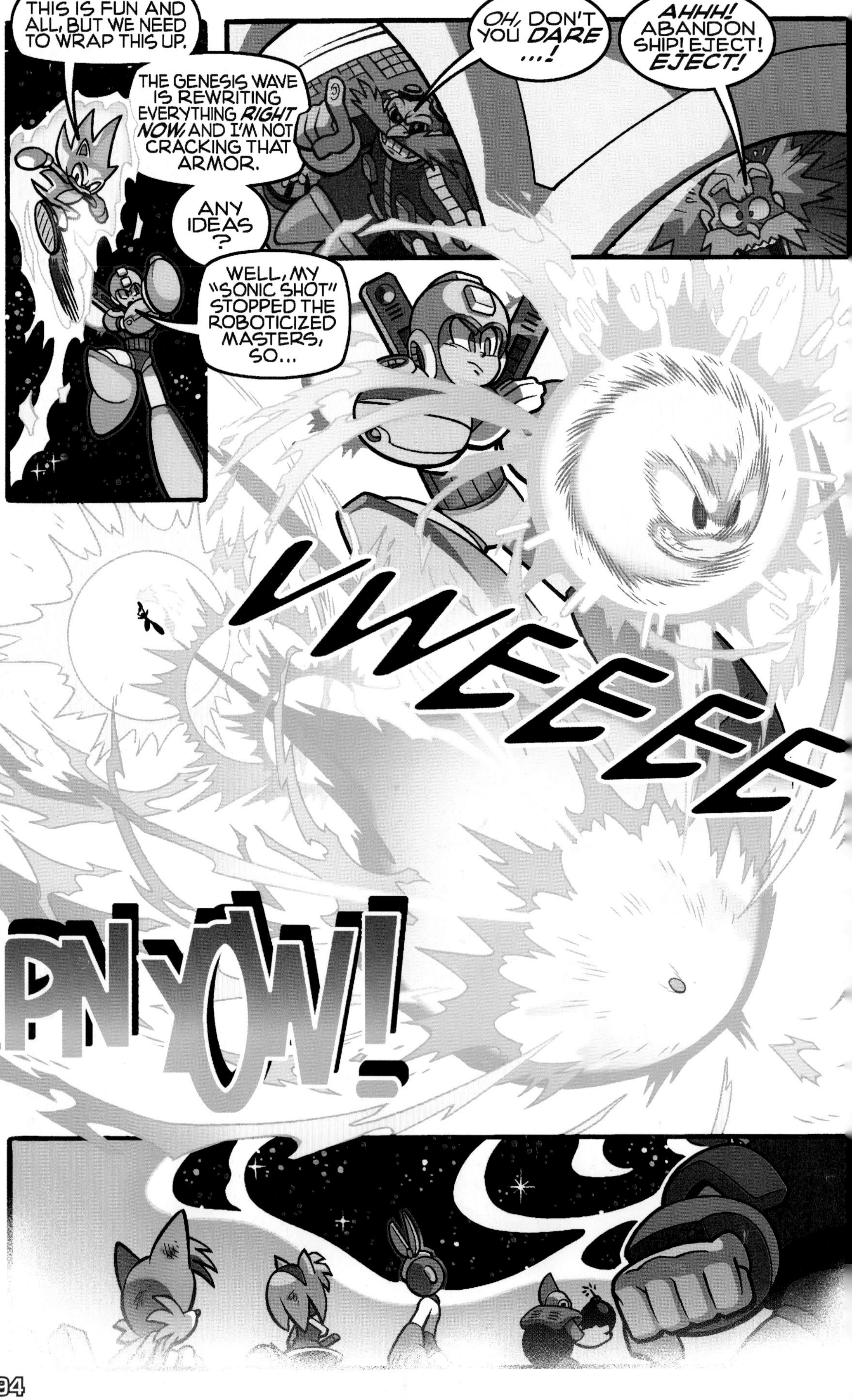
THIS IS FUN AND ALL, BUT WE NEED TO WRAP THIS UP.
THE GENESIS WAVE IS REWRITING EVERYTHING *RIGHT NOW,* AND I'M NOT CRACKING THAT ARMOR.
ANY IDEAS?
OH, DON'T YOU *DARE* ...!
*AHHH!* ABANDON SHIP! EJECT! *EJECT!*
WELL, MY "SONIC SHOT" STOPPED THE ROBOTICIZED MASTERS, SO...
VWEEEE
PNYOW!

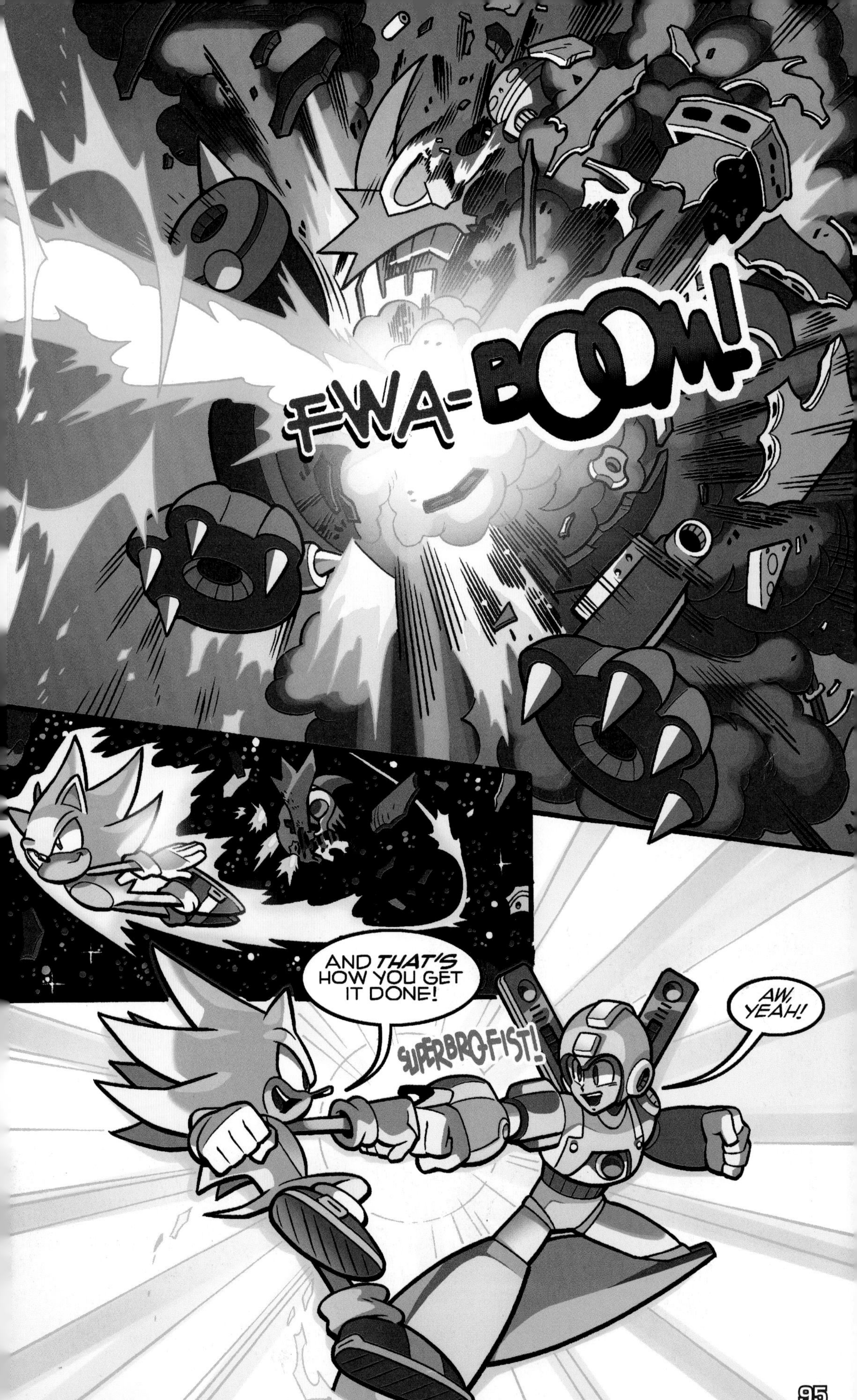
FWA-BOOM!
AND THAT'S HOW YOU GET IT DONE!
SUPER BRO-FIST!
AW, YEAH!

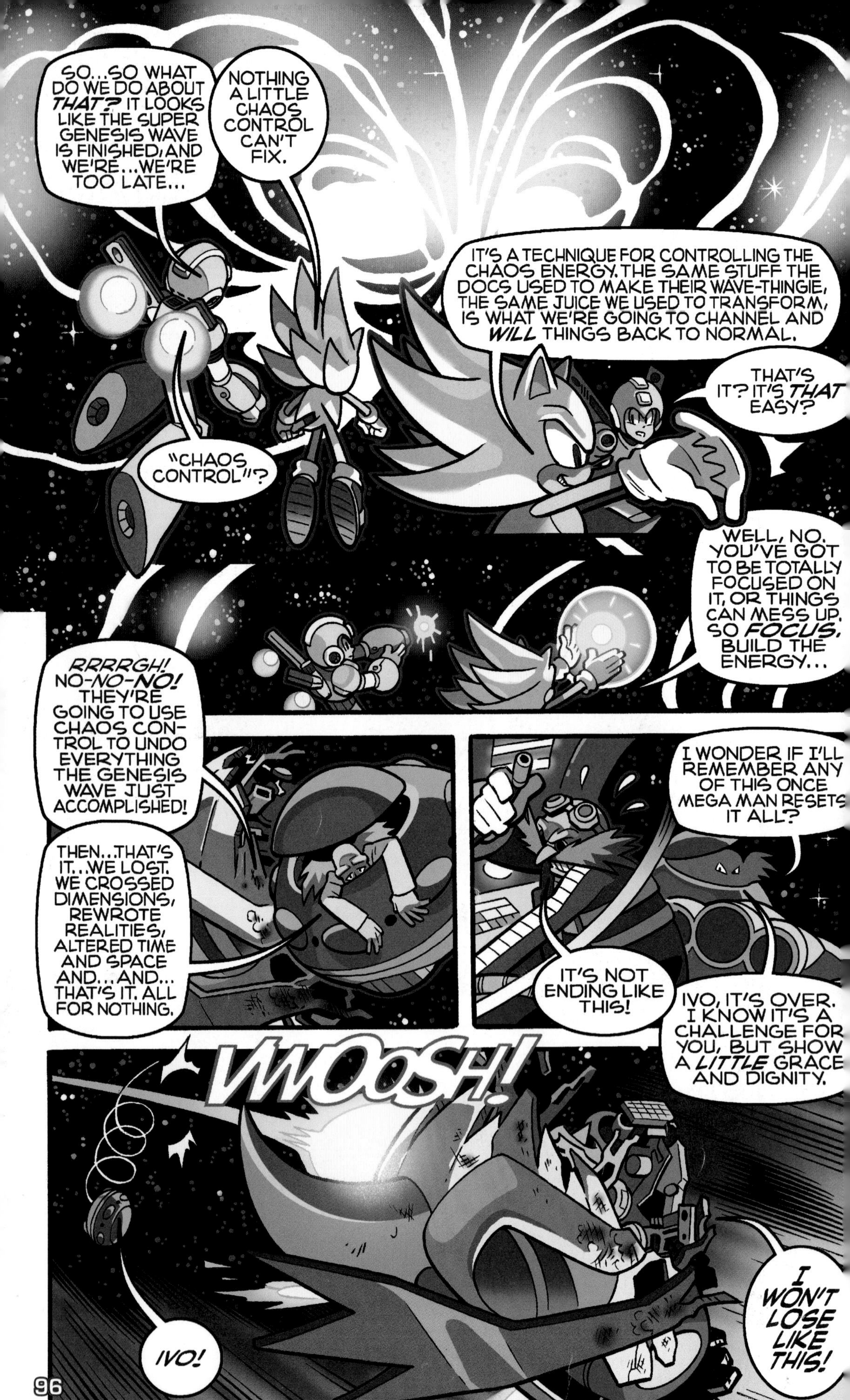
SO...SO WHAT DO WE DO ABOUT *THAT?* IT LOOKS LIKE THE SUPER GENESIS WAVE IS FINISHED, AND WE'RE...WE'RE TOO LATE...
NOTHING A LITTLE CHAOS CONTROL CAN'T FIX.
"CHAOS CONTROL"?
IT'S A TECHNIQUE FOR CONTROLLING THE CHAOS ENERGY. THE SAME STUFF THE DOCS USED TO MAKE THEIR WAVE-THINGIE, THE SAME JUICE WE USED TO TRANSFORM, IS WHAT WE'RE GOING TO CHANNEL AND *WILL* THINGS BACK TO NORMAL.
THAT'S IT? IT'S *THAT* EASY?
WELL, NO. YOU'VE GOT TO BE TOTALLY FOCUSED ON IT, OR THINGS CAN MESS UP. SO *FOCUS.* BUILD THE ENERGY...
*RRRRGH!* NO-*NO-NO!* THEY'RE GOING TO USE CHAOS CON-TROL TO UNDO EVERYTHING THE GENESIS WAVE JUST ACCOMPLISHED!
THEN...THAT'S IT...WE LOST. WE CROSSED DIMENSIONS, REWROTE REALITIES, ALTERED TIME AND SPACE AND...AND... THAT'S IT. ALL FOR NOTHING.
I WONDER IF I'LL REMEMBER ANY OF THIS ONCE MEGA MAN RESETS IT ALL?
IT'S NOT ENDING LIKE THIS!
IVO, IT'S OVER. I KNOW IT'S A CHALLENGE FOR YOU, BUT SHOW A *LITTLE* GRACE AND DIGNITY.
VVVOOSH!
*IVO!*
*I WON'T LOSE LIKE THIS!*

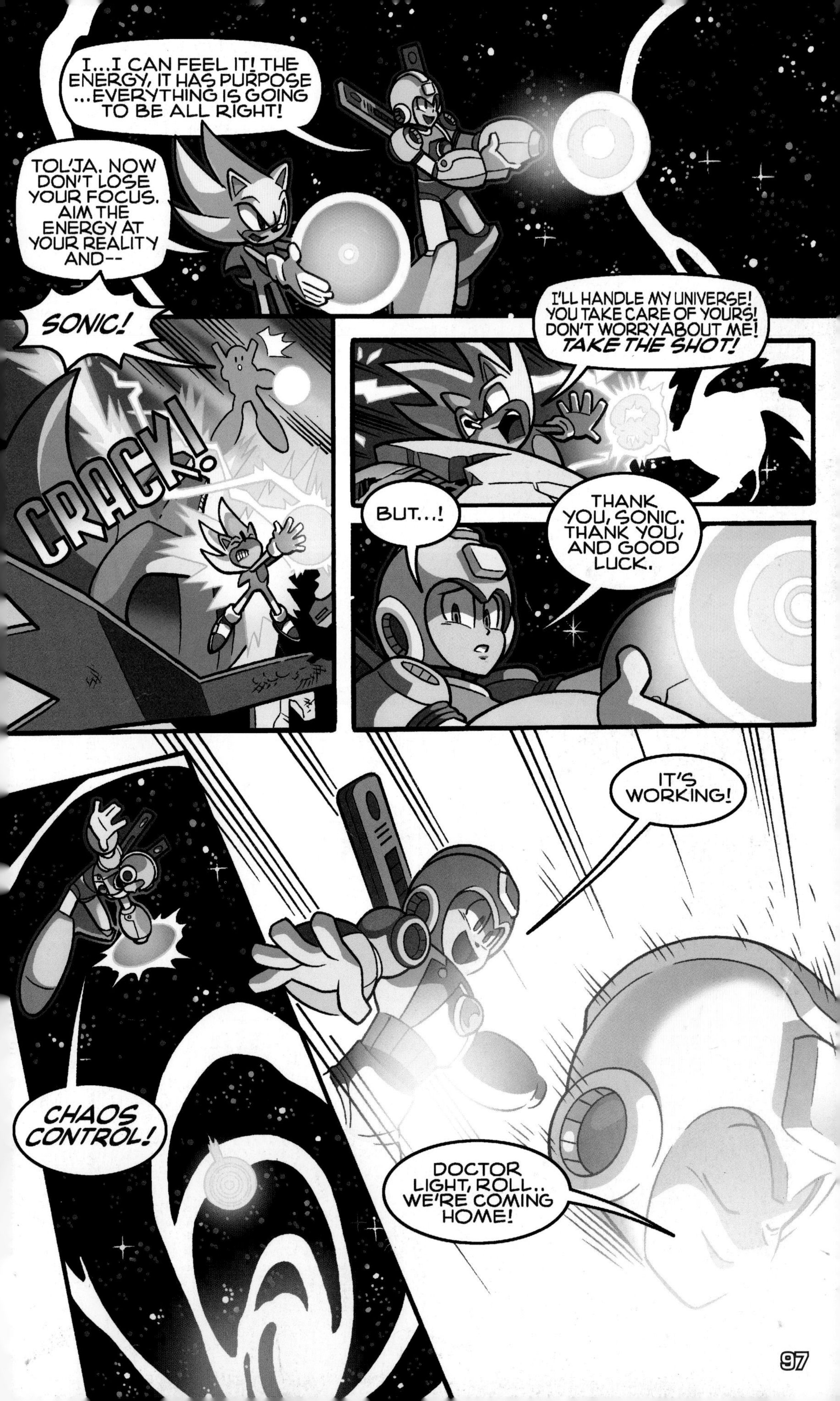
I...I CAN FEEL IT! THE ENERGY, IT HAS PURPOSE ...EVERYTHING IS GOING TO BE ALL RIGHT!
TOL'JA. NOW DON'T LOSE YOUR FOCUS. AIM THE ENERGY AT YOUR REALITY AND--
SONIC!
CRACK!
I'LL HANDLE MY UNIVERSE! YOU TAKE CARE OF YOURS! DON'T WORRY ABOUT ME! TAKE THE SHOT!
BUT...!
THANK YOU, SONIC. THANK YOU, AND GOOD LUCK.
IT'S WORKING!
CHAOS CONTROL!
DOCTOR LIGHT, ROLL.. WE'RE COMING HOME!

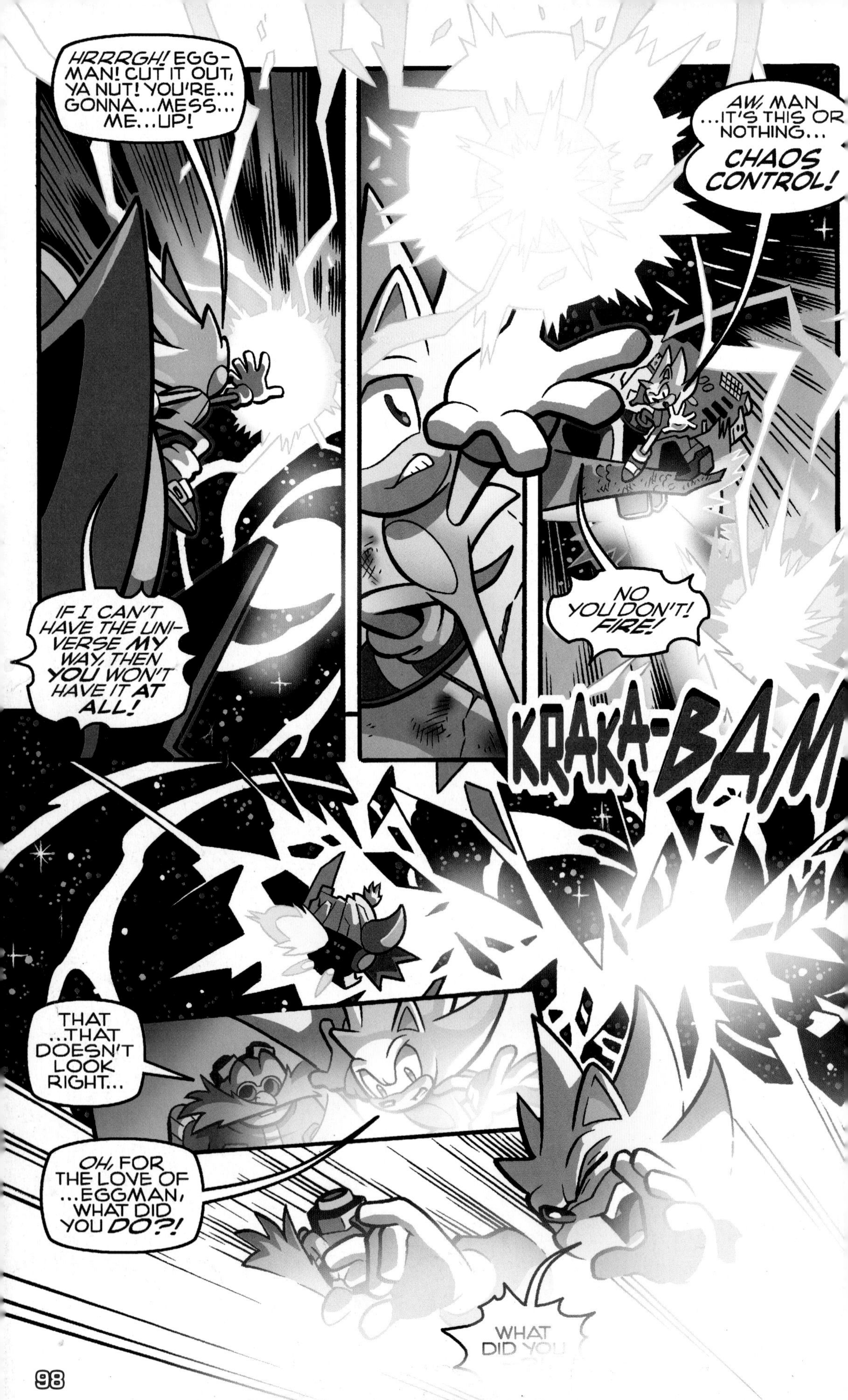
HRRRGH! EGG-MAN! CUT IT OUT, YA NUT! YOU'RE... GONNA...MESS... ME...UP!
AW, MAN ...IT'S THIS OR NOTHING... CHAOS CONTROL!
IF I CAN'T HAVE THE UNIVERSE MY WAY, THEN YOU WON'T HAVE IT AT ALL!
NO YOU DON'T! FIRE!
KRAKA-BAM
THAT ...THAT DOESN'T LOOK RIGHT...
OH, FOR THE LOVE OF ...EGGMAN, WHAT DID YOU DO?!
WHAT DID YOU

# EVIL FRIENDS FOREVER VARIANT COVER

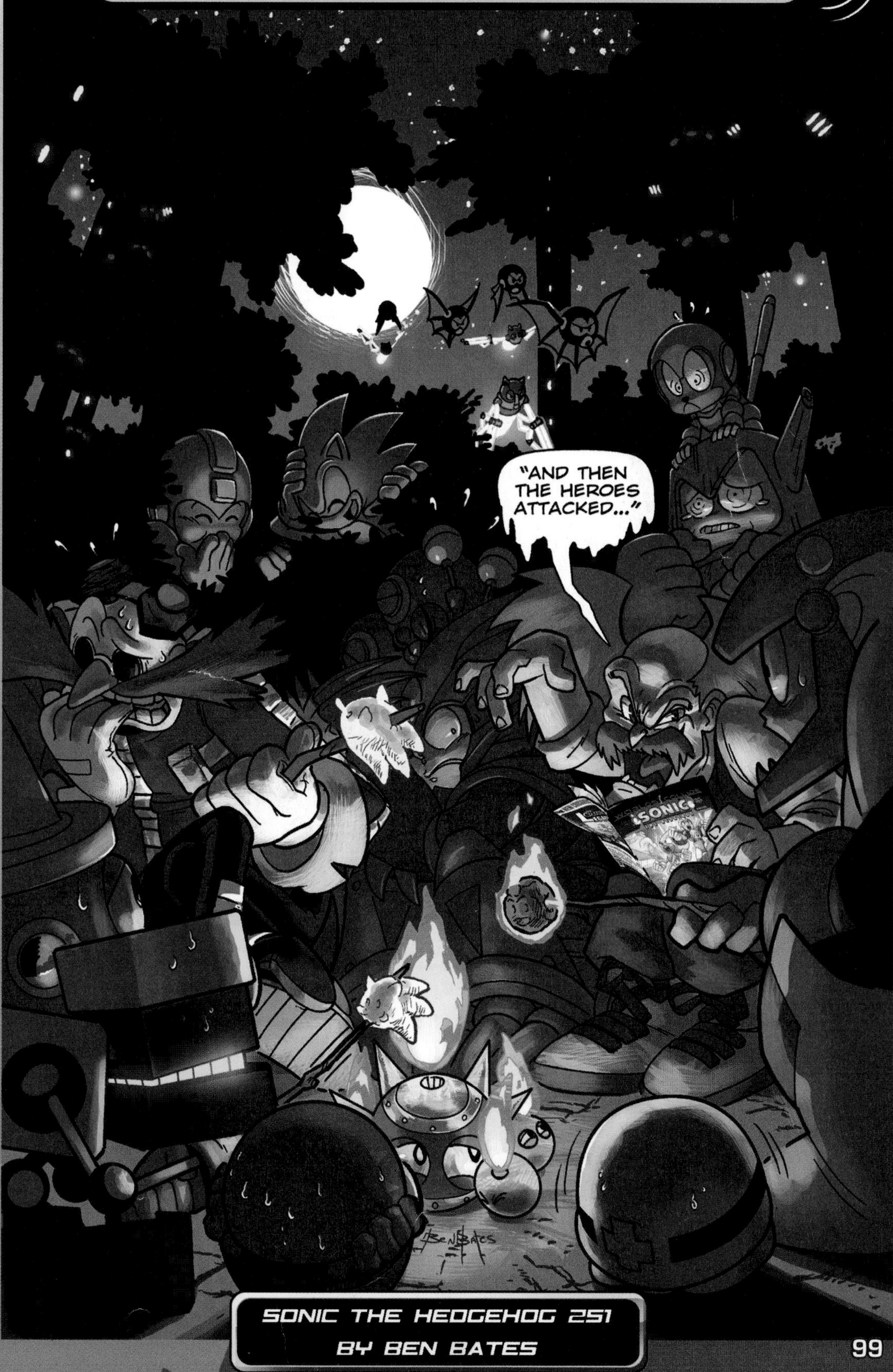

"AND THEN THE HEROES ATTACKED..."
BEN BATES


SONIC THE HEDGEHOG 251
BY BEN BATES

# ORIGINS OF A CROSSOVER
## BY PATRICK SPAZIANTE

**SONIC THE HEDGEHOG 250:** The Sonic 250 cover was a personal favorite of mine, as it was both a compilation cover, as well as a wrap around. It is a rarity for me to get a chance to work on a dual-sided image, and to have the opportunity to have both the Sonic and Mega Man universes involved was a real treat. Paul had suggested the character group on this piece, and it was especially interesting to be able to work some of the Sonic "Badniks" into the mix. (Crabmeat being a familiar face from way back in my early Sonic career.)

**SONIC THE HEDGEHOG 250**

Inked cover art from SPAZ before the piece went to Ben Hunzeker for color.

**MEGA MAN 27:** This cover gave me a chance to pay homage to an older style of classic pulp images; having the protagonist being in imminent danger from an over-powering evil, with panels to show the heroes in the story. Matt Herms did a wonderful job in realizing/enhancing the tension in said image. (I'm especially fond of the lightning bolt that he had added to give that extra tone of danger.) This type of cover is always fun, as I feel that half the excitement of any adventure property is a great villain, and getting the chance to give Eggman a center stage shot, as well as a much more threatening flavor, reinforces the action elements of the book.

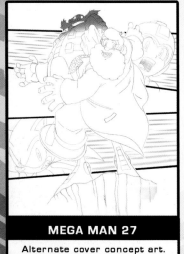

I'm also a big fan of the "bad-guy" cover image. I was always intrigued by a piece that showed the antagonist center stage. The extra tension drew me in and, I hope, draws the current fans to see "what happens next?"

**MEGA MAN 27**

Alternate cover concept art.

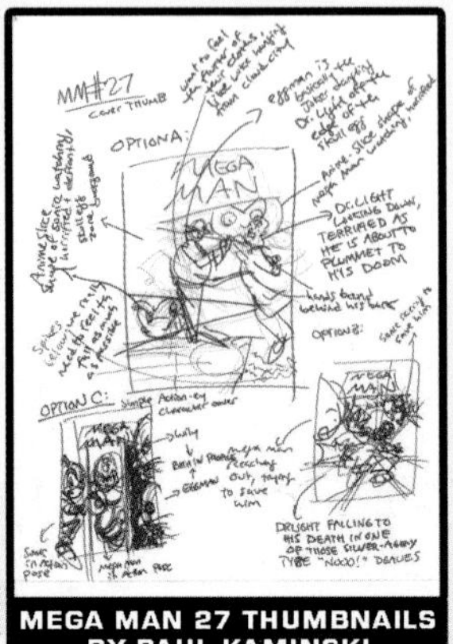

**MEGA MAN 27 THUMBNAILS BY PAUL KAMINSKI & VINCENT LOVALLO**

SONIC UNIVERSE 54

Final ink art from Patrick Spaziante.

ALTERNATE COVER PENCILS FOR SONIC UNIVERSE 54

The original cover pencils were an homage to the "Mega Man Soccer" video game box art.

**SONIC UNIVERSE 54:** This cover, although basic, was a nice return to the classic "Comic Book" feel of the series. Paul had suggested a "coming at you" shot, and although I feel these can get overdone in the Comic Book industry in general, in this case, it felt appropriate. The added detail of the Eggman and Wily faces in the shattered glass shards was something that we both agreed would add some spice to an otherwise standard image. Sonic and Mega Man teaming up is something that many of us at Archie had dreamed about for a long time as a "what if" project, and getting the chance to bring these two icons together has been a real privilege.

**SONIC THE HEDGEHOG 251:** What can I say about this shot... Having Sonic and Mega Man in their respective "powered-up" forms was a cover idea that I felt was truly inspired. Paul had given me the art direction and his goal was to show these characters in their ultimate configurations. This cover gave me a somewhat nostalgic feeling as well, as the layout harkens back (at least to me) to the kinds of comic book covers I loved when I was first starting out. Not to mention as a particular Mega Man freak, getting the chance to draw Duo was especially awesome! Again, as last time, I'd like to take this opportunity to give a special thank you to all the fans of our books. You are the real reason we are inspired to continue creating the ongoing adventures of these great characters!

SPAZ

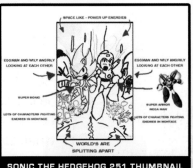

SPACE LIKE - POWER UP ENERGIES
EGGMAN AND WILY ANGRILY LOOKING AT EACH OTHER
EGGMAN AND WILY ANGRILY LOOKING AT EACH OTHER
SUPER SONIC
SUPER ARMOR MEGA MAN
LOTS OF CHARACTERS FIGHTING ENEMIES IN MONTAGE
LOTS OF CHARACTERS FIGHTING ENEMIES IN MONTAGE
WORLD'S ARE SPLITTING APART

SONIC THE HEDGEHOG 251 THUMBNAIL BY VINCENT LOVALLO

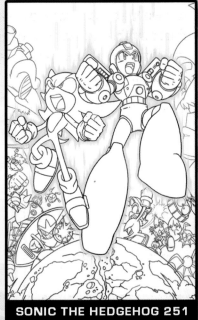

SONIC THE HEDGEHOG 251

Final ink art from Patrick Spaziante.

# OFF-PANEL AND SHORT CIRCUIT STRIPS!

## THANKS TO THE FANS

SCRIPT: IAN FLYNN PENCILS: VINCENT LOVALLO INKS: KENT ARCHER COLORS: JAMES KAMINSKI

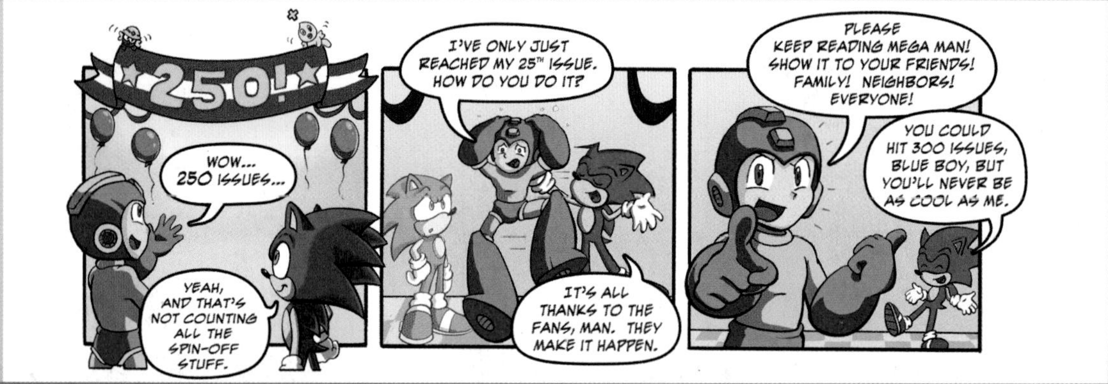
250!
WOW... 250 ISSUES...
YEAH, AND THAT'S NOT COUNTING ALL THE SPIN-OFF STUFF.
I'VE ONLY JUST REACHED MY 25TH ISSUE. HOW DO YOU DO IT?
IT'S ALL THANKS TO THE FANS, MAN. THEY MAKE IT HAPPEN.
PLEASE KEEP READING MEGA MAN! SHOW IT TO YOUR FRIENDS! FAMILY! NEIGHBORS! EVERYONE!
YOU COULD HIT 300 ISSUES, BLUE BOY, BUT YOU'LL NEVER BE AS COOL AS ME.

## ONE BIG PROBLEM

SCRIPT: IAN FLYNN PENCILS: JAMES KAMINSKI INKS: KENT ARCHER COLORS: VINCENT LOVALLO

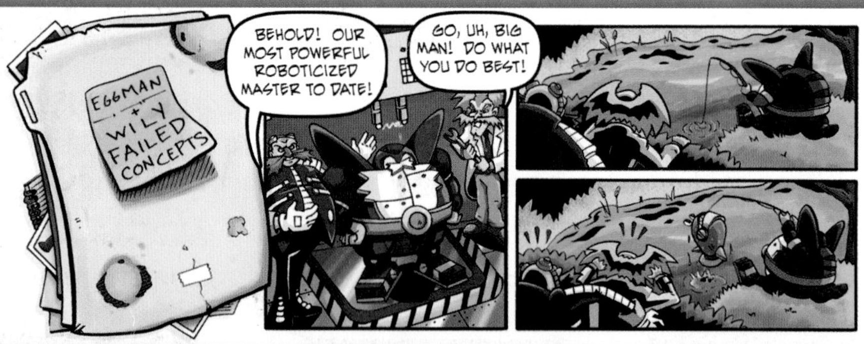
EGGMAN + WILY FAILED CONCEPTS
BEHOLD! OUR MOST POWERFUL ROBOTICIZED MASTER TO DATE!
GO, UH, BIG MAN! DO WHAT YOU DO BEST!

## METAL AND BASS

SCRIPT: IAN FLYNN PENCILS & INKS: JONATHAN GRAY COLORS: ALEAH BAKER

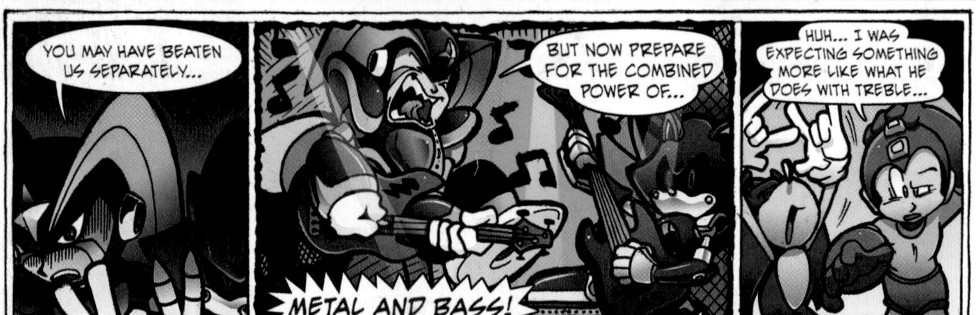
YOU MAY HAVE BEATEN US SEPARATELY...
BUT NOW PREPARE FOR THE COMBINED POWER OF...
METAL AND BASS!
HUH... I WAS EXPECTING SOMETHING MORE LIKE WHAT HE DOES WITH TREBLE...

## THERE-THERE, I UNDERSTAND

SCRIPT: IAN FLYNN PENCILS: VINCENT LOVALLO INKS: KENT ARCHER COLORS: JAMES KAMINSKI

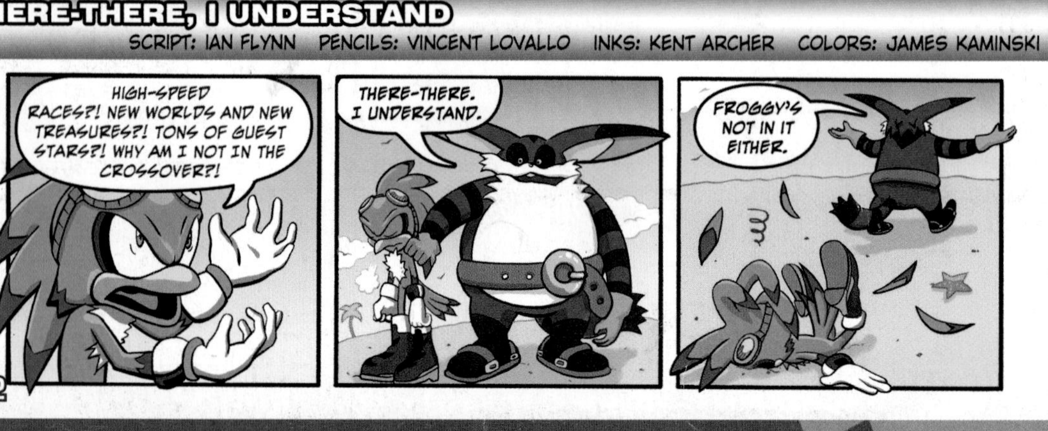
HIGH-SPEED RACES?! NEW WORLDS AND NEW TREASURES?! TONS OF GUEST STARS?! WHY AM I NOT IN THE CROSSOVER?!
THERE-THERE. I UNDERSTAND.
FROGGY'S NOT IN IT EITHER.

# COMING SOON!

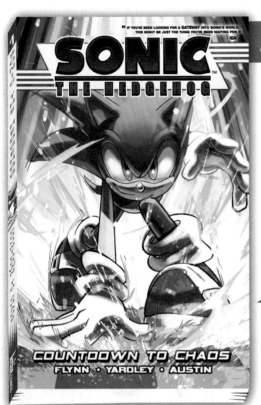